MINDY HAYES

KALEIDOSCOPE

a Faylinn novel

Published by Mindy Hayes
Cover design and photography by Regina Wamba of
www.maeidesign.com

ISBN: 1480012289
ISBN-13: 978-1480012288

To my sister, Heidi Lynn

PROLOGUE

Decisions should be black and white, but there's too much gray area for that, things that tugged at my mind, causing me to question my actions and motives. Where did my loyalties lie? Where were they supposed to lie? Whose lives were supposed to be spared? Who deserved to die? But most importantly, whose right was it to make those decisions?

While watching the scene play out in front of me, the light gradually dimming as sunset approached, I was suddenly aware of the decision I needed to make. She smiled so happily as the swing flew higher in the tree, the wind blowing in her long blonde curls. He stood behind her, his face splashed with that same happiness, those same gleaming green eyes. He encouraged her to hold on tight with fatherly care.

I approached quietly, camouflaged by the trees, weighing my options. My mind knew what it wanted to do, but the consequences would fall on me tenfold. Would it be worth it? Could I get away with it?

Her laughter trailed through the air, filling the outdoors, resonating in my ears, solidifying the decision I needed to make. The consequences suddenly didn't matter. I knew where my loyalties resided. It would be worth it. The grey area separated and all that was left was stark white and solid black.

That was the moment my dagger tore through flesh, cementing my decision.

ONE

The thumping in my chest woke me too early, pulsing so strongly it pounded in my ears. It branched out, streaming down my arms and legs, beating steadily through every vein and artery in my body.

Who needs an alarm clock when yours is internal? But it wasn't just some internal alarm clock. It was a sensation I knew couldn't be normal; shouldn't be normal, and yet it was a part of me. Something I expected every day. It was followed by this strange impulse to get out of my house and be outside. Once I felt the breeze lick through my hair and my lungs filled with the fresh scent of nature, the pulsing subsided, but I still wasn't sure what I was supposed to do. The cool blaze in my veins would diminish and I was at peace.

Momentarily.

I dragged myself out of bed and looked at the alarm clock on the nightstand. Six o'clock. I didn't have to be up for school for another thirty minutes, but it was pointless to go back to sleep. Not that the pulsing would let me anyway.

While growing up I didn't know the pulsing wasn't normal until I mentioned it to Cameron. We were twelve years old and playing cards at my kitchen table when the subtle pulsing started in my veins. I looked over at him and said I needed to go outside for a minute. He gave me a strange look as I excused myself. When I came back inside he asked, "What was that about?"

"The pulsing was getting annoying. I needed some air." I shrugged.

His eyebrows scrunched together as he told me I was crazy. After that I never mentioned it to anyone. My parents never questioned it before so I assumed it was normal.

I know differently now.

As I grew older, the stronger it became. What started out as a subtle itch now felt like another vital organ—only more prominent because it made its presence known in the center of my chest every minute of every hour of every day.

I hopped into the shower, letting the cool water wash away the urge and clear the fog in my brain. It didn't work, but it was worth a shot. When I got back to my room I aimed for the next best thing—the window that overlooked our backyard into a deep forest of Walhalla.

Once I shoved it open and took a deep breath, the thumping began to withdraw, beginning with my fingers and toes, then slowly traveling to the source in my chest. It took a few moments, but finally the pulsing was satisfied.

For the time being.

White light shimmered around his face and a chorus of

angelic voices burst out in a sweet melody when he turned in his chair to face me. Technically, that didn't happen, but it might as well have. That's how my mind saw it. It was that day in my third period science class that I knew I found true love.

A week into our sixth grade year Cameron asked me to be his partner for a science project and I knew there was no turning back. We were going to live happily ever after. Most don't believe you know what love is at the ripe old age of eleven, or that you can even find your true love at that age, but they're wrong. I was living, breathing proof that you could.

Almost seven years later, we stood by our neighboring lockers on the first day of our senior year. I watched him tuck a piece of Isla's golden hair behind her ear and stare lovingly into her annoyingly sparkly blue eyes. His smile spread widely on his face as she whispered something in his ear. Obviously, it was hilarious because he started to laugh that heartwarming, stomach tingling, contagious laugh—a laugh that whether the joke was funny or not, you laughed because it felt good to laugh with him. You wanted to hear him laugh more.

Isla was different from the others he'd gone after. She was real. No fake tans or pounds of make-up. She didn't gossip or flaunt her perfect cheer body. She didn't make you want to poke out your eyes with her abbreviation of every other word.

You know my BFF, Tiff, totally needs a BF for real.

Cameron had gone through many, many... many girls, but none of them were like Isla. It didn't take much to see the difference. I saw it in the way he smiled. We'd been friends long enough for me to know I'd never seen that smile before. And it scared me. I waited patiently for that smile. I knew it was in there somewhere, being reserved for that special someone and had waited years for it to be directed at me.

"Callie." Cameron waved his hand in front of my face.

Oh, great. How long had he been doing that?

"Cal," he said a little bit louder, looking at me like I was an idiot.

I could still see little Cameron in his face. It was all in the eyes. They never changed, still the penetrating sapphire I fell into that first day. Though his baby fat cheeks had thinned out into a chiseled jaw and his light blonde hair was a little darker and a little shaggier, he was still the Cameron I fell for on day one.

"What?" I responded irritably, pretending I heard him say my name over and over again and was agitated to be interrupted from whatever I was doing. Of course, I'd been staring. I cringed inwardly and gave myself a mental scolding for zoning out.

"Isla and I are heading to class. We'll see you at lunch."

"Yeah. Whatever. Cool." I attempted to feign indifference.

He nodded, his hair sweeping across his forehead, and tossed a wave before wrapping his arm snugly around Isla to escort her down the hall. She giggled, her head leaning into him as he nuzzled his face into her neck, whispering sweet nothings.

Well, they were probably sweet nothings.

My heart sank a little.

Isla looked over her shoulder and smiled genuinely at me, delicately waving. "See you later, Calliope."

I despised the fact that I couldn't even hate her. She was too gracious. Nothing like Myra or Dana or Blair or any other skank Cam had been with—girls that made themselves easy to hate.

"Bye, Isla," I said as politely as I could manage.

I couldn't even bring myself to be semi-snarky with her. She didn't deserve it. It unnerved me. She was hard to hate even if she was with the boy I was supposed to spend the rest of my life with. It made me want to gag. I had to believe that I would get my turn. I convinced myself there was still time.

My classes dragged on, as one would expect on a first day, teachers droning over the syllabus and about what was expected throughout the year. I wasn't really worried about not getting into college. I'd get into some college close by. Some place I could keep an eye on Cam.

I was protective of him. Not as a form of jealousy—though I knew it was a tiny part—but because aside from his dad, I was the only constant in his life. And I planned to stay that way. He needed me just as much as I needed him, even if he didn't see it the way I did; even if I were more of a best friend/sister in his eyes than someone he could spend the rest of his life with. I'd never leave him.

My eyes were initially blinded when I walked outside for lunch. I blinked away the brightness, waiting for my eyes to adjust. I breathed in the sunlight, the warmth soaking into my body, nourishing my skin with its touch.

"Hey, Callie," Lia greeted, falling into step beside me.

"Lia," I said. "Hey."

"We own this school this year. Doesn't it feel great? We are no longer the underclassmen. We're finally on top. This is our year. Our *last* year."

"Yeah. Feels good, huh?" I said with half of the amount of excitement she oozed.

Lia sighed happily. "*So* good." She linked her arm through mine. "How's your first day so far?"

"Overwhelming. But I only have one more period and then

I'm done for the day."

"Jealous! I should have taken extra classes with you last year."

"As if you could have added that to your pile of AP classes." She shrugged. "I'm really glad I did though. It'll help this year fly by."

I caught sight of Cameron and Isla sitting under a shady oak tree, playfully shoving each other and laughing. I wanted to throw up. That should be me—but less nauseating.

"I can't believe I dated him," Lia muttered.

It was my fault that they met in the first place. Lia was new our freshman year and I decided to be polite and introduce her to some people to make her feel welcome. Cam, of course, jumped right on that bandwagon. Lia's long dark red hair and big beautiful hazel eyes had him at hello. Half of the school fawned over her, but what I love most about Lia was that the attention didn't faze her. She focused on getting into Harvard or Princeton or one of those Ivy League schools that I could only dream of. Then she was bound for medical school to become a world-renowned surgeon that cured cancer or AIDS or some terminal illness.

"To be honest I can't believe you did either." I chuckled.

"A definite lapse in my judgment, but he looks so happy now." She followed my gaze. "You doing okay with them?"

"Yup."

"All right." Lia knew not to pry. We were close enough that I never had to tell her about my feelings for Cameron. She figured it out on her own. It was also one of the reasons she ended it with him, though it definitely wasn't the only one. And boy, did that throw Cam for a loop. *He* got dumped? That never happened. But he was over it within a week when Blair Vander pounced on him at Jake Winter's birthday bash the following weekend.

"He could do worse," she encouraged.

All I could do was nod. He *had* done worse. I should be happy for him, but I'd never come second to a girlfriend before.

"Shall we sit or...?"

I cleared my throat. "Yeah. Let's go." I thought about sitting with the lovebirds, but I already needed a break. We headed to our own shady spot on the opposite side of the lawn, out of sight from Cameron and Isla.

The bell to my last period class rang and I heaved a sigh of relief. One day down, only one hundred and seventy-nine days to go. Putting it into a number like that made it sound worse.

"Hey, Callie, you headed home?"

I looked to my left side to see Cameron without his second half. "Yeah."

He draped his arm casually over my shoulder and leaned his head down to mine, smelling like his familiar fresh, soapy self. "Can you do me a *huge* favor?"

"That depends."

Cameron had to know I was wrapped around his finger. I tried my best to conceal my feelings, but I wasn't sure how well that act worked. We were two sides of the same coin. We could practically finish one another's sentences. He had to know, didn't he?

He rushed on. "Isla has to stay after school for some mandatory cheer meeting or something, and we drove to school together this morning because my jeep's at my dad's shop. So..."

"You're a little bit stranded." I peered up at him, arrested by his blue eyes. I looked away to break the connection before it was too late and I showed him a glimpse of my feelings.

I could hear the partial smile in his voice. "A little bit."

"What about your dad?" It was a long shot and I knew it.

"He can't leave the shop, you know that. His mechanics are lost without him."

Cameron's dad's auto repair shop became his life when Cameron's mom left. His dad ate, breathed, slept and drank cars. Where did that leave Cam? It left him with me.

Until Isla.

I let out a deep breath. "You want me to go home, and then come back and pick you up just to drive all the way back home," I said dryly.

"C'mon, Cal, *please*? Pretty *please*?"

Cameron only lived a couple streets over from my house. *I* knew I wasn't going to say no. *He* knew I wasn't going to say no, but it was pleasurable to see him beg anyway.

"Fine."

"Thanks!" He planted a quick peck on my cheek. "You're the best."

"Tell me something I don't know."

He laughed. "I'll see you in a couple hours."

I waved him away as I headed for the front of the school to my car.

Throughout our high school years everyone's tried to tell us a boy and a girl can't be best friends without *some* friction between them. "There's always some sort of sexual tension from one or both sides," they'd say. I casually brushed them off because I knew perfectly well they were *right*, but Cameron would laugh and wrap his arm playfully around me, hugging me so close

10

I could melt into him, and say, "Callie and I have done it so far. Haven't we, Cal?" further crushing my heart every time.

I'd nod and wryly say, "Who'd want to date this guy?" while inside I would be screaming, "Me! Pick me!"

So desperately stupid, but such is my life.

Before I went back to get Cameron I figured I would get a head start on some homework. You'd think teachers would at least give you a day to get back into the swing of things, but apparently there was no time to waste in order to get everything accomplished by graduation.

I had the first act of Macbeth to read through; an essay for home economics on what I thought it meant to be a parent; the first chapter of physics to get acquainted with; and my first worksheet of Calculus to work through without any instruction. My calculus teacher wanted to get a feel for what we already knew. As if I would be taking calculus if I already knew the subject.

I spread out a blanket on the grass in the backyard near our gnarly old oak tree to appreciate what sun I had left before evening came. The tree swing hanging from the oak swayed slightly in the light breeze.

Sometimes I could beat the pulsing by going outside before it started and lessen the sensation. There were few places that made me feel as relaxed as when I was near our trees. It could have been the peaceful sound of the chirping birds or the fluttering leaves, but I could never quite place it. It was like the warm river flowing through my veins craved to be among nature. I knew it sounded weird, but I wasn't sure how else to explain it.

I nibbled on an apple slice and flipped through my physics book, scanning the pages on matter. There was a rustling in the woods, which normally wouldn't startle me, but the breeze had stopped and it only came from the left side of the trees. My gaze lifted to the forest lining the back of our property. Our yard backed right up to preserved woodlands. They stood silently now, undisturbed.

I flicked the light of my cell phone on to check the time. There was still an hour before I needed to leave to pick up Cameron. I bowed my head down again, finding where I left off, trying to become enthralled with atoms and molecules and yada yada yada.

It wasn't more than a minute when I heard the snap of a twig. This time I sat up and scanned the grove of trees from one end to the other. Animals heavy enough to snap a twig never came this close to civilization. But everything was eerily quiet again. No motion of the greenery or movement between them.

Crack. My eyes darted to the sound on the opposite side of the forest from where I heard the twig snap, and yet all I saw were the soaring trees and thick shrubbery.

"Hello?" I asked uncertainly. I sounded ridiculous, calling out into the forest at nothing. But I *felt* something there. Tentative footsteps sounded, growing fainter and fainter. But I couldn't see a thing. I stood up to get a better view.

"Hello?" I asked with a little more confidence. There had to be someone there. And most likely I didn't want to wait to find out who, but the curiosity was like a plague, completely unavoidable.

"Calliope?" I gasped and spun to see my dad's curious gaze from the back deck. "What are you doing, sweetheart?"

I fussed with my hair nonchalantly. "Nothing. Just working

on some homework."

He looked at me skeptically, as if he didn't believe me. "Did you hear something out there?"

"It was probably just some squirrels." *Giant squirrels.*

"Come on inside. I really need to build a fence along those trees. I don't like you being out here like a sitting duck. You never know what's lurking in those woods."

I stood up and snagged my books and the quilt from the grass, tucking them under my arms, cell phone in hand.

"Let me help you," Dad offered when I got to the deck, reaching for the blanket.

"Thanks."

"I forgot that you were getting out early this year. I wanted to be here when you got home."

"It's okay," I said. He rested his hand on my shoulder and kissed my forehead.

"I just had to run to the grocery real quick."

I nodded. "What's for dinner?"

"I'm making vegetable lasagna."

"Cool. Do you need help bringing in the groceries?" I asked and dropped my books on the kitchen table.

"I got them all," he said. "Thanks though."

"When's Mom going to be home?"

He opened the fridge and finished putting away the groceries. "She's going to have a late night tonight. Probably won't be home until after eight. She's working on a big case. The trial is coming up in a few months. I don't know the details, but from the sounds of it, she's prosecuting a man for horrendous things... child abuse, battery, murder, you name it." He shook his head and sighed.

Our family defied all family stereotypes. My mom was a

lawyer and my dad stayed home. Not because he had to, but because he wanted to and my mom wanted to work. He didn't go to college. She did. She was in law school when they met.

The lines were still blurry on how they met, exactly. My parents met in some park in North Carolina where my mom often studied during law school. They noticed each other and clicked. Something like that.

I didn't know much about my dad's past. All I knew was that he was an orphan. His parents abandoned him at birth. I guess it was something he didn't like talking about and I didn't pry. My dad did a few odd jobs on the side to keep himself occupied. He designed landscapes in his free time. He loved the outdoors, like father like daughter.

"She'll be pretty stressed out until then, huh?"

He nodded. "She's really committed to this case and getting this guy locked up. But, it just means more time for us." He smiled to try and lighten the mood.

Yay. Not that I didn't love spending time with my dad, but a girl needed her mom sometimes. Moms understood things in a different way than dads. And it'd been too long since I'd actually spent any bonding time with her. I really missed her.

Cam slid into the front seat of my little white Cabriolet. I had the top down to feel the warmth of the sun. She'd definitely seen her fair share of use over the years, but she'd been good to me. Maybe a little beat up, but she was mine.

Cameron and I took turns driving on road trips over the years—half in his old Jeep, half in my Cabriolet. Not cross-country overnight trips, but daytrips to Charlotte, Myrtle Beach and Charleston. We had lots of good memories in this car, blasting music and singing from the top of our lungs with the top down.

"Thanks, Cal," he said. "I know you didn't want to come back."

"Don't sweat it."

Cameron threw his backpack in the backseat and combed his hand through his dirty blonde strands. "Are you as swamped as I am? I feel like I'm drowning in homework. This was supposed to be the easy year. The fun year."

I chuckled humorlessly. "And yet, I get out two periods early and I have twice as much to do as I did with all seven periods."

"It's a joke."

"Yeah, on us."

He slapped my knee coolly and kept his hand there. "We haven't really talked in a while. What's new?"

At that moment I really wished there was something to rub in his face, but I had nothing. We'd spent the first half of the summer together, but he'd spent the second half with Isla.

For whatever reason we'd gone to school with her since kindergarten and he'd never noticed her. Then at one *random* summer party they caught one another's eyes and everything fell into place. As if they were at the right place at the right time. She smiled and waved and he didn't look back. If that didn't feel like complete desertion after seven years of friendship I don't know what did.

The second half of my summer was spent with Lia or my parents. No hot dates or summer romances. No exciting adventures or escapades to relay to him. We didn't even go on a vacation. I should've just lied, told him something. But what was the point?

I shrugged, not at all unaware of the warmth of his palm on my thigh. The simple touch had my nerves darting around my body like a pinball machine. "Nothing really."

His hand squeezed my leg lightly. "Well that's lame. No hot dates or thrilling adventures to relay?"

He knew just how to rub it in. "Nope."

Cameron took his hand back and crossed his arms. "I just don't get that, Cal," he said, perplexed. "You need to relax and stop being so intimidating to all the guys. They want you, if you'll just give 'em the time of day."

"Thanks for the words of wisdom. I'll try harder to change *myself* to be more appealing to *them*."

"You know that's not what I meant," he said. "You just turn the cold shoulder every time any guy wants to talk to you."

I chuckled. *I did not.* "Why do you care so much about my dating life, Cam?" *Did I?*

"I don't," he said, looking away indifferently out the passenger's side. "It's just now that I have Isla, I see what I was missing out on by not being serious about any girl. I can't believe I never saw her before. The blind man can finally see," he exclaimed, his arms spread out above his head.

Cut me while I'm down, will ya? Maybe spit on me while I'm down there and rub a little salt in the wounds to top it off.

"The only guy worthy of my time will be the one who's willing to work for it. I refuse to give this away for free." I gestured to myself to get a chuckle out of him and it worked.

"All right. I see. You're worth more than that. I know. You deserve a really good guy."

If only you could see that guy is you.

I pulled up to his house and let him hop out.

"Thanks for the ride, Callie. See you tomorrow."

I nodded and waved.

It used to be: *I'll call you later* or *let's hang out tonight.* I couldn't even remember the last time Cameron called me just to chat. Gosh, I missed him.

TWO

Pulsating through my body like another heartbeat, the subtle thumping broke my concentration on Macbeth. The sensation beckoned me to my bedroom window overlooking our trees.

The internal thumping started getting a little stronger a few weeks ago. The need; the yearning; the hunger to be outside—it was controllable in the past. Simply being outside used to fulfill the urge. Before, there were times when I could brush it off and go back to whatever task I was doing. Now, I found that it grew stronger every day, pulling me to the trees. It made me feel crazy.

I cracked the window in my bedroom open and skimmed the trees. The sun set behind the grove, generating a grayish blue haze streaming through the branches. I'd never been apprehensive about the vast pasture of greenery before, but as my eyes studied the unknown beyond, I began to question what was out there. I wasn't sure if I was being lured by simple curiosity or something deeper. The only thing keeping me in the security of my bedroom was the coherent side of my brain that screamed danger at the thought of entering a darkening forest alone. But it was so tempting.

My ears perked up at a faint tangle of noises. I lifted the window up a little more, but couldn't quite make out what it was. It didn't sound like birds or squirrels. There were two separate sounds. One was low, baritone almost, while the other was a slight bit higher, but not feminine sounding. I didn't think it was humans, but the sounds were too soft to know for sure. Whatever it was sounded like... arguing? It was probably the next-door neighbors. There was a *crack* and then a *thud*. A tree branch falling?

A knock at my door caused me to jump back. I turned as I let out a sigh.

"Come in," I called.

My mom peered around my door. "Hey, baby. How was your first day?"

I looked to the clock on my nightstand; the bold green numbers showed it was 8:07 pm.

"Long, as yours seemed to be too."

She let out a humorless breath of laughter and walked into my room. She'd already changed into her gray pajama pants.

"Do you like your teachers?"

I shrugged. "They're all okay, I guess. No one is particularly strict or mean, so that's a plus."

She chuckled and sat on the edge of my bed. My mom and I were nearly identical, but she kept her blonde hair short and hid her twinkling green eyes behind brown-rimmed glasses.

"Dad was worried about you today. You feeling okay?"

I nodded without hesitation. "Yeah. I'm fine. Why?"

"He said you just seemed a little on edge." Her fingers stretched out and tucked a few of my curls behind my ear, away from my face.

"It was probably the fact that I got to see Cameron and Isla suck face all day."

My mom wasn't sure if she should laugh or console me so it became a combination of both. "Oh, honey." She pulled me to her chest.

I never declared my feelings for Cameron out loud to her, but I think my mom always knew, as all parents do with that aggravating, built-in intuition they have for their children.

"He'll come around."

I stayed silent in her arms for a moment, contemplating her words of encouragement. Of course, deep down I would always have that hope, but every day it slowly dwindled the more I thought about them together. "I don't think he will this time." I clenched back a tear. I wouldn't let myself cry over him. I thought about what my dad said earlier and realized I'd let my mom pity me long enough.

"Enough about me." I pulled away. "How was your day? Dad said you've been given a really tough case."

She nodded solemnly. "Everything points to this guy, but it's all circumstantial." She explained what she could about the case in her lawyer mumbo jumbo and sighed. "But I'll get him. It's what I do." She smiled and tugged me to her side. "I just need to give it my all."

"You'll get him. I know you will."

"Thanks for your vote of confidence." She winked. "I'll let you get back to your homework. When you're done come downstairs and we'll watch a season premiere of one of the shows we DVR'd."

"Ah yes, let the fall season begin."

Week one of the school year had been conquered. Friday morning rolled around and everyone seemed to be settling into their niches. The freshmen were getting the hang of the layout and weren't as much in the way with being lost. Now they were gaining confidence and big heads because they were big high schoolers. The buzz of coming back to school and seeing friends was slowly fading as people started to feel the weight of the schoolwork pile on.

"Good morning, Calliebug!" Lia beamed at my side as I walked into the school Friday morning.

I groaned, but formed a smile to hide my current state of mind. The pulsing was bad today, fiercer than it had ever been and being outside at school wasn't fixing the problem. "It's still early. Can we keep the squealing to a low decibel?"

"Oh, but it's such a pretty day out!"

"You would think we would have at least one class together," Lia complained as I dug around in my locker for my calculus book.

"You're in all AP classes, Lia. I wouldn't last one day in any of those classes."

"Oh, you'd last just fine if you applied yourself," she said, leaning her back against the lockers. "And you'd have me, which we both know would basically be like a free ride. I could have been your own personal tutor."

I laughed. "I'm good where I'm at. Thanks," I said, shutting my locker. She matched my stride as we shouldered passed people in the hallway.

"I've barely seen Cameron all week. Where is he?"

Thankfully the thumping wasn't painful, but it was

distracting. I was surprised Lia couldn't hear it. It made it really difficult to carry on this conversation. "I'm not the person to ask anymore."

She must have heard the defeat in my tone. I couldn't keep it in check today.

"This phase will pass, you know? They are in phase one. The lovey dovey phase, where no one exists but them. In a month or two they will hit phase two where their relationship will become more comfortable and they will start play-bickering—picking little fights about nothing to keep the relationship interesting. They will be in that phase for a few months and then phase three will hit. That's the phase that will either make or break them."

"What's phase three?" I asked, trying to sound interested.

"It's the confidence phase," she said matter-of-factly. "Where they become so confident in their relationship they don't try as hard because it has come so easy to them before. They will fight all the time over what he hasn't been doing or has been doing that drives her crazy and vice versa." She shrugged as if it was common knowledge.

I peered up at her. "And then…"

"Well… either they will figure out that even though they fight all the time they love each other too much to break up and they will work on being better to one another; or, they will decide the fighting has torn such a huge wedge in their relationship that it's beyond repair and they will decide it's not worth it to fix it."

"So, we've got a few months to see how this plays out," I said, swallowing back the hammering in my ears. Maybe it was like when you traveled to high elevations and your ears needed to be popped. I swallowed again and tried to yawn, but it didn't help.

She nodded. "Six months to a year is the typical natural cycle. Unless the wild card gets thrown in and they break up for a completely different reason, like another guy or someone moves away or someone cheats. Don't worry we already have a month and a half down."

"Oh wise one, how did you gain such knowledge?"

"I read way too many books in my free time."

I laughed as the warning bell rang for school to start, and we split off to our separate classes.

Looking out the kitchen window as I ate my after school snack, I felt the strings dig deeper, tugging me to the forest. The more I watched the spray of ferns and shrubs, the more I was drawn to be amidst the peacefulness in which the leaves rustled and the trickle of flowers crawled under the shade beneath the branches. Despite the warning my internal radar gave to stay away, I couldn't deny the tranquility that spread through me at the thought of breathing in the crisp air, shaded under the awning of green. This time I let it consume me.

I hovered on the edge of the grove of trees where the spongy moss crept up to the lawn, inviting me to take one step. The pulsing was already weakening and calmness was gently seeping in. It was only moments before my body gave into the urge to explore when I felt it.

That sixth sense.

That sixth sense feeling of knowing when someone's behind you or watching you. That tingling feeling that rises up your spine and shivers down your limbs. It felt like I was staring straight at someone in the trees, but all my naked eye could see was the rich woven branches. And yet it was there. Something or someone had to be out there.

The rational part of my brain kicked in and I started to retreat, stepping back. As my foot moved I heard a quiet yet eager step come toward me. I took another step backward and simultaneously heard another step forward.

I swallowed. "Is anyone there?"

As if in response the wind whirled around me, blowing my hair, but no other sound was made.

"Show yourself." It was the next thing that came to my mind. If something was hiding in our trees, I probably didn't want to wait around long enough to find out what it was, but the pull kept my feet planted in place.

A faint trill of laughter echoed from the forest. It was mocking me. I turned on my heel and bolted for the back door to the safety of my home. I got the unsettling feeling that I was being chased, but when I reached the sliding glass door and slammed it behind me, nothing was there. I flipped the lock, sighing in relief and tried to catch my breath.

"Are you okay, Calliope?"

I gasped.

My dad sat in his recliner in the corner of our living room, watching me with a book in his hands.

I straightened up and fussed with the hem of my shirt, pulling it down around my waist. "Yeah." My voice was meant to come off as sure, but I think it fell flat.

"Come here," he urged.

I sat down on the couch across from him; taking comfort in the soft fabric I'd taken many naps on after school.

"Maybe it's better if you stay inside until we get that fence put up."

The thought of being banned from the forest shot a sting of anxiety throughout me. "What? No. I'm fine."

His forehead ruffled in uncertainty. He always made that face when he didn't believe me. "Every time I've seen you out there or coming inside, you look spooked. What are you seeing out there?"

"Nothing," I said too quickly. "I just keep hearing something, but there's nothing there. It's probably just a raccoon or something."

"All right." He closed his book and started to get out of his seat. "I'm going to Andy's Hardware and I'm buying some wood to build a fence today."

"Dad, don't be ridiculous. I'm *fine*. You don't need to build a fence right this minute."

"Yes I do," he insisted. "It should have been taken care of a long time ago. I don't know why I've waited." He shifted once more to get up.

"Dad, you're overreacting. Stay put." I motioned for him to sit back down. "So what if a rabbit or possum shows up in our yard. What harm could they do?" He pursed his lips in contemplation. "Ease up, okay? Don't stress yourself out. It'll get built sooner or later. It doesn't have to be right this instant." I tried biding my time.

He nodded, but wasn't convinced. "I'm having it put up this weekend."

"Okay," I relented.

For whatever reason, the thought of being cut off from the trees made me feel uneasy, though, he did have a point. Not that we'd been bothered too much in the past by wildlife, but something was out there that should be kept out. I felt the hairs on the back of my neck stand up when I looked back to the ominous woodlands; but curiosity still bubbled at the surface, persuading me to let the pulsing capture me again.

When I peered back at my dad, he watched me thoughtfully like he did when he was working on a crossword puzzle, like I was some mystery to be solved.

"Are you feeling all right? You look a little flushed." I put my hands to my cheeks. They were warm, but my heart rate was up from running through the backyard.

"I do feel a little dizzy. I'm going to go lay down for a little bit."

"Good idea," he said. "I'll come get you when dinner is ready."

"Thanks, Dad." I smiled meekly and walked to my room to be alone. I needed to stop acting so out of character. I didn't like to be looked at under a microscope, my every move questioned. I wanted to tell my dad, but I was afraid. The last thing I wanted was to be sent to a therapist because everyone thought I was hallucinating or going schizo.

I was flying. The wind blew over me, the ground far below me. It was freeing. I landed on something that felt like a beam. I looked down at my feet balanced on a rough brown beam covered in leaves. A tree branch? I scoured my location, vines and tree limbs coming into focus, snaking and entwining around each other. I was at least forty feet off the ground.

I leaped from the branch and went soaring through the foliage. A smile widened on my face as a tingling swirled in my stomach. A mix between a laugh and a scream sprang from my lips.

"Calliope!" A voice sang from my left.

I peered over and saw a shadowy figure soaring beside me lift a hand in a wave. We leaped from tree to tree in unison, as if as one, spinning and flipping through the air like acrobats. Our laughter echoed off the branches, bouncing back and forth between us.

I looked ahead to the nearest tree. When I landed I peered over to the tree across where the figure had landed maybe twenty feet away. Sunlight broke through the surface of the trees, cascading rays across his body. Penetrating eyes stared back at me and flipped my stomach.

He laughed, gleeful. "Hi."

"Hi." I smiled, catching my breath.

"You're doing really well," he complimented.

I slanted my eyebrows together, perplexed. "Thanks?" I chuckled.

"Never seen anyone catch on so quickly."

"Catch on to what?"

He spoke, but whatever he said was muffled.

"What?"

He repeated himself, but his words as well as the scene encircling us was taken away by the wind. Beneath me the branch vanished and the forest fizzled away, plummeting me to the woodland soil.

I jolted awake.

THREE

What if I was going mental? I felt it constantly now. It was no longer a lost whisper. It was urgent, persistent. Wednesday morning I woke up and the pull was so strong it nearly shoved me to my window to be closer to the woods. I wasn't sure what I expected to see. It wasn't as if I could see anything beyond the barrier at the end of our property, but it was beginning to frighten me. It didn't seem like something I could hide from. I couldn't bury it deep down inside of me anymore and pretend it was normal to have a persistent urge to be in the forest.

For the first time this year I saw Cameron by our lockers alone. I didn't know how to talk to him about it without sounding paranoid or insane, but he was the only one I knew I could talk to. He was the only one I wanted to talk to.

"Hey, Cam."

"Callie!" He reached out and snatched me into his arms. "How's my number one?" I hated the butterflies for breaking loose and frantically flying in my stomach when I was in his arms.

Was I really still his number one? It didn't feel much like it anymore. "I don't really think you can call me that anymore, deserter," I said, stepping out of his arms, but not in a way that would imply how jealous I was.

"Oh, whatever. Isla knows how our relationship is."

Maybe, but… "Do *you*?" I smirked.

"Cal, I'm sensing a hint of neglect?" He said it teasingly, but I knew he knew I was serious. He might have been oblivious at times, but he wasn't insensitive.

I simply eyed him and that was all it took.

"I know. I miss us too. But Isla is important to me too now." He leaned down and kissed the top of my head, like I was his little sister. "We'll get together next week. Isla has been planning this fundraiser with her mom and it takes place next Wednesday. I'll make time for us. Besides you know how much I love hanging out with a bunch of the PAT moms or whatever they're called."

I laughed. "PTA."

"Yeah. That's what I said."

Please just tell me I'm imagining things and that there is nothing lurking in the trees behind my house.

"You promise we'll hang out?" *Will you tell me I'm not going crazy and that I'm not being lured into the forest by some supernatural force?*

"Cross my heart," he said.

"Cool."

"C'mon. I'll walk you to class." He draped his arm over my shoulder. Instantly I felt safe again.

"Thanks." *But, seriously. What if someone is stalking me?*

My paranoid insecurities could wait. This was the most attention I'd received from him since the beginning of summer.

29

Why taint it with paranoia and make him worry? Or worse… tell me I really was crazy.

Even if I was.

"Have you ever had a flying dream?" I asked Lia, crossing my legs Indian style on the lawn at lunch on Friday.

"Yes!" Lia clapped her hands together. "I love those dreams! Did you have one last night?"

"Yeah, I've never had one before." And it felt natural. *Weird, right?*

"Those ones are so much better than naked dreams."

I cringed and laughed. "You have naked dreams?"

"You've never had one? They are mortifying!" she squawked. "In my naked dreams I always find myself walking down the halls at school, pant-less. Everyone stares, but no one says a thing or helps. They just watch as I walk by trying to cover my goods. It's so much worse than being topless. At least when you're topless you only have one area to cover."

"Wow." I chuckled.

"Be grateful for the flying dreams."

"Someone mention naked dreams?" Cam snuck up behind us, peering between our shoulders.

"Cameron," I heard Isla playfully scold.

"What?" he asked, chuckling. "I love those dreams."

"You would," I said. The tugging suddenly hit me at full force. I arched my back, pretending to stretch and breathed deeply. I turned back to Lia for a distraction as Isla and Cameron got comfortably settled next to us. "How's your brother liking Rome?"

"Apparently it's amazing," Lia sighed. "He says studying abroad is like nothing else. I'm so jealous."

"How's your... your mom handling Matt being gone?" I cleared my throat, to hide my stutter.

She rolled her eyes. "It's like he died. I swear she cries herself to sleep every night. You would think she thinks he'll never come back. He'll be back to visit for Christmas and in the meantime I get the house to myself." Lia smirked, but I knew she missed him. She put up a good front, but when Matt was home he was *her* other half. Most of the time I felt like the third wheel around them, like I'm sure she felt like the third wheel around Cameron and me. Without Matt and Came it felt weird to just be Lia and Callie. There used to always be one of the guys with us at all times.

"The ambition you guys have in your family," Cameron mumbled. "How many Ivy Leagues are you going to apply to?"

Lia shrugged. "All of them, of course."

"Of course," I mouthed to Cam, but smiled at her, admiring her for being unafraid to take what she wanted.

I wiped the pearls of sweat that accumulated on my forehead. The pulsing was taking a toll. There was only one more class for me to get through. *I can do this. I can do this. I can do this.*

"You okay, Callie?" Lia asked.

I smiled again when I looked at her to cover up my discomfort. "Yeah. I'm just really hot." I twisted the cap of my water and took a large gulp, savoring the cool liquid trailing down my throat.

"Huh. I thought it was a nice day today," she said.

"It *is* a nice day," Cameron added, backing Lia. "You feeling sick, Cal?"

"Maybe just a little lightheaded. I'm going to head inside.

The bell's going to ring soon anyway." I snatched my bag. "I'll see you guys later. Lia, I'll see you tonight."

She looked at me with scrunched eyes, not knowing what to make of me. I didn't know what to make of me. How could I even begin to explain it to them?

"Tonight," she confirmed.

"Rest up, Cal," Cameron called and I waved, retreating as fast as I could without making a bigger scene.

"Dad?" I hollered as I walked in the door after school. There was no answer. He must have either been on a job or running errands. The pulsing subsided a little when I pulled into the driveway. The closer I was to home, the easier it was to breathe. It wasn't gone completely though. Not even close.

I plopped on the couch to watch some *brain rotting* TV—as my dad liked to call it—for a cool down before Lia showed up later on to go out. Some romantic comedy was playing that she was dying to see. Girl bonding time—I guessed I could use a little more of it. As hard as it was to get through my last class, I didn't know how I could possibly be normal around Lia tonight.

There really wasn't anything remotely entertaining on. I flipped through the channels, passing over all things boring, trashy, or sporty, which as it turned out was on every channel.

Wait. It was Friday. Dad was going to be building the fence. He was probably out getting the supplies now.

Suddenly, my attention was directed to the yanking in my heart and I couldn't suppress any longer. I shook it off and took a deep breath. I was closer to the grove now. Maybe it would go away. I found the movie channels—sci-fi, western, love, classics…

Nope. The feeling wouldn't subside; it was getting more and more powerful. The overwhelming flame flickered in my chest, heaving me off the couch. I let it push me toward the sliding glass door that faced the woods then shook my head, knowing where my body wanted to go. Trying to conquer the unpleasant feeling overpowering me, I pushed back. *I don't want to go out there*, I told myself. I could beat this. But the pull was too strong to resist it anymore. The greenery swayed back and forth, needing me to be among it, craving for me to be a part of it.

As soon as I slid open the door and walked out, fresh air wafted in, filling my lungs with sweetness. As I reached the forest's edge, my eyes trailed the dark brown columns nearly creating their own fence. *What did we need a fence for?*

I took my first step over the line, gazing through the feathery ferns and felt instant peace. I smiled to myself and walked in further. A butterfly flew in front of my face, its wings a lively blue, fluttering gently, idling in front of my eyes. It was as if it was greeting me, welcoming me into its homeland. After saying hello, it simply flitted away.

I wasn't sure what I was so worried about. It was peaceful in here. Calming. *What could possibly live in here that could harm me?*

The deeper I trekked into the forest, the greener it was. The tree trunks were cloaked in twirling vines and rich green moss. Thick fallen logs turned into hillsides as moss and ground cover crept over them, bringing the dead wood to life once more. The trickle of a stream babbled to my right. It didn't bother me that I didn't know how far I had gone into the canopy of trees. I felt at home.

Without warning a figure flipped down, landing perfectly in front of me.

Startled, I let out a shriek and stumbled back nearly falling to the ground, but he caught my arms easily, steadying me then releasing me just at swiftly.

"Watch your step," he said melodically.

What the...

When I took in his appearance my jaw dropped as my eyes flew wide open to take in every inch of him. His eyes were unreal, a mix between violet and blue, unlike anything I'd ever seen in my life. They were deep blue, yet reflected back in an even deeper purple and bright. His dark chocolaty locks curled right above his eyes, framing them.

Where had he come from?

"You can see me, can't you?" His voice was velvety smooth. Too alluring to be natural. Too silky to be human.

I could only nod. He stood there in all his olive skinned glory with only a pair of dark brown homemade cut offs and a vine twining up one of his sinewy arms. A black band held a small sharp weapon at his hip. *Was this guy for real?*

"That's not possible," he said, folding his arms across his lean chest. Every time he spoke my stomach tingled.

"Well, apparently it is," I said quietly, wanting to flee. I wasn't quite sure why, but a feeling inside of me told me to stay put.

"But you're still human." He started to move toward me, but I stepped back. Being close to him couldn't be smart.

"Typically, that's what we're called," I said skeptically, eyeing him.

His gaze deepened, his indigo eyes staring into my soul. Aside from the color there was something unusual about his eyes. They were... bigger. Not disturbingly large, but definitely not as small as they should be. I took another step back, losing any confidence I gained by passing the property line. This was a bad idea.

"Don't go," he nearly pleaded, speedily reaching his hand out to me. The earnestness in his voice stopped me. "Stay." His voice changed. "I won't hurt you." He was more at ease, alluring. My uncertainty must have been apparent because he tacked on, "Please?" which didn't seem like a word he knew how to use.

"Give me one reason to stay." *Under the shelter of these trees— secluded—with a stranger. An all too fascinating stranger.*

"It doesn't make any sense." The strange boy didn't answer my question. I suppose he wasn't really a boy. He appeared to be a few years older than I was—two or three years, maybe—but not quite a man.

I wanted to laugh. What didn't make any sense was a guy without a shirt, dressed in tattered cut offs with vines spiraling up his arm like some wild man, standing in my backyard. I looked back to a wall of trees and vegetation. I couldn't technically call this my backyard anymore. The reassuring sight of my house was nowhere.

"What are you doing out here?" I asked.

"I should ask you the same thing." He cocked one side of his mouth up in a half-smirk. "Your father is right. You never know what's lurking in these woods."

My stomach churned. How long had he been here... watching me? He took a few steps toward me into a spot where the sun streamed through the full branches, casting light across his perfectly sculpted face. A couple things clenched my breath. One, he was striking, more so than the shadows gave him credit for. His rich indigo eyes were even more vibrantly intense, beautifully peculiar under the glow of sunlight. I couldn't find the words. And two... two was his ears. They were... pointed.

"What *are* you?" I gaped.

Why was I still here?

"Again. I'm the one who should be asking you that question." He was smiling now, overly confident. "You shouldn't be able to see me."

"Of course, I can see you. I'm not blind," I spat.

"You should be." He never took his eyes off of me, certainty in his stance. His toned shoulders pulled back, puffing his muscled chest forward.

"I'm about to start screaming in three seconds if you don't answer my question," I tried to threaten. My backbone was wobbling. I wanted to be strong, but his confidence was unsettling and yet… I wanted to know more. I couldn't break myself away from his hold on me.

He chuckled, unafraid. "Princess," he said, superiority lining his tone. "I don't think you get it. Humans can't see me. If you scream and they come running, they will see you standing alone. I only show myself to those I choose, and if you can see me without my consent, it means there is something not human inside of you."

I'm sorry? There was something not human about *him*. His agile movement. His entrancing eyes. His alluring smile. And those freakishly pointy ears! I was being torn in two directions. One wanted me to run as fast as I could away from the trees, never to return, while the other tied me to him and the nature surrounding us.

"Please," I asked. "What are you?"

"You really don't know?" He looked at me with a curiously amused expression that I wanted to smack off his face.

I stared at him with an agitated edge. "If I honestly knew would I really be asking?"

He chortled. "Well, well, well. Feisty. I knew you'd have to be." I didn't reply. I was waiting and I'd wait all day if that's what it took. He sighed when he realized I wasn't as amused as he was. "A faery. I'm a faery," he said, deadpan.

FOUR

If you're a faery then I'm the Easter bunny." I laughed without humor.

He shook his head and swatted his hand at me. "Don't be absurd. Bunnies are furry and they hop about. You seem to walk perfectly fine."

I rolled my eyes. This guy belonged in a mental institution. "Shouldn't you be like three inches tall?"

"I'm afraid you are mixing faeries with pixies. They're the little annoying ones that buzz in your ears and spread pollen on the flowers."

"I think you are mixing pixies with bees," I stated candidly.

He puckered his lips and thought for a moment. "Nope. Pretty sure it's pixies."

Okay. If we were going to play this game, I could play along. I knew how to play nicely. Sort of. "All right, wild-man-in-my-backyard, if you're a faery where are your wings?"

He walked casually around me, studying me as if I was the

riddle to be deciphered. Though I knew I should be scared, I wasn't. I was curious and confused, maybe a little apprehensive, but he didn't seem dangerous. That nervous intuitive sensation in the pit of my stomach at the presence of danger didn't surface.

"What kind of a man would I be if I had wings? Now that's just silly." He grunted. His light steps circled me, but he kept a safe distance, careful not to startle me.

I folded my arms across my chest, following his every move. "Can you really call yourself a man if you're a faery?"

His electrifying eyes grew puzzled, but the corner of his mouth turned up, smirking again. "I think you're trying to insult me."

I stared him down and nodded. I didn't know what was keeping me here. My instincts should send me running back to safety, and yet there was nothing that could move me from this spot, away from this mind-boggling whatever-he-was.

"Well, Princess," he said, keeping his tone playful. "It turns out you're a faery too, so I suggest you hold off with the insults. You and I are one and the same."

I laughed. I didn't know how it came so easily when he left me feeling so uneasy, but in that moment, even with his arrogance, I felt more self-assured. *Where is his logic?* "If I'm a faery, where are my pointy ears and wings?"

His hand brushed over his chin, the leaves on his wrist quietly flickering as he mulled over my question. "I've been wondering the same thing. You look so naked without your wings."

I shifted my arms back across my chest, feeling exposed. I wasn't a faery. There was no such thing as faeries. And yet, here was a guy who although a little crazy, definitely wasn't human. He carried himself too effortlessly and swiftly. He had

39

unnaturally quick reflexes. And those eyes were unlike any human I'd ever seen.

"The wings are normally the most beautiful part of the fae women. You're probably just a late bloomer." His scrutiny continued as if I was an equation that needed to be solved.

"I can't possibly be a faery. And you can't either. So you have freaky pointy ears. Those could have been surgically altered." Even as I said it I knew it sounded ridiculous, but what other explanation could there be? Surely, it couldn't be his answer.

He stopped and positioned himself easily against a tree, one leg propped up against the trunk. "You think a human would want to surgically alter their ears to look like a faery?" He was trying to rattle me, a teasing smile played on his mouth.

"People do some extreme stuff to their bodies all the time. I wouldn't put it past them," I said. "So, I guess that makes me a regular old human with normal ears and all."

He shook his head at me as if he pitied me, like *I* was being naïve.

"Stop looking at me like that," I demanded.

He looked away instantly, but gradually recovered and said, "You give me no choice."

My stomach coiled.

Before I realized what I was doing, I was standing face to face with the wild boy. I felt this irresistible need to be close to him, to touch him, to smell him. He smelled woodsy, but not in a negative way. It was a citrusy musk, crisp. My heart pounded rapidly in my chest for this boy in front of me. Time stood still. My life paused and everything fell away, but him. *What is happening to me?* My hand reached out to touch his chiseled face. I wanted to run my fingers down his cheek, to feel the warmth of his pulse under his skin. *What harm could that do?*

He smiled mischievously. "Do you believe me now?"

My mind clicked back into play and I was myself again. I stumbled back, righting my footing so I wouldn't fall. "What did you just do to me?"

"It's called Enticement. All faeries can do it," he baited. His smirk never left his face, clearly pleased with his magical luring ability.

"How did you… you… you just crawled into my head? You were in my head?" I asked in disbelief.

"It's a simple trick," he said, nearly sounding apologetic. "No harm done. It's not like I took your memories."

"Don't you ever do that again! My mind is all I can call my own. That should only ever be under *my* control."

"As you wish, Princess." He nodded, a glint of teasing in his eyes.

"Would you stop calling me that?"

He was so smug. It unnerved me. I wanted to strangle this cocky, wild, *beautiful* boy!

"Kai, leave her alone." The voice came from up in the trees. I spun around, searching the limbs above us, but either he was camouflaged or I was blind. Then another figure dropped in front of me. I stumbled backward.

They just kept falling out of the trees! Like acorns!

"I apologize for the fright I might have caused you. Please forgive me."

The fright?

He was undeniably handsome as well. A dark green vine wrapped up his left arm, but he also had something strapped around his bare tan shoulder. A bow and some wooden arrows? And his eyes were richly blue-green, almost aquamarine. How

41

were these eye colors possible? Colored contacts? "You…
you…" His ears were the same as the other one.

"You must forgive us both. Kai was just leaving." He cut
his gaze to the one he called Kai.

"I'm perfectly fine right here actually," Kai chimed, still
casually propped against the tree, scanning me up and down. He
looked at me like no one had ever looked at me before, like I was
the star exhibit at the zoo.

"Are you a…" I broke off, my gaze flitting from boy to
boy.

"A faery as well? I'm afraid so. We're not supposed to toy
with humans. We'll let you be now." He half-turned his back to
me, gesturing for Kai to walk with him, while still keeping an eye
on me, most likely guarding his back. He didn't seem to trust me.
He took one look at Kai and instantly gazed back at me.

I didn't move. There were now *two* wild boys? How many
more were there? What was this? Sherwood Forest? Why did
they have to be shirtless? They radiated this bohemian, carefree
aura. They were unafraid. Though it was *my* backyard, this was
their territory. I was the trespasser. Did they live in this forest? It
was preserved. How could that be possible?

"Human. He said I wasn't human." I pointed accusingly at
the infuriating one. "Which I know is just ridiculous. Faeries
don't exist. I am human. No pointy ears. No wings. No crazy
vines."

He exhaled, running a hand down his face as if it would
wipe away the frustration. "Calliope, will you please just go back
home?"

"How… how?" I stammered, my mind rolling in
summersaults. "How did you know my name?"

Without answering me, he turned. "Now look what you've

42

done?" He snapped at Kai, throwing his muscled arms up in the air. "You couldn't just leave her alone. You had to find out what was so different about her. You couldn't just walk away."

"You know me. Always up to no good. But, I'm afraid you dug that hole for yourself, Declan." Kai chuckled, looking too pleased.

The one who knew my name, Declan, turned back to me. "I'm sorry. I didn't mean to alarm you. Just go back home and forget you ever met us. I can see this was all a mistake. I should have stayed out of it."

"But—"

He eyed me seriously, almost endearingly. "If you know what's good for you, you'll go back. And stay away from the forest. You're not safe here."

"Declan," Kai cleared his throat. "If I may." Declan begrudgingly twisted his head back to see Kai who was now twirling a twig between his fingers. "She's not just some human, not that she ever was," he said under his breath. "I didn't have to reveal myself. She saw me without my consent."

Declan sighed. I wasn't sure if it was out of agitation or relief. "I realize that," he said.

"Realize what?" I asked.

"You started it now," Kai said wryly. It was like his only purpose for sticking around was to irk Declan and rile me up.

Declan ignored Kai. "What did Kai say to you, Calliope?"

I shook my head fervently. "You never answered my question. How do you know my name?"

He ignored me again and spun back to Kai. "Will you just tell her to go back home? She's obviously not going to listen to me."

"And what makes you think she'll listen to me? We've been

43

arguing since the moment she saw me." Kai chuckled and crossed his arms over his pecs. His amusement was unraveling what little composure I had left.

"Hey," I called out, but no one turned my way. I should've just gone home, but I was in too deep now. I was too involved in their little world. Even with them occupied, they obviously knew where I lived so it wasn't as if I was going to be able to escape them. They kept talking over each other. I couldn't really decipher the problem they were trying to work out.

"I realize that," Declan was saying. "It doesn't mean we should be pursuing it. She's safer away from here, safer not knowing we exist."

"I know, but Declan, someone should protect her right?"

"Excuse me," I interjected more firmly.

Declan spoke over me, hardly batting an eyelash at me. "That's what I've been doing for that last five years. Then you come along and everything I've worked for is ruined. I watched from a safe distance. I wasn't completely careless."

Five years?

"It's not as if she's not going to realize it sooner or later," Kai said. "At least this way she'll have someone to go to if she has questions. And she *will* have questions."

"Hey!" I screamed now.

Their heads finally darted my way, at attention. *That was more like it.*

I pointed at Declan. "You are going to tell me how you know my name," I commanded. "And you," I pointed at Kai, "are going to leave me alone."

Kai folded his arms and sat down Indian style against a fuzzy emerald boulder, seemingly unfazed. Uneasily, Declan shifted his stance as if he was a young boy who'd been scolded by his mother.

"Talk," I demanded.

He moved toward me. "I've known you were different for quite some time," he said. "I've been around." His steps were hesitant as they neared me, measuring my range of comfort. "I know your name because I've heard your parents call out to you while you were outside."

"Why were you lurking in my trees in the first place?" I kept alert, watching his light footsteps glide back and forth as he tread through the small clearing.

He sighed. "I'm a faery. I live in the forest. You've been able to hear me for a couple years, but never see me. A twig snap or branch creaking?" He pointed to himself. "I stayed around because I wanted to know the answers."

"And?" I questioned.

He was mere inches away from me now, seeming to guard what he said to me. "You're a faery and that's all you have to know." His aqua eyes searched my face for my reaction.

How was it that if I was truly something mystical I hadn't noticed anything particularly different about myself up until now? If, in fact, these two wild boys weren't psychotic escapees from the nearest insane asylum, why did I feel just like a regular teenager? As bothersome as a mosquito bite, the unnatural pulsing to be in the forest nagged at the back of my mind, reminding me I was disregarding one slight fact. I *did* know something was different. But being a faery? That was a little farfetched. Yes, I knew there was more to life than this. But *this*?

"But I don't have the same features as you," I reiterated. It seemed important to emphasize that I didn't resemble these half-naked men. Last time I checked my features were all very much human.

"That will come," he said easily. "Especially now that you've come in contact with us. The faery inside of you will start to wake up."

"You're insane." I shook my head and stepped away, coming to my senses.

"Call me what you want, but the truth is what it is. The sooner you accept it, the easier this will all be. You can't deny the blood that runs through you," Declan said.

"Faeries don't actually exist. So you have pointy ears and unnatural eye color and he can seduce people or whatever, there's obviously a logical explanation for it all." The evidence was beginning to add up in my head as I prattled off the facts and though they were unreal, they made strange sense.

"I'm not the one who should be answering these questions," Declan said, looking uncomfortable.

I chuckled humorlessly. "If not you, then who? I don't recall meeting any faeries in the past."

He exhaled and lowered his eyes, but didn't answer me.

"Who am I supposed to ask? Please enlighten me," I pressed again, feeling more frustrated than ever. I was minding my own business when I had wandered in here. They were the ones to disturb me and bombard me with illogical information. I wasn't about to let these two off the hook or get the run around. I wanted answers. *Reasonable* answers.

Declan's face grimaced, almost looking pained as if he *had* to answer me. He swallowed and said, "Finnian… your father."

"Why would my dad know anything about you?"

"Because he used to be one of us," Declan sighed.

I shook my head fervently. "You are both *lunatics*."

"Ask him yourself," Kai said, inching closer to me and pointing towards my house. "He won't lie to you. He can't.

There's no way around it now. He was once a faerie just like us. Just like you are now."

My mind clouded and everything started to blur. Their two figures wavered back and forth in front of me, overlapping.

"Now you've really done it."

"Me? I had to answer her. I didn't have a choice. You're the one who ran with my answer. Besides, you even said she was going to realize it sooner or later."

I blinked, attempting to clear my vision, trying to put one foot in front of the other. I wanted to laugh, but I don't think that was the noise that came from my mouth.

"Is she okay?"

"Does she look okay to you?"

The voices fought back and forth, but none of it made sense to me. How did my father have anything to do with this? What could he possibly know about faeries?

"Maybe you should help her sit down."

"I don't think she wants me to touch her."

The trees wavered and then stopped spinning, and I gained my balance.

"There she goes," a voice echoed.

My feet sped over the weaving ground cover, kicking up dead wet leaves as I ran. I heard my name being called over and over, but I didn't turn back. I couldn't.

FIVE

When the need to reach a destination becomes urgent, every other thought escapes you. The destination becomes like a heartbeat repeated over and over again in your mind, rhythmic and persistent.

Dad. Dad. Dad. Dad. Dad.

"Dad?" I hollered as soon as I opened the sliding glass door. "Dad?" I called louder, demanding an answer back, praying he was home.

He came rushing in from the garage, his face coated with worry, a hammer and nail in hand. "What is it, honey? Are you okay?" He must have been building the fence. I'd forgotten all about that.

It hadn't occurred to me how I was supposed to start this conversation. Could I really sit here and accuse him of not telling me about the existence of faeries? Those two guys were probably rolling on the ground now, laughing about the prank they just pulled, the trouble they couldn't help but stir up. But the second one, Declan, he seemed so earnest. He seemed like the type of person I wanted to trust.

"Umm…" I breathed, trying to steady my voice.

"Calliope, are you hurt?"

I shook my head. I had frightened him. Probably not the best way to start this conversation. But really… was there even a good way to start this conversation? "Can I ask you a question?"

He nodded, his green eyes creased with worry.

"Umm…what do you know about faeries?" I asked the question as seriously as I could, but my breathing hadn't slowed down yet. His immediate look of alarm told me all I really needed to know. "Dad," I prompted him to answer, but he stayed silent. "Dad, are you okay?"

"Why do you want to know about faeries, Calliope?" he asked hesitantly. His eyes tensed.

I couldn't believe I was about to ask this question. It was something you asked your parents when you were five years old and questioned every little thing in life, like Santa Claus or the Tooth Fairy. No grown teenager in his or her right mind would question the existence of mythical creatures. "Do they…" I paused. "I mean… uhh…" A short huff of air choked out from my lips. "Do faeries exist?"

He sighed heavily, but didn't answer. His refusal to speak provoked me to further my investigation. *It couldn't be…*

"Dad," I chuckled to myself, still baffled that I was gaining the nerve to ask. He was going to question my sanity. "Are you… are you a… faery?" The words came out as seriously and as cautiously as I could make them. I wanted him to take me seriously, though I could hardly take myself seriously.

"Calliope, where would you get an idea like that?" His tone was angry, but it wasn't aimed at me. He was scared.

"Are you?" I asked quietly, sincerely, though I could barely get the words out of my mouth.

"No." He released a breath of air, placing his fingers over his temples and rubbing like he wished a genie could appear and take away this crazy questioning. Relief washed over me. I laughed in my head and cheered, *I'm not crazy! Just gullible!* He was going to laugh at me now, wasn't he? Instead he turned my world upside down. "But I was… a long time ago."

My lungs choked me. "Was? How—When—How is that— Does Mom know?"

He chuckled, breaking the thick air in the space between us. "Of course she knows," he said.

It didn't make sense. "What do you mean that you used to be? How are you not anymore? How is it *possible?*"

He clenched his lips, either not wanting to answer me or contemplating how to go about explaining his involvement with fairytale beings. "I was stripped of being a faery when I chose to live here. I had to make the transformation from faery to human. By willingly choosing to leave behind that world, I lost my abilities. As you have probably noticed, my ears are just that of a human. I don't have the Sight anymore. I can't see the faery world."

I swallowed. It was true. Those wild boys in my backyard were for real. They were faeries. But I needed the confirmation to come from him. I needed to ask him point blank. "It's true. Faeries are real?"

He nodded slowly, steadily, gauging how I was going to handle the information.

I attempted to measure my breathing, keeping it stable so I wouldn't hyperventilate.

"No. No. I don't believe you. You're just as crazy as they

were." A flash of alarm struck his eyes and I realized my careless mistake. I sucked in a breath and bit my lip nervously.

"Crazy as who? Where did this idea even come from?" The shock written across his face seemed to say he just realized he'd spilled his deepest darkest secret and he didn't even know why.

How was I supposed to answer him? He would kill me if he knew that I had gone that far into the woods. He would be even more furious that I had run into two grown boys and didn't go running for my life the instant they spoke to me. Granted, they didn't look much older than me, but I had carried on a full-blown conversation with them both. And they had actually been armed.

I couldn't speak.

He set his eyes sternly on me. "The idea of being a faery didn't come out of nowhere, Calliope." His jaw clenched as he struggled to control his anger. "Who put the idea of faeries in your head?"

I hadn't thought that one through very well. I couldn't lie to him or keep the truth from him either. What was the point now? If they had known my father, he might have known them as well. And maybe… just maybe he wouldn't completely fly off the handle. "These guys named Kai and Declan."

Dad swiped a hand down his face and looked back at me. "You went deep into the forest, didn't you?"

I swallowed and nodded reluctantly.

"Of course those two would be behind this," he muttered through deep breaths. Before I probably wouldn't have been able to understand him, but my ears were becoming keener on sound. It's not like I could hear the flap of butterfly wings in the distance, but I knew he had barely let those words out of his mouth. A normal person wouldn't have been able to understand him. "How did you see them? Did they just appear or…?"

I recalled Kai's confusion. "Kai said I could see him without his consent."

My father's breath hitched slightly.

I had to know. The question alone made me feel stupid to ask, but it was necessary. I had to know what I was. "Dad, am *I* a faery?"

His cloudy green eyes held concern, the crinkles around them squinting. He didn't know. He really wasn't sure. "Why do you think you're a faery, Calliope?"

I swallowed. "I hear things in the trees. All the time. I'm not sure what it is I hear, but it's not just the birds and the wind. And it's not like what everyone hears. It feels like my ears are extra sensitive to every sound. And I feel this… pull—this yearning to be a part of the forest. It's been happening for years now. I try fighting it, but it keeps bringing me back to the trees. It's become stronger and stronger every day. If I was… normal, like every other human—" I swallowed. "I don't feel normal anymore."

My dad sighed and closed his eyes. I did my best to wait patiently, but this wasn't like just waiting for an answer to go to the movies or to hang out with Lia or Cam.

"Am I?" I repeated.

"Sit down, honey," Dad directed, helping me into a seat at the kitchen table where he sat across from me.

He pressed his lips together, watching me, his arms folded across his chest in near defiance. His eyes closed for a moment and I tried to calm my breathing and appear comfortable with the fact that my dad was about to change everything I ever knew. When his eyes opened back up to me, they glistened. My father's eyes had always been a beautiful green, but now that I knew why, they shined a faintly faded chartreuse color, completely inhuman.

He really had been one of them.

"It appears to me that the changes are starting to take place. So, yes, Calliope," he said. "You are a faery."

I gasped. "How is it possible? You lost your abilities or whatever. And I don't have any of the physical features," I pressed.

"They still might come," he said, anxious. I'd never seen my father physically afraid before. "They come with age. I actually wasn't sure if they would ever come. You are past the normal age of faery maturity, so it's possible that they still might not come. Or you may simply be a late bloomer."

Kai's term came rushing back. The walls of my world had come tumbling down. "What do you mean late bloomer?"

"Faeries get their ears and wings during their adolescent years, which is similar to puberty for humans when you get your," he cleared his throat and tried gesturing to me.

"Dad," I scolded.

"Well... it's sort of a rite of passage," he said. "Your mother and I thought you were out of the woods. But there really is no telling. You don't age like a faery, but you don't age quite like a human. You are in between."

"So I'm half faery."

He heaved out a deep breath. I could tell by the way his eyes grew sharp and weary that his head hurt. "What you are, Calliope... it shouldn't be." He scratched his head the way he did when he was unsure of answers, but wanted to give some sort of information. "I had assumed you would be immune, but the fae blood must still run inside of me. I guess I was wrong. I had a feeling I was going to be wrong."

"You think?" I nearly shouted.

"Please don't be upset, Calliope. There was no way of

knowing this." He sunk further in his seat, troubled. A million emotions passed across his eyes as he sat there, thinking. I wanted to crawl inside his head and know everything he was thinking, everything he was holding back.

I wanted to run. I wanted to get away, to be far from the forest, far from my father, far from my thoughts. I just wanted to be me and nothing else.

"I need some air."

He didn't stop me as I bolted for the garage door and headed for my car. I pulled the top down and started the engine, backing out of the driveway.

The world passed by me as I drove. Wind blew through my hair and flapped in my ears. Where was I even going? I couldn't go to Cameron and I couldn't go to Lia. What would I even say to them? *Hey, guess what? I'm a faery!* I didn't want to go back to the trees with the bickering twins. So I just drove in circles. For hours.

Have you ever had the fear of drowning? I haven't, but I have a feeling it would feel a lot like this. My lungs were closing in, making it hard for me to breathe while my mind was thrashing about trying to keep afloat. On the outside I might have looked calm, probably scary calm like the kind before the storm, but inside I was like a loose cannon ready to blow at any minute. I only required a trigger.

I drove without direction until it was dark out. When I got back home it was after seven and my mom still wasn't home. All of my questions were starting to come to a head like lava in a volcano and if I didn't ask them, I was going to erupt.

I found my dad in the same place I left him, blank stare plastered to his face as he looked out the windows from the kitchen.

"This other world," I said softly, getting his attention. "Your faery world. How long ago did you leave?"

He peered over at me and guarded his words. "When I met your mother, over twenty years ago."

"So you left to be with Mom?" As surreal as it was, it was romantic.

He nodded.

I had so many questions. Everything I wanted to say, everything I wanted to ask jumbled all together, making it impossible to form a logical question.

"How can faeries do what you did? Faeries can simply choose to be human?"

He eyed me, choosing his words carefully. "Under special circumstances," he said in all seriousness. "It's not easy. It's not as if one day a faery can just say, let's be humans now. Most faeries don't want anything to do with the human world. Some faeries find the idea of even becoming a human blasphemous."

I took a deep breath. "What does all of this mean? If I'm a faery, what will become of me?"

My dad patted the seat beside him at the table. Once I was situated, he folded his hands, leaning his mouth against them, contemplating my question. "We'll wait and see."

"Wait," I said. "Wait for what? For me to turn into a freak show? Will I have to live in that world? The faery world?"

"Faylinn."

"What?"

"Our kingdom, our homeland, is called Faylinn," he said.

Anger boiled under my skin when the thought of being lied to my whole life set in. "How could you keep all of this from me?"

"We are humans, Calliope," he said. "Why would I tell you

about Faylinn if I didn't have to? When was I supposed to tell you? You wouldn't have believed me even if I tried. I have no proof."

"Oh, I don't know." *I really didn't.* "Maybe…"

"I didn't know what kind of an affect it would have on you. And obviously it wouldn't have been pleasant no matter the timing." He reached out and set his hand over mine on the table. "The forest calls to you as you call to it, and you can't fight who you are anymore."

My brow ruffled in confusion. "What?"

"The faery world is starting to beckon for you," he said gently. "That feeling you were trying to fight. Faylinn is calling for you to go home." I didn't want to believe him. Logic was in the boxing ring fighting against Dad's confirmation. "I've been watching you watch the trees. I can see the yearning in your eyes. I was afraid that's what it was, but I didn't want to alarm you by forcing you to stay away from it. That's why I figured a fence would help."

Humorless laughter bubbled to the surface. "I can't be a part of that world, Dad. I'm a human. I live in the human world beside other human beings, my friends, you and Mom. I refuse to believe that I'm a fictional being." I wouldn't be freaking out right now if I didn't really believe it could be true, but I was so mixed up in the head that I didn't know what to believe anymore.

"Faylinn doesn't know that. And we are not fictional. As faeries we are drawn to the forest. We are drawn to our home. Our kingdom."

"Will I have to go?" I asked incredulously. That question instantly became the most urgent.

"I won't make you, if you don't want to."

56

At least that was reassuring. "And there's nothing I can do? Nothing I can do to stop it? I'll turn into a faery?"

"We will have to wait and see. The abilities you have now might be the extent of everything. The Sight, your hearing, the pull. You still may be able to live in this world—not pleasantly mind you, but tolerably. You will feel that constant need to be out there. Every day." He pointed to the borderline of trees.

I sighed, trying to alleviate the pressure weighing on my chest. It didn't work. It wasn't just that my world was crumbling down and everything I ever knew to be true was a lie. When the impossible became possible, nothing seemed impossible. Anything was up for grabs. Nothing was for certain. "What are we supposed to tell Mom?"

"Nothing," he decided immediately, leaving no room for argument. "Your mother doesn't have to know anything about this unless it becomes absolutely necessary."

I nodded without question for some reason, wanting to obey him.

"I want you to stay out of the forest, but I know that's not possible or fair of me to demand now." He sat there, searching his thoughts for something… answers… solutions. "And I'd tell you to stay away from all other faeries, but I don't know how possible that is. Declan and Kai," he said. "What did they say to you?"

"Not much. They just kept arguing." He chuckled softly and shook his head as if recalling old friends. "But because I could see them Kai didn't know what to make of me. I don't have my wings or whatever, so he just kept staring."

"Do they know you belong to me?" I nodded. "And they didn't mention anything else?"

I shrugged, going over our conversation in my head. "Just

that Declan has been watching over me for a few years. I've apparently been able to hear them for a while without being able to see them." Which really didn't sit well with me now that I thought about it. What had they seen or heard during all that time?

"So your abilities are coming in gradually," he concluded.

All this time when I heard a random twig snap or a tree branch shake, when I heard low babbling from the trees, it had been them. Through the years of sleepless nights from the subtle unexplainable pulsing, it was Faylinn.

"I'm really a faery," I said it aloud this time, letting it sink in and absorb in my brain.

"You're a faery, Calliope. And with that comes a price."

My stomach twisted. "What more could there be?"

"You can't tell a single soul."

Lia and I met at the theater for her movie after my conversation with my dad, but I wasn't much company. I nearly blew her off and told her I wasn't feeling well, which was the honest truth, but I knew she really wanted to see this movie. During the evening I think she could tell I was a little on edge. Thankfully, she just brushed my behavior off as the blues over Cameron and Isla, which normally would have bothered me. I didn't want to be *that* girl, but it was a better alternative to what was really going on with me.

When I saw Lia was eyeing me as we walked back to our cars, I realized she said something that required a response and I had no idea what it was.

"Huh?"

"Colleges. Applying. Where are you applying?"

"Oh." Of course, it was going to be college application time soon. Was I going to be able to go to college now? "USC, UNC, Clemson," I prattled off some of the universities I'd been thinking about. "I'll apply to a few places in case I don't make it in."

"You'll get into all of them and then you are going to have to make a decision," she stated undoubtedly.

What if in the end the changes became too apparent and I couldn't go to college? I was supposed to get *wings* for crying out loud. How in the world was I supposed to disguise those?

"Yeah," I said, trying to stay focused on the conversation at hand and apparently doing very poorly. "I'll figure that out when the time comes."

"I think you should apply to Princeton and Columbia with me."

I laughed. "Lia, those are colleges you spend your whole life preparing and planning for. I don't have the grades to even be considered. They would laugh in my face."

"Well, it was worth a shot to throw it out there." She threw her arm around me and tugged me to her side. "It would have been so fun to go to college together. Oh. Oh! What if we went and studied abroad with Matt?"

"Lia," I chuckled. "You don't want to study abroad. You want to go to medical school."

She slouched her shoulders. "Well... yeah... it was just a thought. Something we could do together."

"College probably won't be one of those things," I sighed.

I was going to be lucky if I could even go to college.

Becoming a faery changed everything.

SIX

I stepped through the front doors of Walhalla High on Monday morning and felt different instantly. As if a teenage girl needed another reason to feel out of place. It took everything I had Friday night to be normal around Lia. How was I supposed to hide this ginormous elephant that now perched on my shoulders like a parrot? Lia could at least chalk it up to something that was already bugging me, but if Cameron pulled his head out of his butt for more than five minutes to pay attention, he was going to know something was off.

Speaking of the devil, I saw him huddled with Isla by our lockers in a private conversation, their faces so close they might as well be kissing. Like I needed one more thing to distance me from him.

"You look so good today," he murmured.

"You don't look too shabby yourself," Isla giggled.

"I really like this shirt. You should wear it more often."

I realized then that I was going to have to learn to tune out conversations. My hearing was getting too sensitive. The last thing I wanted was to hear every mushy gushy conversation those two had. They could keep those to themselves. *Please, keep them to yourselves.*

As much as I didn't want to tell Cam about me, I felt the same need to tell him. What was the point of a best friend if you couldn't tell him everything? That's what best friends were for. To share your burdens and listen to your dirty little secrets.

Wait. I just had to wait. Maybe nothing would come of it, and I would just have the special ability to see and talk to other faeries. *Faeries.* A disbelieving laugh echoed in my head.

Just wait.

Waiting sucks.

"Hey, Calliope." Isla smiled and lifted her hand in a gentle wave when she saw me approach.

"Hey, you two."

Cameron turned. "Cal, how was your weekend?" he asked.

Oh, you know. I ran into a couple of hot male faeries. Found out that my dad used to be a faery and that I'm half-faery. Nothing too big. Nothing noteworthy, really.

I shrugged. "Not a whole lot. I hung out with Lia and saw a movie. What about you guys?"

"We took the boat to the lake on Saturday. Drank in some rays. Soaked up some sun. Basked in the light," Cam prattled on, closing his locker and tucking a couple of books under his arm.

"You're an idiot," I chuckled. "But it sounds like you guys had fun. A lot more eventful than my weekend." *If only you knew.*

"We need to all hang out sometime," Isla chimed. "We can go out to eat or something." Her smile reached her eyes and they twinkled.

"Good idea, Is." If Cam could find a way to make any name

shorter he would. He might as well have just called her I. As if Isla wasn't a short enough name to say. "It'd be good for you two to get to know each other better," he said.

The three of us. For a whole night together. I could just see it now. Them on one side of the booth, while I sat on the other side. *Alone.*

"How will the checks be divided?" the server will ask. And just to make the distinction even more apparent they'll say, *"We're together."* And I'll say, *"I'm separate."* I was dripping with excitement at the thought.

"What do you say, Callie? You think you're free to go out Saturday night?"

The me on one shoulder said, *"No, just say no, Calliope. Why torment yourself?"*

The me perched on the other said, *"Don't let him see how much it bothers you. It'll only push him farther away. Just go, Calliope!"*

"Saturday. Dinner. You guys name the place," I decided.

"Oh, you should pick, Calliope. What's your favorite?" Isla asked, batting her unfairly long lashes.

"The Green House," Cam said before I could say the same restaurant. "She loves their salad bar."

"Perfect! I love that place, too." Isla smiled at me.

Perfect. I smiled as genuinely as I could muster.

"Are you feeling better today, Cal?" I frowned, trying to place why Cam was concerned about my health. "Friday. You weren't doing so hot," he clarified.

"Oh, yeah. Great." I cleared my throat. "I'm feeling a lot better. Just needed a nap." If only a nap could have cured me.

"Oh, good," Isla sighed. "Cameron was worried about you all weekend."

The first bell rang for school to start. Isla turned to Cam.

"Shall we?" she asked.

I peered over at Cameron who was watching me, and a hint of something in his eyes tweaked my stomach. He gave me a smile from the corner of his mouth before he turned to Isla and accepted her hand. They walked away, leaving me wondering what the crap I had just done. How was I going to pull that night off? I suppose I had a week to prepare.

"What was that all about? Isla was extra bouncy as they walked away," Lia said, her voice sounding over my shoulder.

I breathed out deeply. "We're all going out Saturday night."

"We as in... you, Isla and Cam?" I nodded, shoving my books in my bag. "One big happy family!" she exclaimed.

"Shut up," I mumbled, but put a smile on to let her know I wasn't really mad at her.

We began walking to class when she said, "You don't seem better today."

I looked at her. "What?"

"Friday you seemed off. And today, maybe it's the fact that you just agreed to a night of hell, but you don't seem any better."

I straightened up and plastered on my best *I'm completely normal face*. "I'm feeling good. I'll survive Saturday just fine."

"Sure you will. Because that's the kind of person you are. You'll pull it off without a hitch. And just think... maybe you'll even get another friend out of it. If you spend actual time with Isla maybe you'll decide you actually like her," she said.

"I *do* like her," I countered. "That's the problem. She's actually a decent human being."

"Yeah. It's a real shame when good friends catch a good one."

"Hey," I shot out. "What's that supposed to mean?"

"I'm serious." She held up her hands in surrender. "It's

63

hard. You want so badly to be happy for them because they are happy, but their happiness means they need you less, and it hurts. I get it."

She *did* get it. "Yeah."

The idea of me being a mythical creature took quite a few days to find its way into my brain. It still hadn't truly set in, but it existed in the it's-possible section. I definitely wasn't prepared to venture back out to the wild men before it did. But, now I wanted to know more and I knew my dad and I would just fight back and forth about it. Before when we talked about it, he seemed like he was holding back information. He answered my questions, but he didn't offer anything up freely.

After school I built up the courage. "Declan?" I called out hesitantly as I stepped across the threshold. I thought about calling out to Kai, but he put me too much on edge. "Declan?" I said a little louder.

There wasn't an answer. *What if they were gone?* A sinking feeling washed over me. What if I couldn't ever find them again? I swept aside a few dangling vines and pushed on through the jungle of green. I had gone pretty far in before. Maybe they didn't like loitering on the perimeter.

"Declan?" I hollered this time, being far enough in that neighbors wouldn't question my hollering.

"Hey there, Princess." I spun to see Kai walking out from behind an enormous shrub. "I know you wanted Declan, but you'll have to settle for yours truly instead."

"Oh. Kai." A shiver crawled up my spine. "Where's Declan?" I questioned, forcing myself not to get hypnotized by his luring eyes.

"Back in Faylinn."

"Faylinn," I stated. "So, it's an actual place? It's not just this forest?"

He pounced around the ground, already distracted from our conversation. "You have much to learn, young one."

I begrudging crossed my arms over my chest. "I'm getting a little tired of the nicknames. You obviously know my name. Please call me by it."

He let out a sound of amusement and smiled triumphantly at me before responding. "You're such a faery. It comes out more and more every day."

"What's that supposed to—?"

"Did you get your wings yet?"

"What? No." I shook my head.

"Your ears?" He moved closer to me and lifted his hand up to brush away my hair.

I stepped back. "No," I said, exasperated. Had faeries never heard of personal space?

He frowned at my reaction, but only for a moment, recovering quickly. "Why did you come? You were pretty shaken the last time we spoke. I figured you'd stay far away."

He never answered any of my questions. It was taking everything I had to keep the fight inside of me. I could be mature about this.

"I wanted to know more. I talked to my dad," I revealed.

"And you've come to tell me I was right?" he gloated, smoothly circling me.

"Yeah. Whatever. I'm a... faery, but we won't know the extent of my features until they present themselves. *If* they present themselves."

"So you may never get wings or ears?" His genuine concern laced the tone of his voice. He stopped his agile stride around me, fixing me with a stare that could buckle any female's knees.

"Do I really look that repulsive without wings?"

He cleared his throat. "It simply looks unnatural. Humans are so plain and peculiar looking. But you're not a human so it doesn't mix. My mind isn't comprehending what it's seeing."

"My apologies for being such a riddle to figure out," I said dryly. He ruffled my feathers so easily. Cameron was the only one allowed to do that.

"Why are you apologizing? It's not your fault you're a mutt," he said matter-of-factly, no hint of teasing or lightness in his voice.

I glared at him, holding my ground against his brazen stare then turned and walked away. I didn't come here to be insulted. If Declan wasn't here, I was gone.

"Hey, wait." He appeared in front of me. I still wasn't used to his speed. "Where are you going?" Kai cocked his head to the side, completely unashamed or unaware of his insult.

"Home." I shifted to the side to walk around him.

"Why?" He moved in front of me.

"Why do you care? I'm obviously a burden to you or you wouldn't insist on infuriating me."

"Infuriating," he commented, tilting his head to the other side, studying me. "That's such a big word for such a little girl."

I shouldered passed him. "You've got to be kidding me," I mumbled, walking toward the trees boundary.

"What did I say wrong?" His voice came from where I left him. He almost sounded sincere.

"Really?" I spun around to burn holes in his pretty little face. "Are you dense or simply incapable of being polite?"

He folded his arms over his bare chest and stared unblinkingly, waiting for me to keep talking. He had no manners whatsoever. Did he even have a heart? Did faeries have hearts?

Before I lost my nerve I said, "First, you insult my appearance, then call me a mutt and now I'm apparently stupid. As if I shouldn't know how to use the English language. Call me crazy, but I don't particularly enjoy being insulted."

"I was simply stating facts. I only speak the truth," he said, the corner of his mouth turning up as if he was proud of himself for being honest.

"Yeah, quite bluntly."

"I'm afraid I don't know any other way. Maybe faeries communicate differently than humans." He knew what he was doing. He was trying to be a pain in the butt. This was all a game to him.

"Declan seemed to do perfectly fine a few days ago. A complete gentleman, actually." *If I could call a faery that.*

Kai rolled his eyes. "Yes, perfect Declan. I do strive to be like the perfect Keeper. Only less obsessive." I could hear irritation crawling into his voice.

"I'm sorry?"

"Head on home, Princess." He motioned to the woods edge. "Behind the safety of your walls. Away from a forest filled with the unknown." He turned his back to me and strode away.

Did I miss something? I offended him now? What a girl.

"Maybe you need some wings to go with that attitude, Kai," I shouted out to him. He didn't acknowledge me as he disappeared into the trees.

SEVEN

The wooden swing seat creaked as I sat down and swayed back and forth under the oak in our backyard. I stared out into my new territory, my curiosity like water, drowning me under its influence. My body was numb to everything else but the heartbeat of the trees. I clung a little tighter to the ropes attached to the swing, hoping I could teach myself to control the power, anchor myself and become immune to the pull.

Hands pressed against my back, swinging me higher as my dad's voice broke through the silence behind me. "Remember when we used to come out here and I'd swing you to your heart's content? You'd giggle and smile and—"

"And everything was simple," I finished for him.

He waited and then said quietly, "Yeah."

I let him push me for a little while longer, taking comfort in his silent presence. He'd built this swing when I was ten. I'd begged him almost every day for years to get me this tree swing. Finally on my tenth birthday he nearly had to drag me out of bed to swing me for the first time. Had I known why he was waking me at six in the morning I might have been a little more swayed by the idea. We spent nearly the whole day outside on the swing.

"I don't want you to be mad at me, Calliope," he said after a few minutes.

"I'm not mad at you," I said immediately, and then realized it wasn't completely the truth.

"You haven't spoken to me in days." *I hadn't?* "The silent treatment is getting a little old."

"I wasn't trying to ignore you. I just needed space." I needed time to put all the pieces of my life back together in a different puzzle—a jigsaw puzzle, without the guidance of a picture to go off of.

"How's school?" he asked, changing the subject.

"Small talk? Really?" I chuckled lightly.

He sighed. "Being a faery can't be the only thing we ever talk about now. It's what you are, but it's not everything."

I nodded. Even though it felt like everything now, I knew someday this would be normal. Someday I would wake up and it would be a day just like every other to me. I'd come to terms with my new body.

I let my feet down to stop the swing and then turned to my dad standing with his arms crossed over his chest. "What do you want for dinner?" he asked and I let out a breath of soft amusement. *Someday* this would be normal. I guess I could try to make someday today.

"What about some chicken alfredo?" I suggested, moving beside him.

"That sounds delicious. Why didn't you think of that?" he joked with a small smile.

"Daaad." I nudged him playfully with my shoulder and

walked by his side to the house.

It had been a few days since I let the forest control me. As soon as the urge became too powerful to control, I got in my car and drove away. I never knew my destination. Sometimes I ended up at Cam's house, but I never got the nerve to actually go to his front door. I simply looked at his house, wishing I could just talk to him. But most of the time Isla was there or his car was gone.

He didn't need to declare his love for me. He didn't even need to get rid of Isla. I just wanted someone besides my dad to talk to. Someone that wasn't a part of this new world. Someone who would understand why I was so dang freaked out.

There were times when I ended up at Lia's house. Typically, she was studying or reading, so I'd hop on her bed and click on the TV, if for nothing else but to simply have the noise to drown out my thoughts.

"You all done with your homework tonight?" Lia asked.

"Yup," I lied. I still had a little bit, but I couldn't do it at home and I couldn't tell her that. I guess I could have brought it to her house, but when that pull is tugging at me, nothing logical really crosses my mind.

"Dang my ambition to go to an Ivy League. We have a never-ending pile of homework. I swear I'm never done." She exhaled.

"Oh, but think of the opportunities you'll have because of your determination."

"Yeah, yeah." She nudged me and nestled further into the pillows of her bed beside me. "Matt called home yesterday."

"Yeah? Did he just sit there and rub in how incredible Rome is?"

"Basically."

"Has he gone to the Colosseum yet?"

"I think he did that in the first week."

"Lucky punk."

She peered over at me from her books. "He wanted me to tell you hey and that he misses you."

I nodded. It only took a couple of weeks and my life had flipped to a life so unfamiliar. "I miss him too."

"Me too," she said quietly and nuzzled closer to me, resting her head on my shoulder.

That night I lifted my window open to let in a breeze. It felt so stuffy in the confinement of my little room. I was about to pull the covers over my head to block out the world when I thought I heard my name. I sat up in bed and turned my head to my open window.

"Calliope?" There it was again.

When I got to my window, I lifted it higher and stuck my head out to scan our yard, but there wasn't anyone in sight, only the swing wavering and the leaves rustling.

"Calliope, back here," the voice hissed. It came from the far trees. "There you go," the voice applauded. "Come down." The voice wasn't a shout so I knew my hearing was getting even better.

I wasn't sure why I did it. It could have been anyone out there calling to me. I couldn't really tell whose voice it was, but I had a feeling it was Declan and I wanted to see him again.

71

The floor creaked beneath my feet as I tiptoed to the back door. I waited before going outside to see if one of my parents would wake up, but after a minute there was nothing, so I cracked the door and slipped outside.

When I reached the tree line I didn't have to call out to him. His tall, broad figure appeared and I nearly gasped. I was expecting him, but I wasn't.

"Declan, you scared me."

He chuckled quietly. "I'm sorry. That wasn't my intention."

"What's going on?" I looked him over. His chest wasn't bare anymore, which was only slightly disappointing. It was also relieving that he wore a cream woven top so my heartbeats wouldn't race so swiftly. I hoped that wasn't something they could detect. They weren't vampires. It wasn't as if they could sense the flow of my blood, but who knew?

"I didn't know you came to see us. I thought we truly scared you off, but then tonight Kai mentioned that you came a few days ago and you didn't come back. I wanted to check on you to make sure you were all right." The sincerity in his silky voice was refreshing. I hadn't felt truly cared for in quite some time.

I smiled. "I'm still in one piece. No wings or ears though. Apparently that's just appalling to Kai," I said, shaking my head.

"Oh, don't worry about him," Declan brushed off the comment. "He's like that all the time. You get used to it." His blue-green eyes nearly glowed in the dark.

"I feel like he's someone no one should have to get used to."

Declan chuckled again. It was such a happy sound, but he didn't continue. He seemed content just watching me, the curiosity of the unknown. There were so many things we didn't know about each other and yet, I felt safe. I was outside in the middle of the night, talking to a strange man in my jammies. *I was still in my pajamas.* Shifting, I folded my arms across my tank top, realizing that in a hurry to come outside I hadn't thought to put on a bra to cover myself. The thought instantly made me uncomfortable. I couldn't handle the silence. "Is that all? You were just checking on me?" I prompted.

He shifted from one foot to the other. *Was he nervous?* "Well, yes and... and I wanted to make a meeting time so I didn't miss you the next time you decided to wander in and visit us."

A smile tugged at my mouth. He wanted to see me again. "Well, tomorrow's Friday. I can come after school."

"I'll be in Faylinn again." His shoulders slouched. "What about the next day? Sometime in the afternoon?" he asked, hopeful.

"Okay," I agreed. I was already looking forward to it. *Where did my sudden change in attitude come from?*

"You promise?"

"I promise." I smiled when a pleased grin grew on his face. "I should probably head back to bed. I've got school in the morning."

"I understand. Have a lovely evening, Calliope." He bent his head in a slight bow. "Get some rest."

"Thank you, Declan. I will."

He lifted a hand to wave, but didn't head back into the trees. I scurried away on my tiptoes through the grass in my bare feet. I hadn't even thought about shoes. *Where is my head?* When I reached the sliding door, I turned to wave. He waited by the edge, his tall form shadowed by the trees, until I was safely inside.

73

That night I fell asleep with a smile on my face.

"Are we still on for tomorrow?" Cameron asked as I pulled some books from my locker after school to study over the weekend.

I'd forgotten about our third-wheel date, but I didn't dare let him see that. It wasn't as if I'd made any plans. Well, I did with Declan, but that was earlier. I'd be done with him before it got dark. "Yup. What time am I meeting you?"

"Oh, I'll come get you. You don't have to drive."

Did he honestly not see how awkward that was going to be? Was I really supposed to sit in the backseat while they snuggled up front? I was going to feel more out of place on this third wheel date than I had since I found out about Faylinn. I didn't want him to see my apprehension though, so I agreed.

"Good. This will be fun. Isla's really looking forward to it."

Why? I mustered up my best genuine smile. "Me too."

He nudged my side. "It's okay if you're not, Callie." Though he still had class, he walked me out to my car. "I won't be offended. I'm still making you go, but I won't have my feelings hurt if you don't want to be best friends with Isla."

"What? No. I'm fine. I like Isla," I stumbled over my words. *Why did I stumble?*

He chuckled. "Uh huh… we're best friends, Callie. I read you like the palm of my hand."

I shrugged. *What else could I do?*

I threw my bag in the front seat of my car as I plopped into the driver's side. If he could read me like the palm of his hand then either I hid my feelings for him really well or he didn't reciprocate my feelings and chose to act oblivious. I hoped it was the former.

"I'll see you tomorrow around 6:30ish." He closed my door and leaned through the open window. "Drive safe."

When I looked to him, his face was mere inches from mine, close enough to kiss and for the first time in our years of friendship it became instantly awkward.

"Always," I said as coolly as I could manage, but I didn't turn away. I wouldn't back down.

He blinked. Had I imagined it or had he been thrown by our proximity too? Being close to him always felt natural before, but this time something broke, like the wall of friendship we had been able to uphold all of this time had come crumbling down.

I couldn't do it anymore. I turned back to my steering wheel and twisted my key forward, the engine humming to life.

He cleared his throat, stepping back. "See ya," he said and waved as I drove away.

EIGHT

Saturday morning I woke up and smiled to myself, realizing what day it was. *I get to see Declan today.* I headed to the kitchen for some breakfast before getting ready to meet him. Dad was already at the kitchen table with a newspaper and coffee in hand.

When he saw me he smiled. "Good morning, Calliope."

"Morning, Dad," I breathed. Things thawed out between us since we bonded over the swing. I was grateful for it since he was the only one who knew the truth. The only other person I could rely on.

"How did you sleep last night?"

"Great," I replied as I rummaged through the fridge for breakfast.

He cleared his throat, so I turned to see what he wanted to say. "Have you noticed any…" he broke off and thought about how to phrase his question, but before he could finish Mom walked in.

"Good morning, sunshine!" she sang as she curled her arm

around my waist. "You want me to make you some breakfast?"

"Uh… sure. What are you offering?"

"Well, Dad and I had some waffles earlier if you want the same I still have some batter left over."

"Sounds good to me."

I sat down at the kitchen table and waited until he peered at me over the newspaper. I knew he wanted to ask me if I'd noticed any changes in my appearance so without saying a word, I simply shook my head.

He nodded discreetly and gazed back at the paper.

How was I going to explain where I was going? *Oh, I'm just going to go disappear into the forest for a few hours. Don't worry about me.* No, I had to be secretive about it. I could tell my dad, so at least he knew my whereabouts, but I had to do it when Mom wasn't in earshot.

"No work today?" I asked as I finished my plate and Mom did the dishes.

"I have a few things I need to do from home, but I don't have to go into the office today."

"Well, that's nice," I said. And I did feel that was nice for her, but it was going to make it that much more difficult to get out of the house.

She nodded and smiled. Once she finished the dishes she headed back to their bedroom to work, I presumed.

"I'm going to go see Declan today," I said quietly, wiping my mouth. "I wanted to let you know, so you don't worry about me."

"I don't like it, Calliope." He kept his eyes on his newspaper.

Well, I didn't like that he had kept this gigantic secret for years. *Tough.* "It doesn't matter if you don't like it. After all this time, I deserve more information."

His eyes peeked above the edge of the gray paper. "If you want, I'll tell you what you want to know."

I shook my head. "It's not the same." I knew he would leave stuff out. Declan and Kai were the only ones who had been honest without being haggled. Well, without needing much haggling anyway.

He folded the paper and placed it down on the table while giving me the eye—

that eye parents give when they don't like what they've heard or seen. "So, that's it. You're just going to go hide in the trees all day long? What are those boys even doing so close to here?"

I shrugged. "How am I supposed to know? Are they not allowed to be?"

My dad sighed. "There is no ruling against it if that is what you are asking. I just don't like it. They might have been around all this time, but I never knew and it felt better that way. Ignorance is bliss. I believe that's the human saying. I liked it that way."

I thought *I* was the one who had to come to terms with all of this. "I don't know what you want me to say, Dad. You were the one who was basically telling me I needed to embrace the whole faery thing and now you want to hide it from me all over again."

My dad heaved a sigh as he leaned back in his chair. What did he honestly expect? He knew I couldn't hide from them either. Not anymore.

"It's not that I want to hide it from you. It would simply be easier if you didn't get so involved with them."

"Dad, I've talked to them like once. I'm not running off and

marrying one of them today, just having a simple conversation."
I decided to make nice. "Can I go? Please?"

"Do as you wish. I won't stop you."

I kissed him on the cheek and rinsed off my dish. "I'll be back later. Just tell Mom I went out for some fresh air or something. You've had plenty of practice omitting the truth over the years."

He rolled his eyes, but mustered up a smile to let me know he knew I was only giving him a hard time.

I tried to follow the same trail I took the last couple of times. There was no manmade trail, so I had to follow landmarks that stood out to me before: a moss covered log that looked like an alligator, the tree that looked like it was dancing. The sound of the stream needed to stay at my right.

"Calliope." When I heard my name I spun around to see Declan smiling at me. "You came." He sounded relieved as if he hadn't believed I would actually come.

"Of course I came. I don't back out of promises."

He smiled, disrupting my heartbeat. Very few people had ever caught my attention. Maybe I was oblivious or maybe they simply weren't that interesting. Declan was definitely interesting. Today rather than the bow and arrows slung across his shoulder, he had a thin belt with a sharp off-white dagger attached to his hip. It looked like the tooth of a large animal. The cream top was gone, baring his tanned skin once again. I don't think the fae men knew the kind of effect a topless man could have on a girl. Or maybe the fae women were so used to it that it had little or no affect at all on them.

I noticed a certain body wasn't lingering around and I hated myself for not feeling relief, but disappointment. "You alone today?"

He raised his hands to his hips and scanned the branches above us. "I don't know where Kai is. We don't always have the same schedule. I was getting so used to it only being me until he found his way over a few months back. I'm sure he'll show up when he feels like it."

I nodded, not really sure where to go from here. There were so many questions I wanted to ask, but it felt strange to just dive in.

"Come," he said, pointing to a gigantic rooted tree. "Have a seat." He perched himself on one side, folding his legs under him and offered me the other root for a chair.

I chuckled. He was so nimble, which amused me because it wasn't as if he had the body of a skinny dancer. He was tall and burly. But, I suppose if they lived in trees they would have to learn to adapt to their surroundings. *Did they live in the trees?*

"What?" he asked, perplexed by my amusement.

"Nothing." I bit back a smile.

His pitch-black lashes fluttered, contrasting with the vibrant green-blue in his eyes that still captivated me. "So, you seem to be adjusting a little better than the first time we met," he observed.

"I'm definitely not completely adjusted, but being the daughter of a faery isn't something you can hide from. I guess you could say I've... come to terms with it."

"So, you are happy to be a faery?" Declan tilted his head, hopeful.

"I wouldn't go that far. I'm... learning to adapt," I said.

He nodded, but didn't speak. His eyes didn't shy away from

me. They stayed focused and inquisitive as if I was the only thing that mattered.

I decided to start with the questions. We had sat awkwardly for long enough. "Why are you here? Why aren't you in Faylinn all the time?"

Declan blew air from his lips. "Faylinn is ruled by a faery that isn't the most... pleasant faery." He chose his words carefully. "Not that many faeries *are* pleasant, but he's brought a whole new level to faery cruelty. Quite honestly, Faylinn is falling apart and he doesn't care. He doesn't realize it's his fault it's falling apart."

I resituated on the root, getting more comfortable. "What's happening to Faylinn?"

"A lot of Faylinn's faeries are slowly dwindling away. Some just disappear without a trace and others are dying, younger than they should. The longer Favner rules the fewer there are of us." He scratched his head. "No one wants to live under a malicious king, but most don't want to live in the human world. To have to wear such confining clothes and speak as you speak. To have to learn the ways of money and your human jobs. It terrifies us. Some try to leave, but if they don't truly want to be human... they don't survive. And no faery can live in the human world unharmed." The angst in Declan's voice was apparent. "And those that do survive... the ones that come crawling back to Faylinn aren't forgiven." He paused as if not wanting to continue. "They are tortured and do not survive."

I cringed at that morbid thought. What kind of a place did my father come from? "What does he do to make them want to leave in the first place?"

Declan looked sorely thoughtful, trying to decide where to start. "We used to be equals. No matter the season we were born. No matter where we lived. No matter the gender or outward appearance. There was a time when we got to be with our families and thrive in the jobs we were born to do. We were able to pick when we wanted to reproduce, where we wanted to live. We had freedom. But Favner," he said, taking a breath. "Favner split us up. He tore apart our families and divided us into separate colonies. Now, we are told what to do and when. We are required to do as he commands. Eat, sleep, work, and reproduce."

"What do you mean by colony?"

"We were each born into a colony: Sowers, Craftsmen, Keepers or Weavers. We were raised in those colonies and taught the ways of each trade. When he became king he created a new colony: The Nesters."

"What are the colonies for?" I leaned forward now, immersed in the world of Faylinn. Declan looked too upset to talk about it, so I stopped him before he started. "I mean… you don't have to tell me if you don't want to."

"No, it's okay. You'll need to learn about it sooner or later." He paused before continuing as if debating how to reveal the information. "The Sowers are the gardeners and hunters so to speak. They produce all of our food by hunting or farming. But instead of farming when it's time, they are forced to harvest from dawn until dusk so there is always an abundance of produce. Not that an abundance of food is a bad thing, but a lot of it goes to waste. To a faery, being wasteful of nutrition is almost sacrilege."

Being wasteful of nutrition should be sacrilege to anyone.

"The Craftsmen build the dwellings and repair them. They construct whatever the king wants. And it must be done rapidly. If the king wants a new tower on his castle, the Craftsmen are commanded to build it in a day. Granted faeries are swifter than humans, but they aren't *that* swift. Which causes more issues."

"So, the Craftsmen are basically the manual labor." I grew tired at the thought of physically working constantly. "They must be exhausted all the time."

He nodded. "They are. They are worked to death. That is the only way we are allowed to stop. We serve until death takes us."

I had to lean back against the tree now for support. "What about the rest of the faeries?"

"The Weavers provide clothing, blankets, curtains, all things that require material. They weave the fabric and create anything you might need. They always supply things like jewelry, wreaths and baskets. They are very good with their hands."

"Like a seamstress."

He nodded. "The Keepers are the protectors. They keep the boundaries of Faylinn guarded to ensure no one intrudes and they keep the peace inside the kingdom. The Keepers have the most leniencies with their job. They are allowed to have the most rest because Favner wants his guards alert at all times. They can rotate more often and have a little more flexibility for free time. He really wants his guards well taken care of. Apparently, we have something important to protect. I think Favner is just worried someone will come and overthrow his reign as king." Declan bowed his head and focused on the ground. He shook his head and blew out a huff of air.

"What about the Nesters? The new group Favner formed," I prompted.

"Nesters." I could tell this was the one that bothered him the most. "The Nesters bear seedlings. No other colony is allowed to reproduce because *apparently* the other jobs are too important to be put on hold for reproduction. But as a result the

Nester fae are dwindling away. Bearing a new seedling is tiring. It takes only a month not nine months like humans. And as soon as one seedling is born, another must be created. The process is repeated until the faery can no longer handle carrying another. They don't survive long. Nesters are never not expecting."

"So not every woman gets the opportunity to have children?" That thought churned knots in my stomach. Declan shook his head without meeting my eyes. "How did Favner decide who was meant for each colony?"

"He needed to keep our kingdom populated so there was one Nester selected from every family. They were the first to be picked. And then he divided us up from there as he saw fit."

Divide them, as if they were game pieces to be dispersed among players.

Another thought twisted my insides as I thought of the possibilities. "How are... seedlings...?" I didn't know how to phrase this. Did faeries procreate the same way we did? And if so, did that mean they were forced to create with one they didn't love?

"How are seedlings created?" Declan let me off the hook.

I nodded, trying to keep the blush from my cheeks.

"How is anything reproduced?" *Did he really want me to answer that question?* "The fae are made the same way that a human is," he simplified.

"So they have to... with others that they don't..." I couldn't bring myself to follow-through with my questions.

Declan merely gave me a look, affirming my now deepest fear. "They do get to choose who they create with, but I suppose that doesn't really make it any better. There were many couples who were separated, forced to create with another."

I shook my head. I was specifically stuck on the Nesters now because unless I had a sibling I didn't know existed, which was highly unlikely, I was the last in my family. The only one who could... create.

"Each colony used to bond within their own colony, but since Favner forbids bonding..."

"Bonding?" I questioned.

"Marrying," he clarified. "I believe that's what humans refer to it as."

"You have to marry within your own colony? You don't get to choose from anyone in the kingdom."

He shook his head. "But there is no bonding anymore. Bonds have been torn apart."

I didn't like the sound of any of this. "Do they create seedlings with the same faery every time?"

"Yes."

I sighed, feeling a small weight pulled off my chest.

"But those who created before were separated from their partners and have to create with someone else now."

He nodded. "Those that were chosen as Nesters, yes."

My stomach was churning, sick for the people of Faylinn. "And how old do you have to be to begin having seedlings?"

"It depends on the physical maturity of the faery, but sixteen is the average age." My stomach sank. I felt like I might puke. "Favner wants them creating life as soon as they are capable."

I swallowed. "And before that age... what do the Nesters do?"

"They assist those carrying. They learn how to nurture a new seedling and prepare their bodies to be ready to carry when it is time."

I cringed. The thought of living in Faylinn petrified me. If I had been born in Faylinn I would have had to start reproducing seedlings almost two years ago. It was decided. I was never going to Faylinn. My body belonged to me, not Favner. He wasn't about to start making those decisions for me.

"I'm sorry, Calliope. I should have been more considerate." He reached out to me, but his hand never quite touched mine before he pulled it back. "I know you're the last of your family."

I could only nod, and then paused. "How did you know that?"

He looked at me for a moment before answering and then said, "Like I told you earlier. I've been around. I hear things. I know more than you probably think I do."

A chill ran through me. His words were not comforting.

He reached out hesitantly. "Oh, I… uhh… *Pixies*… I didn't mean for it to sound like that. I'm sorry. I've never invaded your personal space. I've only been here as a protector. A Keeper. My job."

"You're a Keeper."

He nodded and plucked at a piece of bark he picked up from the ground.

It made sense as to why he was able to come so frequently. "So, when you're not here chilling in the trees, you're protecting Faylinn?"

He nodded again. "I take my shift and then I escape away to make sure you're still okay."

I turned my face away to hide my blushing cheeks. When I peered back at him he looked helpless, idly fidgeting with his hands. I gave him a sympathetic look.

"You've all become slaves. You're treated like machines. But everyone has a breaking point. So, what's being done to stop him? I mean… he can't reign forever."

Declan gazed at me unblinking. "Unfortunately, he could be

king for several hundred more years. We don't live forever, but we age very slowly. About a day to every month a human lives."

"So that means I have to live... what..." I was trying to do the math in my head, but it was hurting my brain to try and calculate it without a calculator.

"A human would have to live for about thirty years before I became a year older. But even then we don't die at the normal human age. We live to be hundreds of years old. Some of the fae even thousands of years."

"How old are you?"

"In fae or human years?"

I chuckled. "Both."

"In fae I'm nineteen. In human years I guess I'm about... 150 years old."

My thoughts stopped, trying to grasp the concept. "But I thought that..."

"The aging process starts to take effect when our fae features come, as soon as our features are fully matured."

"So what... you aged normally until you hit puberty and then it slowed down?"

"Basically. But time is different in Faylinn. It also doesn't exist the same way it does here."

"This is all too complicated to wrap my head around."

He chuckled and smiled coolly. "The fae aren't supposed to make sense. There is a reason why humans don't believe we exist. Nothing about us could scientifically be proven or be logical to the human brain. The makeup of our bodies is completely different. Our blood is different. Our organs are different." He shrugged. "We don't have to make sense. We just are."

"How many of you... of us are there?"

"Thousands. But like I said, we are fewer than before. Before it was tens of thousands."

How could a colony of faeries that large go undetected? How could they live freely in the woods without being disturbed? That had to cover a lot of forest.

I watched Declan. He spoke with an ease that calmed me. Even though he spoke about something I couldn't grasp and was still forming its own place in my mind, I felt content being here with him, listening to him explain the fae ways. "Then what about me? Since I'm half, will I age half as slowly?"

"You…" He sighed and looked puzzled. "We will only know your aging process with time as your other faery features show themselves and as the years pass us by. As I'm sure your dad mentioned, there aren't many like you, if any. You're the first half-fae that I've ever known."

I took a deep breath. "The first?" I asked. "How could I be the first?"

He chuckled, amused by my disbelief. "I didn't say you were the first, simply the only one I've ever come in contact with. I'm sure you're not the first in all the centuries of faeries to exist."

That was only semi-comforting to know I wasn't just some mutant, but I still wished I had someone else to learn from. To have somewhat of an idea about how I would grow and exist throughout the years. The uncertainty left me unsettled. I would constantly be in search of what I should expect.

A thought formed in my mind. There were only five colonies. "No two family members could be a part of the same colony, could they?"

"No," he said quietly and shook his head, pressing his lips together in frustration.

"Were there any families with more than five members?"

Declan nodded stiffly and spoke quietly. "Those that were left were not allowed to live."

I felt sick. I swiped my hand across my ears and through my hair as if I could wipe away his words.

I was afraid to ask. "How many were in your family?"

He grew solemn and I realized I should have been more sensitive. I shouldn't have pried.

"Thankfully, only four." Declan looked to the moss beneath his legs.

I thought about comforting him, but he looked more uncomfortable then I could have imagined him ever being and it made me angry. Angry for him. Angry for Faylinn.

"Why did he separate you? If Faylinn already had a good system, what was the point of reassigning and forcing everyone into a job they weren't familiar with? And then disposing of extra fae." Like they were garbage. As if their lives meant nothing.

"He wants our loyalty," he said without inflexion. "Families create unity and loyalty to one another. He wanted to destroy that. We are no longer allowed to bond because it creates ties of loyalty to someone else other than him. He wanted to weaken our influences and diminish any possibility of retaliation against him."

"Did he say that?"

Declan shook his head. "No, he gave some speech about the importance of learning new trades and expanding our knowledge of other colonies which makes sense, but no one believed that was his goal. As soon as he separated us we were no longer allowed to live with our families. He said it was important for us to connect with our new fellow colony members to create stronger colonies."

"But wouldn't the division of families cause a rebellion to

begin with? Why hasn't Favner ever been overthrown? Why doesn't everyone create a rebellion and retaliate?" It made perfect sense to me.

"Ahh… that would be nice," he agreed. "But unfortunately that's impossible."

"Why? Nobody likes him. Everyone obviously agrees on that. Just get together and fight back."

"No, I literally mean it's impossible. Royalty have a special ability, an extra special ability." Declan stopped and sighed, lifting his gaze toward the sky.

"And what's that?" I prompted.

"Giving away our faery secrets now are we, Declan?"

My ears perked up. I heard his voice coming from up high. When I gazed above us Kai was perched on a limb several feet up. One leg was pulled to his chest while the other dangled over, bobbing up and down. He was shaving the tip of a twig into a point, making an arrow. How long had he been there?

Declan lifted his head to Kai. "They aren't secrets to her, Kai. And I'm only answering what she asks. I'm not going to throw out information that doesn't concern her or worse— frightens her. I'm not you."

"Can you blame me for wanting to live on the edge?"

After Declan's explanation of Faylinn's troubles and our aging process, I didn't have the energy for their bickering.

"Thanks for telling me about Faylinn, Declan." I got up from the roots to leave.

"Leaving so soon, Princess?" Kai dropped from the branches, agilely landing on his feet in front of me, keeping me in place.

I glared at his attempt to perturb me. "Not everyone can laze around in the trees all day long, Kai. There's important work to be done in the world."

"Oh, I think I do very important work," he contended.

I put one hand on my hip, observing him, hoping to intimidate him at least half as much as he intimidated me. "It's true, you do keep the peace in Faylinn. Speaking of which, shouldn't you be doing that now? The precious king couldn't possibly last another minute without you, I'm sure."

He didn't answer, but a momentary look of pain flickered in his eyes before his mask was back up. He scoffed and began walking away, disappearing into the trees.

"What's his problem?" I asked Declan.

Declan shrugged and shook his head as if he never knew what was going on in Kai's head. When I turned back to Kai, he was gone. "I wouldn't worry about him. He gets his feelings hurt easily."

I heard a distant offended noise coming from where Kai had gone.

Declan and I laughed quietly. "Apparently," I said, but I may have taken it too far considering what I just learned about Faylinn. Life wasn't easy for any of them and I practically rubbed it in his face.

I grabbed Declan's hand resting on his knee and squeezed it. "Thank you for talking with me today. It really means a lot that you trust me with all this information."

He shrugged as if it were no big deal. "You deserve to know."

"Thank you anyway."

NINE

I showered off the day after spending the afternoon in the woods and blew my hair dry, letting it fan down my back in light wavy curls. After brushing a little mascara on my lashes and gloss on my lips, I was set.

It was Saturday night and Cam hadn't forgotten about our plans as I hoped he and Isla would. But tonight the heavens opened up and the angels sent me mercy. Isla was sick and couldn't make it. I almost thought Cameron was going to cancel, but then he said, "So, it's just you and me. I'm coming to pick you up now."

"Cam, we can wait for Isla. She was the one who planned this night." Why I said it, I wasn't quite sure. I should have taken this night like the gift it was.

"Why? I owe you a date anyway. Besides, Isla insisted we still hang out. She feels bad for ruining our plans."

I wasn't sure if I felt more dejected that this wasn't Cameron's idea or if I was more frustrated that Isla was still so perfect that she practically pushed him to keep the plans rather than flaking on me.

"Well, isn't she a keeper."

"I think so." I could hear the smile in his voice and a little piece of my heart broke off.

Cam drove, which was a nice change. I hadn't ridden in the front seat of his jeep for quite some time. Now that I thought about it, the last time I rode in his car was to the summer party at Jake Winters. After the party, I ended up needing to hitch a ride home with Lia because Cameron left with Isla.

"Do you mind?" he asked. "I really want to take her home." I knew that look in his eyes. He wanted to do a lot more than just take her home.

I tried to keep the hurt out of my voice. "No, it's fine. Lia will take me home." I prayed my voice hadn't failed me.

"You're one in a million, Cal," he'd said, and kissed my cheek.

Yeah, that's what they all tell me before leaving with another girl.

"You're still up for the Green House, right?" he asked, bringing me back to the present. I looked over at him peering at me from the driver's side.

All he needed was one look from me.

"Of course you are. What was I thinking?" He chuckled, keeping an eye on the road.

"You weren't." I smirked. "That is unless you really need a hardy steak dinner tonight."

"Nah. We'll let tonight revolve around you."

I punched him in the arm as he laughed.

The salad bar greeted us as soon as we walked into The Green House. After piling our plates, we reached the register and Cameron said, "Two."

"Cam, you don't have to pay for me." I reached into my purse and pulled out my wallet.

"Whatever, Cal, this night's on me. You're not paying."

I offered him a smile and thanked him.

The restaurant wasn't as packed as I assumed it would be on a Saturday night. They seated us in a booth off to the side, in a quiet corner, obviously thinking we were on a romantic date. I wasn't about to correct them.

"What bug has Isla caught?" I asked, situating myself in the seat across from him.

"A stomach bug. I'm keeping my distance until it passes." He stuffed in a bite of his Caesar salad.

"What. You don't want to endure the bug just to be near her?" I smirked.

He gave a look that was not amused and I laughed. "Ha-ha. No. I'll survive a few days without her just fine."

I smiled and popped a cherry tomato in my mouth. It felt weird sitting across from him and not having him know everything about my life. We never had to have catch-up conversations before. We always knew what was going on in each other's lives. And here I was with the biggest, most outrageous news and I had to keep it to myself. He'd never believe me even if I could tell him.

I spent the afternoon with Declan. A faery guard. How could I ever explain that to Cameron? I learned about a kingdom that apparently I belonged in. No, I didn't feel like I belonged. I felt left out, but not as if I was missing something. Or maybe that's what it was. Was it possible to miss something you never knew existed in the first place?

"Callie?" his voice held concern. "Cal, you okay? What's on your mind?"

"What?" I shook out of my daze.

"You look lost. Are you feeling okay?"

"Yeah," I said as reassuringly as I could. "Yeah, I'm great. I'm at my favorite restaurant. Eating my favorite food, hanging with my favorite person. What could be wrong?"

He tilted his head to the side, scrutinizing me, having forgotten about the plate in front of him. "I don't know. But it's something."

I shrugged.

"Talk to me." Cameron peered at me over the table. His familiar blue eyes captured me and I nearly poured out my heart. How did he do that? This part hadn't occurred to me when I agreed to a night alone with him. Without the distraction of Isla, Cameron could observe me. What if he could see a difference? What if I was starting to look different?

"It's just good to be here with you," I said, munching on another bite of greens to deflect the topic. "I've missed this."

He nodded, hesitantly accepting my answer. It wasn't as if I was lying. I did miss this, the casual comfort of being near him. He was my other home.

"I'm glad we did this too. I still want for us all to get together, but we have to make our nights too. There's so much less pressure when I'm with you, you know?" He looked down at his plate as if he finally remembered it was there. "I mean, don't get me wrong, I'm definitely not tired of Isla. I don't think I'll ever be, but—"

"I get what you mean, Cam," I cut him off before he could ramble on and on about how perfect she was. I hoped it wasn't too obvious. "You don't have to explain yourself. I know you. You know me. It's easy."

"Yeah," he agreed and smiled easily.

I didn't want to be easy for him. Comfortable, yes. Happy, yes. Effortless, yes. But easy... I never wanted to be someone's choice because it was simply easier. I'd never let myself be that to him. I needed to accept that our relationship would never be romantic. I was just his best friend, Cal. Someone it was easy to spend time with.

We didn't speak for a few minutes, eating in a comfortable silence. After several rounds back to the salad bar, the food hit the spot, totally satisfying my Green House craving. When I looked up from my empty plate to him, he was watching me. My stomach twirled under his scrutinizing ocean eyes.

"Do I have something on my face?" I asked, wiping the corners of my lips.

"No." He looked thoughtful, gazing at me as if I were someone different, like he'd never looked at me before. I cleared my throat and tried to keep confident eye contact, but failed a couple times and dropped my eyes back to my empty plate. He blinked and shook his head. "Did you get enough to eat?"

I grinned. "I'm stuffed. Completely content." I leaned back in my chair, stretching out my stomach. "You?"

"Yeah." He nodded. "The night's still young. Do you want to do a movie or something?"

Did he really need to ask? "Sure."

We pulled into the parking lot of the movie theater and Cameron said, "I have to pee."

"You should probably do that in the bathroom," I advised.

He nodded. "The parking lot might cause a little bit of a scene."

"These people came to see a movie not a peep show."

He chuckled. "Dangit."

Cameron paid for the tickets without question or comment

96

and I thanked him again.

"You do the bathroom," I said. "I'll get popcorn and meet you in the theater."

"Deal." He nodded once.

When I walked in, snacks in one hand, drink in the other, Cameron saved me a seat next to him in the back row, our usual spot.

"Light butter?" he asked.

I nodded as he held his hand out to me. He didn't have to ask. I knew he wanted the chocolate covered raisins I hadn't shown him yet to mix in the popcorn. He knew just how I liked it.

Once the lights in the theater lowered to a dim glow an unusual tension encompassed Cameron and me. I wasn't sure if he felt it, but I definitely did. Going to the movies had always been casual before, but now that he was with Isla it felt like we were crossing into enemy territory, a boundary that shouldn't be passed. It wasn't unlike him to curl his arm around me during movies in the past, but now it seemed like he didn't know what to do with himself. The entire time he was shifting in his seat, situating and resituating the placement of his hands. He'd rest his arm on the armrest between us then shift to the other side, then cross his arms in front of his chest and sigh. After finishing the popcorn I stuck with the arms across the chest approach. It made things easier. I didn't know why he was so anxious.

When the lights came up, he let me pass in front of him and followed me to the exit. As we walked to his jeep, he wrapped his arm across my shoulder, enfolding me close to his warm body. "Thanks for coming out with me tonight."

"Thanks for not ditching out on me." I smiled and nudged my head into his shoulder.

He squeezed my shoulder once and slowly trailed his fingers down my arm, tickling my stomach uncontrollably, before releasing me as we approached the jeep.

The ride to my house was silent as we drove through the still darkness, which normally wouldn't bother me, but it wasn't our typical comfortable silence. We had a thousand pound mammoth in the backseat peering over our shoulders as we awkwardly tried to act natural. Cameron pulled into my driveway as the digits on his clock above the stereo read 10:57 pm.

I hopped down from the passenger's seat. "Thanks again, Cam. I had a lot of fun."

"Me too, Cal." The look in his eyes changed again, like he was trying to figure me out which was the last thing I needed right now. Having Cameron dissect my appearance now was dangerous. He might notice something about me before I did. But there was something more in his eyes, something that resembled longing.

"I'll see you Monday," he said after clearing his throat. He had to feel it too. It couldn't just be me. There was no way he couldn't detect the difference.

I nodded and closed the door, waving as I walked away. Once I was safely in the house, his car pulled away.

At the sight of my bed, I could instantly hear it calling my name. The exhausting day hit me. I sat at my armoire and put my curls into a messy bun on the top of my head, pulling the strands away from my face before putting on moisturizer.

After leaving Cam though it felt strange, I felt satisfied. I had my Cameron fix. I could probably let Isla take my best friend for a few more weeks before I felt neglected again. At least now I knew he still cared. He still wanted me in his life.

When I turned my face up to the mirror, taking in my

appearance, my eyes bulged and I stifled a scream. I frantically turned each side of my face to the mirror, examining the foreign growth. It was really happening. It wasn't as if I could turn back now even though I wanted to.

My ears had begun to form delicate points.

TEN

I dodged my parents all day Sunday. My excuse was that I had a ton of homework I needed to concentrate on and shouldn't be disturbed, which was a bunch of bull. I locked myself in my room. What I really needed was to test different hairstyles to figure out the best way to cover up these babies. There was no way I could do that if my mom was constantly coming in and out of my room. With every creak and every thud, I jumped, thinking there was someone at my door.

At midday I heard a faint knock on my door and the sound of my dad calling my name. It nearly made me fall off my chair.

"Come in," I said and pulled my hair down around my ears in case Mom was with him.

He peered around the door and stepped inside alone. "Is everything okay?" I gave him a helpless look and he rushed to my side. "What changed?"

I pulled my hair behind my ears to reveal the tips. Of all things I was expecting, a smile was not one of them, but it formed on his face as if I just told him I got a 4.0. Was that pride in his eyes?

"Dad?" I prompted.

His voice was quiet as his bottom lip quivered. "I haven't seen those in so long I almost forgot what a faery looked like," he said softly

Sentimental. Really. He was getting sentimental on me? "Dad," I repeated, my voice reprimanding him.

"I'm sorry." He swallowed, blinking back tears. "Right. Your ears." He couldn't stop looking at them. "It won't be easy to hide those."

"You think? I can't keep these from Mom."

A deep breath of air flowed from his mouth as he ran a hand over his face and his faded green eyes finally met mine. "You're going to have to try."

"But, Dad—"

"She's got a lot on her plate right now, Calliope," he interrupted. "I cannot add this to it."

"You say that as if it's *her* burden to bear." I threw my hand to the closed bedroom door.

"This affects us all, Calliope," he chastised.

"Oh really. Because the last time I checked, your ears looked pretty rounded and normal to me."

The stern look that crossed his face made me shut my mouth. I'd never seen my dad so wound up. He was normally the laid back one in the house. Zen. Which made sense now that I knew he lived in a forest for the majority of his life. But why was it so important to keep this from my mom? I understood that this case was a big deal. I understood that it could completely rock her world, but this was a lot for me to process on my own. And I didn't want to live a lie. I wanted to be able to live and talk freely in my home.

"I'll tell her. Just not yet. We have to wait for this case to be over. If her concentration is tampered with, she could lose and this vile criminal could get off. This case is really important to her, Calliope."

I sighed. I knew it was. She'd been building this case for months and months. It was *the* case. The one she had fixated on for years, doing everything in her power to keep this man behind bars before his trial. I saw his point, but it was going to be far from easy. Not that any of this had been easy thus far. Nothing was easy anymore. Everything was complicated. I was spinning more webs full of lies and if I wasn't careful I was going to get caught in one of them. I didn't want this.

"Just give it a few more weeks," he pressed.

"As if I have a choice."

"Thank you, Calliope." He leaned down and kissed the top of my head. "Hair looks good by the way."

I laughed without humor and offered him a smile. "Thanks."

Luckily, the next morning I slipped out of the house undetected and made my way to school. If my mom had been around, she would have figured something was up. I hadn't gained control of myself yet. I needed to get my bearings before being able to confront her without suspicion.

I made my hair extra curly and braided it in two, making sure not to tuck it behind my ears. I hadn't braided my hair since I was twelve. It was probably a horrible idea to go to school in the first place, but I had to go. I couldn't not go to school ever again. I still had a life, a human life that I was going to cling to for as long as I could. I would *not* go to Faylinn and be forced to live among the Nesters as a slave to Favner. My body was not his to use as an instrument for reproduction. That was going to be decided by me and the future Mr. Whoever when the time was right.

My nerves were spiraling in chaos underneath my skin. Every eye that I caught in the hallway was judging me. Examining my every move. I touched an ear nonchalantly, self-consciously. It was safely nestled underneath my nest of hair, as I was sure it would stay if I would just stop touching it.

I saw the back of Cameron's head by our lockers. Maybe it was because I was so conscious of my ears now, but when my eyes found him they went straight to his perfectly round ears, his blonde hair brushing the tops. Isla wasn't with him, thank goodness. The fewer people I talked to today the better, at least until I figured out how to hide these things better.

"Hey," I said, breathless, and hid behind my locker door, searching for my English book.

"Mornin'," he replied, still rummaging in his locker.

I focused on my breathing. That was where I would keep my composure. If my hyperventilation didn't slow down, it was going to make me faint and cause a very unnecessary scene in the middle of the hallway. I was being paranoid. Cameron wasn't going to notice anything was different if I simply acted natural.

I heard him close his locker door. "Isla's still throwing up."

"That's disgusting."

"Tell me about it." He sighed and came to stand on the other side of my locker door, in view of me. I could feel his eyes on me, but I didn't want to seem flustered or out of character. I continued to sort through my locker, hoping he'd leave so I wouldn't have to have an actual conversation with him. "Calliope, you've got something in your hair." He lifted his hand, pointing.

103

My hands flew to my ears, fluffing my hair out over them. *My other ear.* The wind had moved my hair just enough for a point to barely poke out through the blonde curls and I missed it. I knew people were looking at me funny. This was going to be harder than I thought.

"Cal," he prompted. "What was that?"

I attempted to play stupid. I knew it wouldn't work for long, but I stalled to think. "Oh… I don't know," I said, clipped, closing my locker. "Must have been a leaf or something."

He chortled. "Oh, c'mon. That didn't look like a leaf." He reached out to touch my hair and I stepped back.

I was supposed to keep this world from Cameron, but he was making it very difficult. And I was doing a terrible job at seeming normal.

He laughed again. "Take a chill pill. What's up with you today?"

I'm becoming a faery. There wasn't any denying it anymore, as much as I wanted to. As much as I didn't want it to be true, it was happening, just as Declan and Kai predicted. If there was one person I needed more than ever now, it was Cameron. I had proof now. He'd probably scream like a girl at first, but he would know what to say to me. He would know what to do.

"Cam, meet me after school."

"What?"

"Just meet me after school," I persisted.

He sighed and pressed his shoulder against the lockers. "Cal, I told my dad I would head straight to his shop after school. Just tell me now."

"This is important, Cameron," I said seriously. "Please?"

His misty blue eyes grew uneasy as reached his hand out, setting it on my arm and rubbing reassuringly. "Are you okay?"

Hearing the worry in his voice made me want to cry, a feeling I stifled until now. I'd been tough, but no one had shown any sympathy until now. I'd simply been expected to accept this. Why was it that sympathy sparked the need to cry?

I bit my lip. I didn't want to make him anxious for the rest of the day, but I couldn't say I was perfectly fine either. He could read the discomfort clearly on my face.

"Cal?"

I shook my head and tried to assure him. "It's nothing that can't wait until later. I just really need you to meet me. Say you will, please?"

"Of course. I'll tell my dad I'll be a little late."

"Thank you." I gave him a quick peck on the cheek. "Just meet me at my car."

He nodded, but the look of concern never left his face as I walked away.

The end of the day couldn't come fast enough. I was constantly fussing with my hair, making sure my ears were covered at all times. When I awoke this morning and checked my ears, the points had become more prominent. They were definitely faery ears now. I wasn't even sure when they started to form. I don't think Declan would have missed them if they were there Saturday morning, but maybe they hadn't been big enough to notice. Cameron wouldn't have known to look for them at dinner. It scared me how fast they grew. Were my wings going to be the same way?

"Is it just me or did Jake Winter sprout into a Greek god over the summer?" Lia asked as she took a bite of her sandwich at lunch.

"Jake, really?" I followed her gaze to a group of guys punching each other and goofing off without a care in the world.

She shrugged meekly, so unlike her.

"I'm sorry, but do you remember what Jake said to you the first time you met him?" She rolled her eyes, knowing exactly what was coming. In my best Jake Winter voice I said, "Hey, are you lost? Because heaven is a long way away from here."

"Winter is such a tool," Cameron said as he plopped across from me on the grass. I hadn't noticed him coming up to us.

"See, even Cam remembers that fateful day," I said, feeling validated.

He shrugged. "That's only because that was the day you chopped off all your locks, Cal, and you were bawling your eyes out next to Lia when he came up. He was so oblivious and insensitive that he didn't even see you crying. He just proceeded to gawk at Lia."

I looked up at him, speechless, but he wasn't looking at me. His were eyes locked on the ground, holding something I couldn't read. Frustration? Uncertainty?

He remembered that?

"Okay. Okay. He's a tool and I'd never give him the time of day," Lia said, conceding. "Does that make you feel better?"

"Thank goodness," I said and turned my attention back to her. "But don't let me stop you if he's the man of your dreams."

She glared at me, but gave a small grin. "Speaking of hair. Yours is especially nice today, Callie. I'm digging the braids," she teased.

"What's wrong with the braids?" I lifted my hands to my hair, double-checking my ear's whereabouts.

"Nothing. I've just never seen you wear braids before. It's very Britney Spears."

"I was thinking the same thing," Cameron cued in at the wrong time. "You haven't worn braids since we were in middle

106

school, Cal."

"I just felt like changing things up a bit. There's only so much you can do with curly hair." They eyed me, questioning my poor excuse of an answer. "Lay off the hair," I commanded jokingly, but I think it came out more like pleading.

Cameron's eyes read my lies. "Huh, you sure there's no other reason?" he asked.

I eyed him, warning him not to go any further and mention our earlier conversation. This ended with Cameron. I was not going to tell Lia. If he wanted to get on my bad side he'd keep up with the questioning, but he knew better.

He averted his gaze. "You going to finish that sandwich, Lia?" he asked.

She looked at the unfinished sandwich in her hands and then back at him, handing it over. I didn't think he even wanted it, but it ended the conversation about my hair.

When the final bell rang I waited in my car for Cameron, more anxious than I thought I was going to be. I shouldn't tell him. It'd been a battle in my head all day. As much as I wanted to tell him, I could still back out and make up some bull crap story about why I was on edge. I should want to hide this from the entire world, but I felt a lighter thinking I was only moments away from sharing this huge secret with my best friend.

I put the car in drive as soon as he sat in the passenger seat.

"Where are we going?" he asked after closing the door.

"Away from the school."

"Why?" he pressed. "Callie, you're killing me here. You can't even tell Lia? Why can't you just tell me now?"

"Because I have to show you and I can't show you in the middle of our school parking lot. We need to go somewhere private." I pulled out of the parking lot and headed toward the canyon.

I looked out of the corner of my eye to see him with lifted eyebrows and a hint of a smirk on his face. "What are you going to show me?"

"It's better if we don't talk about it and you just see them for yourself." I kept my eyes back on the road.

"Them," he said flatly. "Calliope, are you going to show me something dirty?" he teased.

"What? No, you perv!" I punched his shoulder. "Just prepare yourself, okay? Open your mind to all possibilities. It's going to be really hard for me to tell you this and I need all of your support." His stare was even more skeptical now. Before he could say anything, I said, "Don't ask any more questions. Just sit there. Please. I don't have the patience to argue with you right now."

He was silent for a minute, a serious expression on his face. "You're not dying are you?"

Breathless laughter escaped my lips. It kind of felt like it, but... "No," I amended.

He sighed. "Gosh, Callie. Don't scare me like that."

"You thought I was dying, really?"

"Well, you're being so secretive. It's making me really nervous."

"Then think a little less depressing and more unbelievable, okay?"

He shifted and peered over at his anxious face. I could see the wheels turning in his blue eyes as he tried to piece together what I told him so far. Whatever was flipping through his mind, it wasn't going to be remotely close to the truth.

"At least give me a hint."

"Nothing I say to you will hint at what I'm about to tell you, okay? It'll only confuse you. Now hush. You're making me more nervous."

I drove into the canyon. It wasn't more than fifteen minutes from school, giving us seclusion and practicality so he could get to his dad before he started to question his whereabouts.

When we pulled up to the trees, Cameron didn't move. "C'mon," I prompted as I got out of the car. He slowly exited the vehicle, apprehensive, as I knew he would be. He paused by the passenger's side of my Cabriolet. I snatched his hand and pulled him into the trees. He unwillingly dragged his feet along the dead leaves and grass. My patience was being tried.

"What? Are you scared of me now? It's just me. C'mon, Cam."

"Callie," he murmured. "Where are we going?"

"To a place where we can't be interrupted," I said without looking at him. "Or seen."

"You've officially freaked me out," he emphasized.

We were deep enough now. I was praying Kai or Declan wouldn't show up. Not that I'd ever seen them anywhere in the trees except for by my home, but I wasn't prepared to show them my ears yet. I needed my human moment to freak out first. I faced Cameron. The look on his face wasn't making this any easier.

"Please, Callie, the suspense is killing me. What's so important that you had to isolate us from the rest of the world?"

I took a deep breath, unbraiding one braid at a time as I tried to calmly explain. "There have been some changes in my appearance over the last couple days. Some changes that aren't exactly *normal*." I kept my gaze firmly planted on him and gained the courage to pull my hair back, unveiling the new addition to my body.

Cameron's eyes swelled out of his head. "Calliope, what happened to your ears?"

I dropped my hair and took a step toward him. "Cam, I'm just as freaked as you are right now, so I'd like you to tone down the piercing shrieks just a notch."

"Calliope," he said it this time in awe and amazement. "How? What did you do to them?" He gently pushed my curls back, revealing them once more.

"Me?" I pointed at them crossly. "You think I would have done this on purpose?"

Cameron looked at me blankly, completely speechless, but he didn't retreat. He stayed standing in front of me, my unwavering constant. I prayed he would stay that way after this.

"Cameron, what has pointy ears, wings and is about three inches tall?" His expression twisted as he tried to put together what I was telling him. I waited for some recognition to appear on his face; something to tell me this wasn't *that* farfetched. But who was I kidding? This was *crazy*.

"Are you seriously trying to tell me you're a faery?"

I sighed; relieved I didn't have to say the words myself and nodded.

He laughed humorlessly. "You've got to be kidding me! What?" Cameron looked at me with a puzzled smile. "Callie, you're joking with me, right? You got me real good." He didn't wait for me to correct him. He laughed easily now, his expression relaxing. "You really had me going. Those are some *amazing* costume ears. I really thought—"

"Cameron," I asserted. "Touch them. These are my real ears."

His face fell and his laughter became uneven huffs of air. I took a hesitant step toward him, measuring his degree of uncertainty, hoping he wouldn't run away from me and he didn't. Slow even breaths calmed his amusement. His laughing stopped altogether and he bit his lips. One of his hands slowly lifted to my face. The touch of his fingertips softly trailed up my cheek to my ear. They were cautious as they inched their way up and around the curve. I watched his eyes, so unsure and nervous. He pinched the point.

"Ouch!"

"Holy crap!" He jumped back, stumbling over his feet. "Whoa, whoa, whoa…"

"Cameron," I cautiously said, his name the only familiar thing that fell from my lips.

His breathing accelerated, his eyes were wild with uncertainty. "I… I… You… You…" He couldn't speak. He couldn't look me in the eyes. Maybe this wasn't the wisest decision. He blinked as if he thought every time he reopened his eyes my ears would be gone. "Cal," he breathed, shifting one step back. "What in the…"

"Cameron, please don't run," I begged, hands outstretched to him. I couldn't bear to see his back fleeing away from me.

He shook his head and finally met my eyes. "Run? Callie, I wouldn't ever run from you. But I mean… C'mon… This is *insane.*" Cameron's light sapphire eyes traced every feature on my face.

I stayed quiet. If I gave him a little more time to let his mind process this, just maybe, he could think it was possible. I needed him to believe me. I needed Cameron.

"You have pointy ears," he said slowly.

I nodded, but he shook his head.

"How… What… How…" I swallowed ready to start explaining when he slowly said, "Your eyes." His eyes bore into mine. "They are *really* green. I've never seen them so bright." His eyes squinted as they explored me. The only sound I heard was his quiet quick breaths. "And they're... *bigger*."

My heart jolted. "What?"

"Your eyes. They were never this big. They're not unnaturally big, but they were definitely smaller before."

"My eyes?" My eyes had changed, too? Oh no... *What if my wings started to grow in?* I reached back, but felt nothing, only the smooth cotton of my sweater.

"I noticed something was different on Saturday, but I couldn't quite put my finger on it. And I've never seen them so green. Maybe it's the lighting." He closed his eyes, shaking his head once more. "But you're not three inches tall..." Cameron was even more baffled now.

"Well, technically no faery is. Or so I'm told. Those are called pixies."

He didn't look amused. "Well, thanks for the term rundown. Callie, how is this even possible? How do you know that you're a faery? Maybe it's just some rare human deformity."

"It's not a deformity, Cameron," I assured.

"You don't have wings," he fought back.

"They aren't far behind these." I pointed to my ears. "And who's to say what features a faery possesses anyway? No one actually believes they exist. The only knowledge everyone goes by is in storybooks and Disney movies."

"How..." He wasn't grasping this. I couldn't blame him. But at least he wasn't running.

"Would you believe me if I told you my dad was a faery? That he could back up my story. Although, if he knew I revealed this to you, he'd probably kill me."

"Your dad," he said skeptically.

112

I nodded, letting him soak in the information. This might take more convincing than I thought. Maybe I shouldn't have told him so soon. I should have waited. He couldn't deny it if I had wings. *I* couldn't deny it if I had wings. But had I revealed myself in full faery form he probably would have fainted and that wouldn't be safe this far up the canyon.

Cameron didn't speak for what felt like an eternity. In reality it probably wasn't more than a minute, but time wasn't flowing normally in my mind.

"Cameron, speak," I pleaded.

He breathed out a low huff of air. "Whoa... So what? You're like half faery, half human? Are you even human at all?"

I lifted my shoulders meekly. I didn't even know anymore. Was I still a human? Gosh, I still wanted to be human. Even just to keep a sliver of who I thought I was. But as I thought about being human, standing in the shade of the forest, I felt less human than ever. The trees fought for my allegiance.

Cameron must have seen something in my eyes. He stepped towards me and cupped my face in his hands. I wanted to touch him back, but I didn't want his hands to leave my face. "Callie, you've been my best friend for years. Though this makes me question your sanity, I see that you believe what you're telling me. I want to believe you."

I felt hope and it pricked the back of my eyes, glazing them with moisture. He pressed his lips together and fixed me with a sympathetic gaze.

"You can't expect me to take in all of this and automatically accept it, but I'm willing to try," he said.

I nodded and reached one hand to rest on his waist to save me from my weak knees. "I know... okay." I could live with that. I could live with even an ounce of hope that I had someone

I could go to who never lied to me, who never kept anything from me, someone I could trust one hundred percent.

I swallowed my emotions, reigning in my tears. He must have noticed my shaky emotional state and our very close proximity because he looked down at my hand on him and then went comical on me.

"Callie, this is cool. Own those pointy ears. You're a faery!" He threw his hands in the air.

"Shut up," I laughed.

"What else do you want me to say? My best friend is a faery. Who else can say that?"

"Nobody and neither can you," I stressed.

"Like I would actually tell people. I'd rather not be sent to the loony bin with you."

"I wouldn't be sent to the loony bin if anyone caught sight of my fae features."

The significance of my words flashed in his eyes and he nodded. "You're right." He looked at me in all seriousness. "You'd become someone's science experiment."

The thought made me cringe. To think of myself as anything but normal—human. And to think if my identity was put into the wrong hands that my own kind would turn against me and view me as a freak, merely *something* to experiment on. I would no longer be a *someone*, but an *it*.

He said firmly, "I won't ever let that happen to you. You don't have to worry, Cal. You know your secret is safe with me."

I nodded and breathed through my consuming panic. I knew I could count on Cameron. It was touch and go for a moment, but I knew I loved him for a reason. "Thank you, Cam."

His eyes drank in my appearance, studying all my new

features. I couldn't say I hadn't done the same thing to myself. Every time I looked in the mirror I stared for a few moments before it clicked that it was me, like a drastic new haircut you're not used to. When his eyes met mine again he asked, "Now what? How long have you known?"

"That faeries exist or that I am one?"

"Both! How long have you kept this from me?" He was offended now. I hadn't expected that emotion.

"Well... I've known about them for a little less than a month now. They've been telling me I'm one for about the same time, but I didn't truly believe it until Saturday night when I saw these." I gestured to my ears.

"Saturday? I was with you Saturday," he realized.

"My hair was down. I didn't notice them either."

He shook his head. "You can't hide those forever, Calliope. Someone will eventually see them."

"I'll just have to be very careful. I was able to do it all day today. I'll figure out how to do it every other day."

Cameron looked unconvinced. He folded his arms across his chest, taking a strong stance. "I don't like the sound of that. That wouldn't last forever. *I* noticed them this morning. There's no telling who else could."

"I know," I sighed in frustration, throwing my hands up. "But what am I supposed to do?"

"You're a faery. Can't you disguise yourself or something?"

"No," I said, discouraged. "At least not yet. But if I did I would have to make myself invisible. You wouldn't be able to see me unless I wanted you to and what's the point in that? I wouldn't be able to live a real life."

"There are others," he stated, deadpan.

It didn't surprise me that Cameron trusted me enough to

believe me, but it was unexpected how well he was taking it. He accepted it a lot better than I did, that's for sure.

"I've met two so far, but supposedly there are thousands more."

A blank stare crossed his face as if he'd just seen a pig fly and then he was back in problem solving mode. "Don't they know anything you can do? Can't they turn you back into a human?"

"They are faeries, Cameron. Not wizards."

"But your dad... he looks human. Why can't that be you?"

My dad. *Why hadn't I thought of that?* He left the faery world to be human. I just needed to ask him how he did it.

"That's it, Cam. You're a genius! I don't know why my dad and I hadn't put that option together." Surely, we were smarter than that. But maybe he didn't put two and two together because it wasn't possible. My hope instantly dwindled.

"Let's get you back. Your dad is going to wonder what's taking you so long. I don't want you to have to lie more than you already are."

"My dad can wait. I want to help you."

"I mean it, Cameron," I said, walking back toward my car. "We'll set up another time to talk about this. If you don't make it to help your dad, he's going to want to know why and I don't want to be the reason you have to lie."

He snagged my arm and turned me to him. "C'mere." He grabbed my shoulders, pulling me to his chest and enveloped me in his warmth. "Take a breather, okay? You've got yourself all wound up."

I chuckled. "You try finding out you're a faery and take it completely rationally."

He laughed into my hair. "I'll try that."

When I got home, all was quiet. It was a little after four and I hadn't expected to see my mom, but after just getting my ears I wouldn't have put it passed my dad to be sitting at the kitchen table anxiously waiting for me to come home. Maybe he thought better of it today and decided to give me more space. Since I couldn't ask my dad about getting rid of the faery genes, I turned to the next best thing. I just hoped they were around.

ELEVEN

When I reached the small clearing that had become our mutual meeting ground, I saw Declan perched on a boulder, his stare drifting back and forth, surveying the area. He was a still silhouette of muscle and dominance. After the conversations we've had over the last few weeks, I knew better. He wasn't all-intimidating or a threat... to me anyway.

"Declan?" He turned and smiled gently down at me.

"You can't get enough of us, can you, Princess?" Kai emerged from behind a tree, causing me to jump back.

"Must you always appear out of thin air?"

"I like to keep things interesting." That impish grin formed on his striking face, but rather than irritating me it caught me off guard, causing my breath to catch.

I swallowed and gained my composure before it became too noticeable that he ruffled me. "Well, I guess it's my turn to make things interesting."

Declan's face tilted, intrigued, while Kai cocked an eyebrow

118

as if he didn't believe I could possibly entertain him. I did what I did for Cam and pulled my hair back.

"I knew they'd come in," Kai said smugly. "It was only a matter of time." He leaped behind me, but I chose to ignore his whereabouts and turned to Declan for guidance. He hopped off the boulder and meandered gradually over as if measuring his steps one by one. His cautious strides evoked the nerves in my stomach to run wild.

"Declan," I encouraged him to say something, anything. He was still too quiet for comfort.

"You're finally starting to look like you should," Kai spoke up over my shoulder, covering the silence. "You still look half naked without the wings, but you're getting there." He materialized in front of me. I controlled the urge to step back. Of course he'd be the first to check my back for wings. "You'll get there." He moved away from me and dropped to the soil, propping his lean back up against a near tree trunk then pulled out some sort of flute, blowing into it, creating a flowing erratic melody.

When I looked back to Declan he didn't look happy. I sort of expected him to be happy about this. I was becoming one of them. It was difficult to read his expression. Although he wasn't happy, he didn't look mad either. He looked... melancholy, as if my turning into a faery was a negative thing.

"Declan?"

"Kai is right," he agreed. "You're starting to look like you should. They look as if that's where they always belonged."

Declan's face didn't look very convincing, unless looking like I should was a bad thing.

"When should I expect my wings?" I shifted my eyes between the two Keepers, steering the topic.

"Beats me." Kai stopped his melody for only a second and shrugged, then instantly went back to playing that irksome flute.

"There's no way of knowing," Declan replied evenly.

"So, they could just show up while I'm at school?"

"Well, I assume it will be a gradual thing like your ears," Declan said. "How long did it take for your ears to become full size?"

"About a day."

He nodded. "You'll be able to feel a difference when your wings come in. It won't be the same as your ears. You've always had ears. You've never had wings. I'm not sure you'll be able to hide them as well as you've hidden those, though."

"What about my dad?" I questioned. "Since he's not a faery anymore, can't I do what he did? Can't I stop the process? Kill the faery inside of me?"

Declan's face contorted in pain and I realized how morbid that sounded. "I don't think so," he said softly. His arms twitched at his side as if he contemplated reaching out to me, but thought better of it. "You're in transition. You can't stop the transformation from happening. If you tried, you'd die. Once it's finished—most likely months from now, maybe longer—if you decide you don't want this life, you could probably transform back into a human." The look on his face revealed he hated that idea, but he was trying to remain neutral. "But, Calliope, everything is so unknown with you. It's possible being half and half keeps you from transforming to one or the other at all. Even if you tried you might not survive the transformation. Would you really want to risk that?"

The flickering hope that burned like a flame inside of me was immediately extinguished as I shook my head. "There's really no other way."

Declan was silent now.

Kai got to his feet and walked to me, casually draping his arm around my shoulder. "Oh, it's not so bad, Princess. It's actually kind of a thrill to be a faery. You'll see."

I did my best to ignore his closeness, the warmth of his sinewy body at my side. "How does Faylinn make decisions anyway? I thought Faylinn was a place," I said.

I watched Declan look to Kai and his arm around me, sharing a stare that seemed meaningful somehow before he found my eyes again. "It is, but it's more than just a place. It's the enchanting power over all the faeries. Faylinn makes us what we are. It's like the all-mighty power. We answer to it."

Kai gradually removed his arm as if finding himself and stepped far away from me. I fought against the initial void it left me with.

My eyes flickered to Kai, but he wasn't looking at me, so I turned my attention back to Declan. "It talks?"

"No. No, it's nothing like that," he chuckled lightly. "It's simply a state of being. It's just there, like the wind and the air we breathe. You can't see it, but you can feel it."

"Are you guys a bunch of hippies?" It would make sense as to how they dressed, all natural and simple.

"A hippie?"

"Yeah, you know… love, peace and harmony." I held up two peace signs.

"Well, of course we want all those things. Who wouldn't?" Declan held up his fingers and Kai followed, trying to make sense of my hand gestures.

"What are you trying to do with your hands?" Kai asked. "Bunny ears?" He wiggled his fingers.

I shook my head. "Never mind. You two are hopeless."

"Calliope, we're from different worlds," Declan said, dropping his hand. "Of course we're not going to understand every little detail about one another, but that's what we're here for. We want to help make sense of our world, so you know what you are. Where you come from."

"But I don't want to be what you are. Doesn't anyone see that?"

"Hasn't anyone ever told you life isn't fair?" Kai sounded like he was scolding me. "Get over it, Princess. You're a faery."

I wanted to scream, but I held it inside. I could be mature about this. But he was just so… so…

"Calliope," Declan prompted before I punched Kai in the face. Good timing. "I'm sorry this isn't what you wanted. I understand that it's hard to accept something that your whole life you've been told is a tale. But, I would like to help make it right, help you understand that being a faery isn't a curse."

It was easy for him to say. He hadn't been told he was faery only a few weeks ago. But I kept my negativity to myself. He was right whether I wanted to admit it or not. It was time to start learning about faeries. It was time to stop wallowing in self-pity and accept what I was.

"Thank you, Declan."

He shrugged. "It's what I'm here for."

"I told my best friend Cameron," I blurted. I wasn't sure why I felt like I needed to confess that, but there it was. Out in the open.

"Calliope." Declan placed his hand over his face and sighed.

"Faery basics, Princess," Kai said. "You don't reveal our species to humans. Has your dad taught you nothing?"

"No, he did," I rushed on. "But Cameron saw my ears and I couldn't hide them from him. He won't tell anyone. I know it," I tried to plead my case. "He'll do everything he can to protect me."

"Did you tell your dad that you told Cameron?" Declan asked.

"I haven't gotten the chance yet, but I don't think he'd be too happy with me if he knew."

"How do you know Cameron can be trusted? Humans can never be trusted," Kai emphasized every word.

"My mom's trustworthy. Why do humans have to be deceitful? It's not as if you faeries have been the most forthcoming."

"It's not that they are all deceitful. It's that they can't grasp the idea of our existence," Declan intervened. "They could become fixated or violent. It's not pretty either way."

"You sound as if you know from experience," I said.

Declan rubbed the back of his neck, seeming uncomfortable. "I've heard stories. We've had a few situations occur with male faeries luring human woman. They didn't do it maliciously, only out of curiosity, but things got a little out of hand."

"Well, that was the faeries own fault for using Enticement," I exclaimed.

"Enticement doesn't work on humans. Humans simply can't resist us," Kai said.

"Cocky much?"

Kai chuckled, but didn't deny it.

"It's true, Calliope," Declan backed up Kai again. "Or from what I've heard anyway. It's why we tend to just stay away. It's safer for all parties."

"Well, Cameron is different. He hasn't become fixated with me." I would have noticed and I wouldn't have minded.

123

"You forget. You're only half. It might make you affect humans differently or not have an effect at all," Declan said.

"Can't you put on some enchantment that does the opposite of Enticement or something?"

They both chuckled, which made me feel foolish. They couldn't expect me to know everything. "We can do a ruse here and an enchantment there, but we're not all-powerful. We can't do whatever we want," Declan clarified.

I sighed. "Well, I told Cameron and I can't take it back, so now what?"

"Nothing," Declan said. "We just have to hope that he's one of the few humans who can be trusted."

It really got under my skin to hear them question my best friend. They didn't know him. They didn't know me. It didn't matter that they watched me for years or whatever. That meant they knew my routines and basic information, but they didn't know *me*. I knew they had their reasons, but if anyone could be trusted with my secret it was Cameron.

"So, this is it? For the rest of my existence, I'll be a faery and no one else can know about me?"

Declan solemnly nodded his head. "I'm sorry, Calliope," he said.

I clenched my fists and exhaled. "All right. Teach me everything I need to know."

TWELVE

I noticed that the more time I spent in the woodlands, the easier it was to keep the yearning at bay. It was satisfied as long as I made an appearance in the trees. That discovery was a relief, but it also made me feel trapped. I'd never be able to live a day without the trees. I was tied to Faylinn for better or for worse.

Every day I anticipated my wings' arrival, but they didn't show. Would they look like butterfly wings? Or maybe a flower? Were they going to glitter or shine? Or would they be gossamer and sheer? What if they were going to be too huge to cover up? If they were, my dad would surely be more worried about it and have said as much. But then again, there really was no telling what information that man was going to give up.

The four of us sat on the lawn for lunch. Cameron and Isla sat next to one another, cross-legged, sharing chips and whispering to each other. The whispering stopped getting old and now it was just another day with the lovebirds. It'd been a week and Cameron kept my secret so far.

Out of the corner of my eye I saw Lia snag a hand full of grass and yank, tearing the strands to bits.

"Don't pick at the grass," I reprimanded.

Lia looked at me, puzzled. I wasn't sure why I said it. It wasn't as if I thought plants had feelings or anything, but the thought of nature being torn and picked apart twisted my gut. Nature was my home no matter where I went. I was turning into such a faery.

"Whoa, hadn't realized I would offend anyone."

"You didn't," I retracted. "I don't know why I said that. Pick all the grass you want."

Lia eyed me curiously. "I have to go to the bathroom." She sighed, getting to her feet. I wanted to follow, but at the same time I knew I needed to keep my distance. Why did I have to say that?

"Oh, me too," Isla chimed in. "Wait for me." She stood up and grabbed her backpack. They walked side by side to the school doors.

"Do you plan on ever telling Lia?" Cameron's voice was slightly reproachful, as if he knew he was treading treacherous waters.

I looked over to him. "Cameron, I wasn't even going to tell you. I can't keep telling people."

"But you spend more time with her than me now. And you don't really hide the fact that you're changing very well. It's not just your appearance anymore, which by the way, is definitely noticeable. Half the guys in the hall are stopping just to watch you walk by." There was a tone in his voice I couldn't place. A tone he'd never used with me before.

Was it jealousy?

"Whatever," I said, blushing a little, but brushing him off.

And he was wrong. I hadn't been spending more time with Lia than him. I'd been spending more time with the Keepers, but I didn't correct him. "It's a need to know basis. I'm going to involve the least amount of people necessary. The necessary being my dad, you and the Keepers. It's safer this way."

"The Keepers?" Cameron squinted, unfamiliar with the term that had become a part of my daily vocabulary.

"Yeah, Kai and Declan," I said. "They're the faeries that introduced me to this world in the first place."

"A couple of dudes, huh?" he said, half chuckling.

"Well, someone's got to help the women procreate. Did you think all faeries were just a bunch of girls flitting about in frilly dresses?"

He shrugged sheepishly. "I just never pictured a dude with wings."

"They don't have wings," I retorted. Since when did I become so defensive about the fae?

"How do they fly then?"

"Faery magic," I said blandly. "I don't know. I've never seen them fly. I don't think they do fly. They can just jump really high and far, like an acrobat or something."

"Will you be able to fly?"

It suddenly dawned on me how little I knew about being a faery. Did they fly? Would I be able to use Enticement as well? Did they have any other abilities? What kind of houses did they live in? The questions were piling up and I knew my head would explode if I kept thinking about them.

"I don't know. We haven't gotten that far in my faery education," I said dryly, but my weariness shined through.

Cameron chuckled. He could obviously see my discouragement because he said, "Callie, it'll all come to you.

You'll learn everything eventually. Give it time."

I heaved a sigh. "It's like being born all over again, but instead of having years to learn how to walk and eat and talk, I'm being throw into a world that I know nothing about and am expected to know everything right away."

"I wouldn't be too worried about it. You have time, right? It's not like you're being quizzed about it or have to move to your faery kingdom tomorrow."

I glared at him, silencing him just in time for Lia and Isla to come back.

"It's getting chilly, Cam. Can we go inside?" Isla asked.

"Sure." He stood up and dusted off his pants. "We'll see you ladies later."

"See ya," I said.

"Bye," Lia said. When they were back in the school, Lia turned to me. "You and Cameron have been getting chummier since they started dating. I told you phase one would eventually start to fade."

I almost forgot Lia's relationship theory. "He's still head over heels, but it's okay." I shrugged, taking a sip from my water bottle. "I'm getting over it." And I was. Well, at least to the point of realizing I had bigger things to worry about than my love life.

She laughed. "If that's not the biggest load of crap I've ever heard come out of your mouth I don't know what is." I shifted my gaze to her. "I might not be telepathic, but I wasn't born yesterday either. You still look at him the same way, Callie. You're still one hundred percent smitten."

"Great," I said. "Glad I haven't miraculously been nominated for an Oscar for my acting skills."

She snorted and shoved me. "Don't worry. As obvious as it is to me, I don't think he knows. He's charming, but he's not a jerk. He wouldn't string you along if he knew about your feelings."

"I know. How else do you think I've been able to keep my friendship with him for this long?"

"He loves you, you know?"

I nodded. *Just not in the same way I love him.*

"Going with pigtails today. I like it," Dad said when he materialized in my doorway. I leaned against my headboard, working on an assignment for calculus.

"I figured Pippi Longstocking wanted her braids back."

He chuckled. "I don't mind the braids. They remind me of when your mom braided your hair when you were little." He regarded me with that you're-growing-up-too-fast look before breathing a sigh. "Your creativity is becoming noticeable though. Mom mentioned it last night," he said regrettably.

"Well, I can't risk just leaving my hair down like I used to, Dad. You know that."

He came to sit at the end of my bed by my feet. "Have you put any more thought into going to Faylinn?"

"No. Why would I?"

He sat wordlessly for a moment, considering something before he spoke. "It might make things easier," he commented softly.

"Easier for who? Don't you think Mom would notice if her only daughter went missing?" I expressed myself with a little more attitude than was probably necessary.

"Easier for you," he said gently. "And I would obviously tell your mother before anything progressed that far."

He didn't know what he was saying. He couldn't possibly think I would want to live in Faylinn under the ruling of someone like Favner. It was no wonder my dad left in the first place. It wasn't just romantic. It was smart, maybe his only way of survival.

"Dad, Favner… Favner is evil. I don't want to live in a place that—"

"Favner?" Dad said the name like it was foreign on his tongue. "Favner is ruling Faylinn?"

"Has he not always?" Did I know more about Faylinn than my dad?

Dad shook his head, but didn't say anything more.

"Well, Favner is ruling now and everyone is divided up and forced to work these tiresome jobs—day or night, rain or shine. They're slaves and I would have to become a Nester."

"What do you mean have to?" The look in my dad's eyes was unreadable. "What's a Nester?"

"How do you not *know* this? Nesters are ordered to carry the seedlings. Do you know what that would mean for me?"

The look on my dad's face shifted from unreadable to furiously confused. "What do you mean Nesters are forced to reproduce? What about Craftsmen and Keepers? What about Sowers?"

Why didn't he know any of this? What had it been like when he was in Faylinn? "They have their duties to focus on. Favner couldn't afford for all jobs to be overlooked, I guess."

"What if a member of another colony gets pregnant?" he asked, a heated undertone lacing his voice.

I hadn't thought far enough to ask that question. But if Favner's way of ruling was any indication, I didn't want to know because I could only imagine the measures Favner would take for

130

punishment. I shrugged timidly and shook my head.

"I don't know," I said.

He stood up from my bed and began to pace. In all the years of my life, I'd never seen my dad this angry. He didn't say anything more. I sat silently until his pace slowed and his breathing was back to normal. My dad finally looked at me, and if I wasn't mistaken I saw his eyes glisten as if tears were threatening to spill over.

"Dad, I can't live in a place that would turn me into a slave," I said quietly.

"And I wouldn't ask you to. We'll find a way to keep you safe." He turned to the door, but before he exited my room he said, "Don't stay up too late, Calliope. Six thirty will come around before you know it."

I nodded even though he couldn't see me because I couldn't force my mouth to make any more words. I didn't know what to make of his reaction. What had it been like when my dad lived in Faylinn? Who ruled then and why wasn't he ruling now?

THIRTEEN

Several weeks passed and the paranoia began to wear off every time someone looked at me. Either that or I stopped paying so much attention. I think I'd mastered the art of ear coverage with my creativity. It was even a little comical the way I was complimented by others at school when I came with a different style. If I were smart, I'd tone it down to keep the attention from me—period.

"Do I get to meet your faery friends or are you ashamed of your human friends?" Cameron asked, matching my pace as I strode down the crowded hallway to English.

"Meet Declan and Kai?" I stopped, stepping to the side of the hallway and out of the way.

"Yes. Meet them," he said as if I was slow, as if it shouldn't make me uncomfortable.

I shifted from one foot to the other. "I don't know. I guess you could, but I'm not sure if it's all that good of an idea. They might not even want to show themselves to you."

"They make themselves invisible to humans?" I nodded. "But they appear to you," he clarified.

"I'm not completely human," I said, hushed. "They don't have to show themselves to me. I just see them like I see you."

"Cool. So when do I get to meet them?" he persisted.

It was one thing to reveal that I was a faery to Cameron, but it was a whole other story to combine the two worlds. They would crash and burn.

"Are you sure you want to? I mean, they aren't exactly the friendliest and I'm not sure bringing an outsider into their territory would make them very comfortable." I tried to deter the idea in his head. I could only imagine the remarks Kai would make and the look on Declan's face.

"You spend all your free time with them," Cameron said. "Of course I want to meet them. I want to know who you deem worthy of spending time with. I want to make sure I can trust them."

I rolled my eyes and started to make my way toward English again. "It's not that I deem them worthy. They're just the only ones I know."

Cameron and I walked side by side down the hall, hips bumping, as we squeezed through others' conversations. It felt so good to be just him and me again. This was how it was supposed to be. Just the two of us.

"Fine, but to be on the safe side would you park your jeep down the road from my house? If my mom comes home while we're out there and sees your car I won't be able to explain that."

He chuckled. "Why don't you just tell your mom, Callie? She's going to figure it out sooner or later. She *did* fall in love with a faery," he said under his breath. "It's not as if she won't believe you."

"I know, but my dad asked me not to. And even though he kept this from me, I want to do as he asked. She's dealing with a huge case right now. And when she does find out, it'll fall on his shoulders. I'm only obeying him."

"Oh, so that makes it okay," he teased.

That *did* make me sound a little shady. "No, it's just—"

"Cameron!" Isla called out from down the joining hallway and smiled widely.

Cam looked at me apologetically. "Duty calls." He smirked. "I'll be at your house no later than 4:00."

"All right," I surrendered. "But I still don't know if it's the best idea," I said uneasily. "And they might not even be around. I didn't tell them I would come today."

"Live a little, would ya?" He winked at me before turning back to Isla.

Why couldn't I have told him no? I breathed heavily and turned to head off to class.

Earlier that morning Dad told me he had a job so he wouldn't be home waiting for me after school. That was a relief now with Cameron on his way, though if Dad was home it could have been my escape for the afternoon. But knowing Cameron, he would have just pressed and pressed to meet the Keepers until I let him sooner or later.

"They're not going to lash out and challenge me to a duel of sword fighting, are they?" Cameron asked as we stepped out onto the back deck.

"What world do you live in where faeries are like medieval knights?"

134

"Hey, like you said... who's to say what faeries are like? The only faery I've ever heard of is Tinkerbell. I'm giving your Keepers the benefit of the doubt, all things considered."

I chuckled. "They won't *challenge you to a duel*. But they probably will keep themselves invisible. I don't know why I let you talk me into this."

Cameron took hold of my hand when we reached the trees. I wanted to make a snarky remark about him being scared, but instead I invited the handholding and kept the remark to myself. I led the way without a word. He stumbled a few times on fallen logs and inconveniently placed rocks, but I kept him upright.

"How are you not tripping all over the place? It's like a freaking maze in here."

I shrugged. "I come out here a lot. I know where to step?" I offered.

"Yeah. More like you're a faery and Grace should be your new name." I smiled to myself at what appeared to be a compliment.

When I found our small clearing in the woods, Kai was the only one in sight. He sat with his back toward us on the fuzzy green-cloaked boulder; the ripple of his muscles emphasized with the way the sunlight hit him. The wooden flute played a beautiful melody from his position. He'd only ever played pointless notes and sporadic tunes before, but this was like a hauntingly soothing lullaby.

I wanted to stay quiet, listening to his music making, but Cameron look a step and snapped a twig, causing the music to stop and Kai to turn. Realization set in that I'd let go of Cameron's hand and left him several feet behind me, having been pulled toward the music.

At first I couldn't read Kai's expression. He almost looked

135

relieved, but then his expression changed back to unnerving Kai. "What an unsuspected surprise." He hopped off the rock and sauntered over to us. "Who do we have here?"

I motioned between the two of them "Kai, this is Cameron. Cam, Kai."

"You're Cameron?" Kai laughed instantly. "I don't understand what Declan was so worried about."

"Shut up, Kai." *What did he mean by that?*

"He's here?" Cameron asked. "You see him?" His eyes drifted over the greenery, probing it from side to side, blinded because Kai obviously had kept himself hidden.

I sighed. "Kai, will you please show yourself so I don't look like a crazy person staring off into space, talking to myself?"

"Only because you said 'please.' That's all you had to do."

Cameron didn't say anything. I wasn't sure if he could see Kai until I turned back and saw the look on his face. Cameron's eyes were wide, his mouth slightly hanging open. "*You're* a faery?" he said disbelieving.

"In the flesh," Kai remarked. "Declan will be sad he missed you," he said, peering back at me with those arresting eyes.

"Where is he?" I asked, trying not to seem disappointed that he was missing.

"In Faylinn," he said, matter-a-fact. "You should know the answer to that by now, Princess."

"Princess?" Cameron chimed over my shoulder. He stood awkwardly hesitant. He pretended like he was all cool and comfortable with this world, but I knew him better. If he felt completely at ease I would have been worried.

"He likes to provoke me, and calling me princess does it pretty well."

Cameron laughed. "My kind of guy." He took a step

forward and lifted his hand to high-five Kai, but Kai merely stood there, which in turn made me laugh. Kai looked to me for guidance. That was a first.

"He's a faery, Cameron. They aren't really familiar with human hand gestures."

"Well, don't leave me hanging," Cam said, turning to me, so I smacked his hand to show Kai what Cameron had wanted.

"And what exactly was that?" Kai asked irritably, feeling left in the dark.

"A high-five. It basically means that you agree with what the other person is saying, or it's a way of cheering and congratulating someone. We, humans, use it for acceptance, camaraderie."

"Oh, like a Root."

Cameron and I raised our eyebrows and shared a look.

Kai walked over to me and took my hand in his without hesitation. My heart sputtered. His hands were strong and, although a little rough from living outdoors, they were gentle. He glided his hand up and laced his fingers around my wrist. I mirrored him, wrapping my hand around his wrist. When I lifted my eyes from our intertwined hands, Kai's deep eyes stared back at me. They were an ever-changing form of purplish blue. Today purple won over the blue. His eyes never left mine as he spoke.

"It signifies unity, support. The Keepers use a Root whenever we relieve another Keeper of duty at the end of the day. Sometimes it's used when a deal is made or when meeting before or after a long journey." A small smile tugged at the corner of his lips as his thumb lightly brushed the inside of my wrist, sending shivers down my body. "It was also used during the ceremony of bonding. One faery to another." A twinkle danced across his eyes, jolting the beat of my heart. "I believe humans call them weddings."

"That's cool," Cameron said, unaffected.

I, however, was trying to recover.

Kai didn't let go, but I didn't feel like we could stay that way without it getting awkward, so I reluctantly released myself from his soft grip, feeling a little piece of me slip away as I did it.

"It's kind of like that, but a little more casual," I said and shook off my initial reaction. *Stupid Kai.* He'd done that enchantment thing or whatever on me. I scowled at him, but he didn't seem to notice.

"Why is it called a Root?" Cameron asked.

"Do you know how redwood trees grow?"

Cameron and I shook our heads.

"Roots are the lifelines of a tree, their heart. While most tree roots grow downward deep into the soil, the roots of the redwood grow outward, intertwining with their neighboring roots as if holding hands. As they entangle around one another they strengthen, anchoring themselves, giving such solid support to each other there's no way they could fall."

"Why the holding of the wrists. Why not just a simple handshake?" I asked.

"You have major arties in your wrists. Lifelines. We're holding one another's lifelines in our hands. Don't humans have a term 'my life is in your hands'?" I nodded once. "Well, we use it in the literal sense."

My heart sped up as I watched Kai. His gaze never wavered, steadfast and confident as he watched me. I felt so small and insecure in that moment.

Cameron rested his arm around my shoulder and pulled me to his side, almost possessively. "So, when Callie gets her wings, will she be able to fly?"

138

Subtle, Cam.

"Callie?" Kai seemed perplexed and agitated by Cameron's nickname for me. As if everyone should call me princess to infuriate me. "Fly? Faeries don't fly. We're agile. We can climb great heights, leap far distances, and balance on a thread. Because of the wings it sometimes gets mistaken for flying, but the wings have no special abilities. They are merely one more way to define a female from a male."

"So you spring from tree to tree like that one movie." Cameron pointed with his free arm to the branches weaving above us. "Crouching tiger something or other."

Kai, of course, had no idea what he was talking about and I'd never really seen a faery in action so I didn't know, but to break the tension I said, "Yeah. Just like that."

"Cool." Cameron bobbed his head. "So, do you sleep in these trees or do you have houses?"

Kai made a face, a cross between amusement and annoyance. "I don't mind sleeping in the trees, but I do have a bed that I go home to."

"So, why are you here?" Cam asked bluntly. I nearly cut in because Kai's face immediately closed off, obviously uncomfortable with Cam's questioning, but I was curious too. I knew that he and Declan wanted space from Favner, but why always come to my backyard? I'd never asked why I needed protection.

"Why not?" he finally retorted.

Cameron didn't have an answer. He shrugged, his arm never leaving my shoulder.

"It seemed a place better than any," Kai said.

There was a silence between the three of us, only the soft breeze and rustling of leaves to break the silence.

I cleared my throat. "What are the houses like, Kai?"

"Well, it has four walls and a roof."

"Wow," I said. "How insightful of you? Do they have doors and windows too?"

He smirked out of the side of his mouth. "They even have walls inside to divide the rooms apart."

I rolled my eyes. This was exactly why I never came to talk to Kai. He was *so* forthcoming with *heaps* of information. It was time for me to take Cameron home. "Well, Kai, thanks for the riveting faery lesson today. Tell Declan I was sad we missed him."

"You can bet I will," he said all too enthusiastically. I knew he wouldn't.

Cameron didn't want to leave, so I had to wrap my arm around his waist and lead him away as he watched Kai.

"Later, dude," Cameron hollered.

Kai didn't say anything and when I looked back he was gone. As always.

When we were close to the border Cameron said, "He wasn't at all what I had expected. He was like a mix between that elf from Lord of the Rings and Tarzan."

"Tarzan?" I said, laughing.

"Well, the whole bare chest thing. Do faeries wear shirts? Or are all the faeries topless because if that is the case you're taking me to Faylinn right now."

I shoved him. "I've seen them in shirts before. I think it just comes with the territory. It's not as if they have air conditioning. They're outside all the time."

"You've never seen any female faeries before?" he inquired.

With a shake of my head I said, "They aren't actually supposed to leave Faylinn, I don't think. Declan and Kai get special permission or something." I shrugged. I'd never really thought beyond that.

"Don't you want to go to Faylinn?"

The mere thought of it terrified me. "Yes, in theory it's intriguing, and, sure, I'm curious, but with the way Declan described Favner... what if he never let me leave once I set foot on their soil? I can't take my chances with that. And I don't want to be what Favner would make me."

We reached the perimeter of my yard and he stopped. "He's that bad, huh? You couldn't just say, hey I'm visiting."

I chuckled. "I don't think it works like that."

"That's too bad." He smirked.

I looked through the branches and vines toward the back of my house. "We need to do this very carefully and nonchalantly like we didn't just walk out of these trees. I'll go first." I checked my phone. The light flashed on that it was 4:48. "My mom and dad shouldn't be home yet, but if one of them is, I don't want to get you tangled up in this, too. Once I reach the house I'll signal to you, okay?"

Cameron agreed.

I walked up the back steps of our deck and peered into the window of my house. Mom was at the kitchen table with her back to the window. *Crap.* She was home early. She hadn't seen me, but if she looked outside at all and hadn't already seen me in the back she would wonder where I was coming from. As if sensing my presence she started to twist in the chair toward me. I dropped to the ground, out of sight and crawled away as fast as I could, which turned out to be pretty swift.

When I looked out to the trees Cameron wasn't in view, but I knew he could see me, so I pointed to the side of the house and motioned for him to stay put. If I could get in through the front door and distract her to keep her from looking outside, he could get away.

I steadied my breathing before opening the front door. "Hello?" I called out into the house.

"In here," she called back from the same place she had been, thankfully.

I strolled through the hallway to the kitchen. *Be cool.* "Hey, Mom," I said. "You're home early."

"Hi, Calliope. Yeah, I finished all I needed to get done today and there was no point in starting on another project, so I came home. Are you just getting home from school?"

"No, I was running some errands with Cameron," I lied as I made my way to the window. If I could motion for him to book it to the side of the house we would be home free. "Where's Dad?" I asked to distract her from my nervous behavior. I knew I wasn't doing a very good job at being discreet.

"He had a job. He'll be home later this evening, so it's just you and me. Want to go see a movie or something?"

That actually sounded like a really good idea. My mom and I hadn't hung out for a long time. I couldn't even remember the last time it was only the two of us.

"I'd really like that."

She smiled. "Let me get my laptop. I'll check the movie times."

"Okay."

As she walked away, I swiftly turned to face the woods and waved my arms to have him head to the side of the house, but there was no movement from the trees. How could he not see me? I probably looked like a giant monkey jumping up and down and flailing my arms.

Great. I hadn't thought this one through. There must have

been a glare on the window. Cameron couldn't see me. Just as I was about to open the sliding glass door, Mom walked back in.

"You have any preferences on movies?"

I spun around to her. "Umm… anything funny." Cameron was probably wondering what the hold up was.

She sat back at the table and scrolled through the movies. "Jackpot—that new romantic comedy came out today. 6:15, 7:45 and 9:30," she read off. "If we go now we can grab a quick dinner and do the 6:15 showing."

"Great!" I said, too enthusiastically. She looked at me and laughed.

"Okay," she said slowly. "I'll go grab my purse."

As soon as she was out of the room, I threw the sliding glass door open and pointed for him to make a run for it. Thankfully, he listened and booked it out of the trees. He smiled goofily as he held up his hand to his ear in an I'll-call-you gesture before he disappeared around my house. I closed the door and breathed a sigh of relief. *Phew.* I raced to the garage door so I looked like I'd done something while she was gone.

"You ready?" She smiled as she turned the corner.

"I was born ready."

She chuckled and we headed out for our first girls' night in months.

"Why don't you wear your hair down anymore, Calliope?" she asked as we drove down our street.

I shrugged, figuring indifference would work in my favor. She lifted her hand from the steering wheel, her hands outstretched to touch my hair and I pulled back, barely dodging her touch.

"Oh, come on. It's my favorite when you wear your hair down," she whined.

"I like changing it up, trying out different hair styles. I've never really done that before. I needed a change."

She reached out again.

"Mom," I said more firmly, shifting out of her reach. "You'll mess it up and I'll have to do it all over again."

"Oh, who do you have to impress? It's just me tonight."

"Well, it would just be a pain." My arms curled in front of me, seeking comfort close against me.

Mom chuckled. "Okay, Miss Defensive. I'll leave the hair alone. It does look cute today," she amended.

"Thanks," I said, biting my bottom lip. I was going to eventually mentally beat my brains to a pulp if I didn't get a better hold on not getting defensive.

My life depended on it.

That night I lay in bed unable to find the peaceful serenity of sleep, tossing and turning as the floodgates opened in my mind, pouring out the countless issues I couldn't find solutions to. It wouldn't shut off. I jerked when my phone began to ring and Cameron's face glowed on my screen. He'd actually called.

"Hey," I answered warmly.

"Hey, you in the clear?"

I chuckled quietly. "Yeah. My mom was home, but I played it off and we went to the movies."

"Oh man. Good. I've been stressing about it all day. I thought we were toast when you didn't come out. It felt like an eternity."

"My acting skills have improved since all this started," I yawned.

"You in bed?"

"Yeah."

"I didn't wake you, did I?" he questioned with a weird hint of concern in his voice.

"No, I was just laying here. Got a lot running through my mind." I twirled one of my curls through my fingers and played with the point on my ear. There were times when the tips would still catch me off guard and other times when it felt like they had been there all along. They'd become a part of who I was.

"You want to talk about it?" Cameron's voice interrupted my wandering thoughts.

"Talk about what?"

"I don't know. Whatever's running around in that head of yours." His familiar voice was soothingly soft. It reminded me of the Cam I used to know, who never missed a goodnight call before this last summer.

I sighed, relieved I was slowly getting my Cameron back. "It was just something my dad said the other day. He questioned what happened to the fae from other colonies that got pregnant and weren't supposed to."

"Did you find out the answer from your fan club?"

I chuckled lightly, not in the mood to contradict him. "Not yet." I exhaled. "What kind of a kingdom do I belong to? Where no one gets a choice. Where fae disappear and die for no good reason. The Keepers are there to protect them from invaders and keep the peace within, but who's there to protect them from the inside, from the one they really need protecting from?"

Cameron remained quiet for a moment. I could hear him considering his answer. It wasn't as if I really expected an answer. People searched for the answers to world peace and the end of hunger, but they couldn't solve problems bigger than themselves.

Was this just one of those problems that could never be resolved?

"It's not your burden to carry, Callie. I think what's important is that you are safe here, away from the tyrant who will never lay a hand on you."

I nodded without answering. If only it were that easy. If I felt comfortable with that answer I wouldn't have been lying in bed, searching for solutions in my head all night long.

We sat in silence for a few minutes, listening to one another's breathing. There was a time when we would stay on the phone all night long until one of us fell asleep. I remembered several occasions waking up with my phone either drained of battery or Cameron's shallow breathing on the other side.

His breath was becoming shallower now.

"Are you falling asleep?" I quietly questioned.

"Maybe." He yawned.

"Go to bed. I'll see you tomorrow."

"Sure thing," he said softly. "Good night, Cal. Sweet dreams."

"You too."

FOURTEEN

To keep from having any more awkward situations with Kai, Declan and I set up a schedule for when he would be in Faylinn. Of course, I didn't tell him why I wanted to know when he would be around, but I think it was implied. For weeks I went to the clearing to get what I liked to call my Faery 101. It was essentially a question and answer session where I asked all the questions and Declan answered them.

Declan never acted put out by my incessant need to know everything and always answered to the best of his ability. Kai showed up less than half of the time, which left me feeling a million different ways, but I chalked it all up to nerves because he was a wild card. I never knew what to expect with him, so obviously my emotions had a wide range of highs and lows. I didn't really care whether he was around or not—or maybe I did. Ultimately, I wanted to be prepared for one or the other.

Clearly, the fae didn't have technology, but it baffled me to think of living in such simplicity: living off of the land and eating only what was grown or lived in the woods. They weren't vegetarians as I imagined them to be. I learned that they might not sleep on tree limbs, but that some of their homes were in the trees, like tree houses. They were allergic to all things metal. So, everything they built was from nature—all things from their surroundings—wood, bone, clay, animal teeth, and rocks.

"It's a common misconception that we're allergic to only iron. Though iron does block our magic, we're affected by lead, steel, and silver just the same as iron," Declan explained.

"So, is that why you stay in the forest? You're invisible so it's not as if anyone could see if you wanted to leave."

He nodded. "We don't have to actually touch metal to be affected; simply being in the proximity of it weakens us. But since you're only half, I assume you're immune to it. You are lucky."

That *did* make me feel lucky. If I became allergic I would be forced to leave. That was one power I hoped would stay the way it was.

"How about the eyes? Why are they so vibrant?"

"Why are human eyes not?"

I shrugged. "DNA?"

"Who's to say what is normal? The faded green, blue, and brown might be normal to humans, but it's perplexing to us. Just as the make-up of a human's DNA and so forth creates eye color for them, it does the same for us. It's just in the fae DNA. Maybe it's what we eat; maybe it's fae magic. It's just the way it is."

I knew being a faery was never going to truly be logical to me. They could teach and try to explain until their cheeks turned blue, but it wasn't going to make sense. I just had to accept that.

"You two travel from Faylinn every day. How far away is it?"

Declan stood from the roots and began to roam the area. I noticed neither Kai nor Declan could ever stay in one place for long. It made me wonder, if they got restless so easily, how they managed to keep themselves entertained in these trees every day.

"Well, it takes about an hour with our speed. It's probably about 200 miles away," Declan replied.

I looked up and saw Kai resting on his usual limb in the trees, a large fig leaf placed over his eyes as his bobbing foot crossed over the other. He remained silent, most likely ignoring us down below.

"How is Faylinn protected? You said there were thousands of you? How can an area that's inhabited by that many faeries be overlooked?"

"Faylinn is guarded by wards, like an invisible fence. When humans pass by they don't even see it. In actuality, it doesn't even take up any part of the forest. Once you pass into Faylinn it's like passing into another world. The passageway just happens to be placed in this forest."

I was quiet for a moment, drinking in the knowledge. Once my head wrapped around the idea I threw out the next question.

"Is anyone else allowed to leave? Or is it just you two?"

Declan didn't answer right away. And he wouldn't meet my eyes either. "Honestly, we shouldn't even leave, but it hasn't been an issue thus far."

"What if Favner finds out?" The thought of either of them getting into trouble worried me. Well, the thought of Declan getting in trouble bothered me. I might revel in the thought of Kai being put in his place.

"He'll kill us," Kai's voice drifted down from his branch. My head jerked up to the tone in his voice, so straightforward, not a hint of fear or concern.

"You don't know that, Kai," Declan lectured, leering up at him.

"It doesn't mean I'm not right," he replied with the same casual tone.

"He would really kill you for leaving Faylinn's boundaries?" My eyes flickered from Declan across the clearing to Kai above.

"No. He wouldn't kill over that," Declan confirmed.

Kai mumbled something from his limb. A look of frustration crossed Declan's face as he glared up into the tree.

"What?" I asked.

"Kai is just being a tyrant."

Kai scoffed, but said nothing more as if he couldn't be bothered with us or our conversation anymore.

"Declan," I prompted. "My dad brought something up the other day that I hadn't thought of before and it really bothered me."

"What was it?"

I bit my lower lip. "What happens if a faery from another colony aside from the Nesters gets pregnant?"

Declan pressed his lips together. I'd seen sorrow in Declan's eyes before, but nothing like the anguish that masked his gaze now. "They're terminated," he said softly.

"The faery or the seedling?" I murmured, matching his tone.

"Sometimes both. The termination is meant for the seedling, but sometimes the mother doesn't survive." I swallowed and he turned his head away from me, looking to the soil.

"Why?" I asked.

"Declan," Kai cautioned, but I didn't understand. "You don't have to—"

"No, it's okay," Declan said, gritting his teeth before carrying on. "You see, the connection between a mother and her seedling is very strong. I've heard the bond is like no other sensation. Of course, when a mother is with child she can sense the baby. She can feel its movement and so forth. For fae women that sensation is heightened. They can sense what the seedling wants, what the seedling feels. It has to do with the accelerated process of the pregnancy. So, when a seedling is terminated, the mother feels their pain, their loss and…" he trailed off and I didn't have to ask him to finish that thought. I didn't want to ask him to finish. "Most times it's too much for them to handle."

Tears pricked my eyes, but I kept them from falling. "But if termination could mean losing a faery, why would Favner risk it?"

Declan peered back at me under that thick gaze of his lashes as if I should know the answer to this by now. "It's punishment, Calliope. A deterrent from thinking they could somehow hide it. A lesson to be taught to those who think they could get away with it. 'If death is the outcome, so be it,' I once heard him say."

I should have thought better of my question before I asked it, but I didn't. "Do you know someone that this happened to?"

"*Don't.*" Kai landed at my side, finally making an appearance, warning me. I overstepped, but I couldn't take it back.

Declan answered me anyway. "My mother was passed her seedling bearing years, but apparently the fates didn't feel she was finished. Favner found out a week before the seedling was ready to come."

My chest ached, compressed under the weight of his words.

Why had I asked? Why couldn't I keep my curiosity to myself?

"Declan." I swallowed. "I'm sorry. Had I realized…"

"Calliope," he murmured. "It's okay. It happened a few years back."

"How many?" I asked hesitantly.

"A little over six years." He looked back to the ground, surprisingly keeping his composure.

I winced. That must have felt like months or less in Faylinn time. I reached out and rested my hand over his. He flinched slightly, but didn't move his hand. There were no words I could say. I didn't know loss yet. I'd never lost anyone that close to me before.

The sun started to set, dimming the natural light in the grove of trees. "You should probably get back home, Calliope. It's going to be dark soon," Declan encouraged.

I nodded reluctantly. If only I could've kept my lips shut. "I'll be back tomorrow."

"I'll be gone tomorrow," Declan replied, then hesitantly said, "If that's a factor in you coming or not."

It was. "The next day then?"

"What am I? Mud beneath a toadstool?" Kai asked, positioning himself against his tree and finally smirking at me, sending my nerves frantically in every direction.

I cleared my throat. "Kai," I said surprisingly even. "Would you like me to come see you tomorrow?"

Please say no.

It wasn't because I despised him, but the idea of being alone with him actually terrified me; and not in the I'm-terrified-of-the-things-that-go-bump-in-the-night terror, but because he stripped me of my confidence and relentlessly tormented my vulnerabilities without even realizing it. Or maybe he did and that's why he did it: to purposefully fluster me.

"I'll pass," he said, disinterested in our one-on-one conversation already. "I do have a life apart from watching Declan's back."

"Do you now?" Declan asked, humored, pulling himself back together. "Please share. I'd like to know what you do when I'm not here to keep you in check."

"Wouldn't you like to know," Kai said and turned his back on us, traveling into the woodlands.

"Yeah, I would." Declan replied, watching him, but Kai didn't answer. He once again shot off his feet without as much as a goodbye.

"Why does he always do that?"

Declan chortled and moved his aqua eyes back to me. "Do what?"

"Just walk away without any explanation."

"He's all about the dramatic exits. I stopped questioning why Kai does the things he does a long time ago." Declan scanned the trees around us. "It's almost sundown, Calliope."

"Right. I was leaving." I started to back away and waved. "I'll see you on Wednesday."

"You know where to find me." He offered a small smile and my stomach tingled.

The house was dark when I got home. Mom obviously was caught up at the office, but I didn't know where my dad was. We hadn't talked much aside from the casual greetings and polite conversation about our days since the day I told him about Favner. Though we hadn't spoken, I was comforted by the fact that he wanted to keep me at home. Safe and sound.

I fell asleep that night with the reassurance that no matter what happened I would be looked after. I would be protected.

FIFTEEN

The tingling woke me that night. My spine tingled like it had fallen asleep. I sat up and rolled my shoulders around, trying to get rid of the feeling, but it wouldn't let up. I reached my hand around my back to scratch when I felt them.

My wings.

Flipping on my nightstand light, I got to my feet and hurried to my mirror. I pulled the hem of my shirt up and spun my back to the mirror, peering over my left shoulder. It looked like two small rolls of creamy yellow fabric budding from in between my shoulder blades. I reached back and stroked the delicate buds. The soft wings tucked snuggly in themselves as if unready to hatch. Breathing in and out, I watched them in the mirror.

In that moment everything clicked. Everything I'd been fighting or wanting to deny was becoming a reality as I examined the yellow bundles poking out over my spine. *When it looked you dead in the eye how could you reject it any longer?* It was like I was in an

AA meeting and I was finally coming to terms with my life.

My name is Calliope Willow Holbrook and I have wings. I am a faery.

I couldn't tear myself from the mirror. I knew I needed to sleep, but I had freaking faery wings! Every couple of minutes that thought triggered and I was reminded that I was looking at *my* back, not just watching some fantasy movie play across the mirror. Their appearance altered subtlety as I observed them, but nothing drastic happened. After about an hour the weight of my eyelids began to sag and I dragged my legs back to bed, compelling myself to sleep.

When I woke up the following morning, I raced to the mirror to check the progress of my wing's development. The rolls had grown, but they stayed curled neatly inside like a bear hibernating in the winter. Even after watching them all night long it still hadn't registered that they'd grown out of me.

Suddenly, it dawned on me. How was I going to hide the Hunchback of Notre Dame? I looked like a hump was growing on my back. My backpack would cover it while I wasn't in class, but what was I supposed to do when I took it off? It was only October. It wasn't cold enough to wear a hoodie inside, but I would simply have to suffer the heat. With the bulk of the material and the hood resting against my shoulders, maybe it would distract the eye.

I threw on my thickest sweatshirt and checked my back. The bulge was still visible, but not as noticeable. It wasn't ideal, but it would have to do. I rolled my ringlets into buns on either side of my ears, settling for Princess Leia style—going for a grunge look and praying I pulled it off.

Cameron must have seen it in my eyes the moment out eyes met. When I walked up to our lockers, he scanned my body up and down and knew. "You got them?" he whispered close to my ear.

I nodded once, discreetly I hoped, pretending that he didn't say anything to me.

Isla was busy on her phone, thankfully overlooking our small interaction as Lia walked up.

"Good morning, all," she said.

"Good morning," Cameron and I said in unison. Isla barely lifted her head and muttered something resembling, "morning."

"I'm dying to go swimming. You want to head to Lake Keowee and go for a dip after school?" Lia asked.

Cameron and I shared a quick look and glanced swiftly away, but I don't think it was fast enough.

"I'm going to have a lot of homework today. Maybe I'll catch you next time. How about a movie tonight?"

She glanced between Cameron and me. Isla was oblivious as she finished writing a text. Cameron caught onto the immediate awkward silence, but rather than saving me he bailed. "Isla, we're going to be late. Let's go." He escorted her away from our crowd.

"Bye, guys." She waved over her shoulder.

"Bye, Isla," I said.

They weren't gone for more than five seconds when Lia cornered me.

"What's up with the secrecy?"

"What secrecy?" I shifted my backpack. The weight was pinching my buds.

"You and Cam." She gestured to him walking down the hall. He looked over his shoulder, an anxious look in his eyes. *Poor timing, Cam.* "You're hiding something."

"I'm not hiding anything," I said, shaking my head and

chuckling breathlessly.

"Are you and Cameron..." she let her question trail off, alluding to something sketchy behind Isla's back. "You know..."

"No," I said adamantly and started walking to class.

"What is it then?" she persisted. "Why can't you tell me?"

"There's nothing to tell," I chuckled to make light of things. I did not need her thinking I was doing the dirty with Cameron behind Isla's back. How could she think so low of me?

"Oh, there definitely is," she insisted.

Lia wasn't going to make this very easy on me. I hated lying to her, but I couldn't tell her. "There really isn't, Lia. We're just finally back to the way it was before."

"No, this is more," she challenged.

I sighed. "Enough detective for one day, yeah?"

She eyed me, knowing I wasn't being completely honest, but she let it go. "Whatever you say, liar. Keep your secrets to yourself. I'll let you for today."

The last thing I needed today was for Lia to start a fight and abandon me. I felt alone enough as it was. Losing a best friend on top of my human genes might actually put me in a mental institution.

"I saw you with Jake yesterday," I deflected the conversation from me. "You looked awfully chummy by his locker."

She stood a little taller, closing off her expression to me. "I was talking to him about our life skills project."

"You did *not* tell me you had a class with him. And you have a project together?"

She shrugged, trying to feign indifference. "What's there to tell? He's in a class with me. He sits across the room and I actually listen during class. No one else exists in there, but me and the teacher."

I smirked. "And you have a project with him?" I egged her on. It was probably a bad move, but the distraction of simple life issues was refreshing. I actually missed them. When all I really had to worry about was my unrequited love for Cameron. I'd gladly welcome back my human problems if they would take away my new genes.

"Mrs. Jennings paired us against her better judgment. I did not willingly go into the partnership and I set ground rules on day one. If he causes me to fail this project I will make his life a living hell."

"I can imagine that was only more of an incentive to screw up. Some attention is better than no attention in some people's minds." I chuckled.

Lia wasn't amused. "He's actually deemed himself to be a worthy partner, contributing and pulling his weight on his part of the assignment. I've been quite impressed."

"Apparently," I said, nudging her shoulder. "I don't recall mere school project partners smiling the way you did at him." She grew quiet and shifted uncomfortably. "I'm only giving you a hard time, Lia. If you really like him don't let me—or Cam, for that matter—hold you back."

Neither of us spoke for a moment.

"He's really not some dumb jock," she said timidly. "He's actually really smart. And nice."

I grinned. Though Jake was that last person I pictured making Lia happy, I wasn't about to be the one to stand in her way.

"I'm glad you're happy, Lia."

"Thank you." She finally smiled at me.

"Would Matt absolutely flip if he found out about him?"

The idea made me chuckle. Cameron wasn't the only one who wasn't a fan of Jake.

"Oh, Matt's living up his life in Italy. I couldn't care less what he thinks," she said. But I knew she was speaking through her teeth. Matt's opinion meant everything to Lia.

"Can I be there when you tell him?"

Lia shoved me and I nearly tripped over myself, laughing.

By the end of the day my back was throbbing. It felt like I had a charley horse the size of Texas between my shoulder blades. My backpack was not helping the situation at all. I dodged everyone I could on my way out of the school doors and raced home as fast as my car would take me. Lia would have questioned me further, seeing the apparent pain in my eyes and Cameron would have begged to see them.

When I stormed through the garage door my dad was there to greet me, hunting in the fridge for an afternoon snack.

"Is everything all right, Calliope?" he asked, closing the door.

"No, it's not all right. They came in." I arched my back, dropping my backpack on the kitchen floor and tugged my sweatshirt off. "I have to get to my room." He stepped to the side and let me run down the hallway, swinging my door shut.

I tore my shirt off and instantly the wings uncurled from their cocoons, stretching like a limb after being in one position for too long. I immediately felt freedom. When I peered at myself in the mirror, four long daisy-like petal shapes fluttered behind me as if they were waving, greeting me for the first time.

They felt strange as if they didn't belong to me, like they

159

weren't attached to my body. It was like an out of body experience. I was above myself watching these wings branch out of someone else's back. And yet they felt more a part of me than anything else, like my arms, just another limb that moved without thought.

The top wings peeked about a foot and a half above my shoulders. They weren't as big as I pictured them being and that was fine by me. I just hoped they didn't plan on getting any bigger. These were controllable. Now the struggle was to figure out how to plaster these babies to my body and hide them under my clothes.

I fiddled around with their movement, testing how they fluttered and my ability to shift them. It turned out I could get them to curl around my torso, but they didn't want to stay that way for long. I suspected it was like trying to stay in a position for any extended amount of time. They needed to stretch. I let them spring back out behind me and the relief was instant.

They really were beautiful. Their soft yellow tint gleamed in the reflection of the mirror, a soft reminder that they were there, a soft reminder that they grew out of *me*. After admiring them for who knows how long, it dawned on me that I was running out of time for solutions. I needed something for school tomorrow.

It really was unfortunate that I had to find something to hold them down. I dug around in my drawers, throwing out tank tops, underwear and bikinis. Then something caught my eye— my leotard from ballet. I couldn't wear it every day because number one, it was from like three years ago and two sizes too small; and number two, it would be too noticeable under my clothes. But it would give me something to go shopping in in the meantime.

It took a lot of restraint to keep the wings down without

snagging them in the spandex. I pinched them a couple times and winced from the pain. *You are smarter than the leotard.* I stretched the straps over my shoulders, feeling the indentation they were already leaving in my shoulders, but I finally managed to conquer the leotard.

"Where are you going?" Dad asked when I passed through the kitchen on my way to the garage.

"To buy something to hold these down," I said, slipping my purse over my shoulder.

When I looked to him there was a haze over his eyes, making him unreadable as he scanned my body.

"Dad?"

"What?" He gazed up at my eyes, finally acknowledging me again.

"I'll see you later."

He only nodded as I waved.

After searching through way too many stores to count for my wing restrainer I finally found a viable bustier. I suppose it was more of a tight tube top. There was no boning or wires that could jab my wings. It was stretchy, a soft comfortable material, and, most importantly—form fitting.

By the time I purchased the wing restrainer and got in my car to go home, it felt like I'd been tightening my abs all day and could barely hang on a minute longer. The wings began to cramp. I raced home, blaring music, summarizing Macbeth, trying to think of Cameron, and solving math problems in my head all at the same time, attempting to keep my mind off of them. When I pulled into the garage it was seven-thirty and Mom was home.

She and Dad danced around the kitchen, opening and closing drawers, working around one another to get dinner ready as I raced by, trying to slip by without them noticing.

Success! They didn't even as much as twitch, too consumed by each other and the meal. I reached my bedroom door, closing it behind me. I tugged off my shirt and struggled with the leotard, moving as cautiously as I could around my wings. When they finally unfurled I let out the breath of air I held. Never had anything felt so good.

There was a knock at my door. "Calliope?" Mom called.

Crap! "Just a second!" I looked to the door handle and realized I hadn't locked it. *Crap! Crap!*

I reached for my shopping bag, tearing the tags from the bustier. What was I thinking? There was *no* time for the bustier!

"Honey?" She rattled the door and I heard the click as she turned the knob.

"Hold on, Mom! I'm naked!" I hollered in a panic. I might as well have been naked. I was completely indisposed. Under the pressure I concentrated as much as I could, but they didn't want to lie down. Who could blame them? They'd been trapped for enough hours as it was.

"What's taking so long, Callie?" she questioned through the crack in the door.

"Just give me a second," I pleaded, hoping she couldn't hear the distress in my voice. I sighed and closed my eyes, reaching for the nerve endings in my back. Thoughts of the trees and the cool breeze running through my hair fanned across my mind. Leisurely, my wings glided around me, wrapping snuggly around my torso. And stayed. I threw on my shirt.

"Come in."

"You snuck right by us." She smiled, but I saw the suspicion in her eyes as she scanned my body as I fidgeted. "You hungry?"

162

I nodded. "Starving." Not really, but it was something to say.

She looked to the shopping bag on my bed. "Did you go shopping?"

Dad saved me when he appeared behind her. "What's taking you girls so long? Dinner is ready," he said, kissing Mom on the neck, distracting her on purpose. She giggled and spun to him, smacking him in the arm. "Finn." She grinned.

He looked to me. I thanked him with my eyes and he winked, but I could see the unrest in his eyes. He thought we were going to be discovered.

I asked them to give me a minute and then I would be there. Dad closed my door with a relieved look on his face. He couldn't have closed it fast enough though. I tore of my shirt and released the wings and stretched them wide. These things were not meant to be confined.

This was going to be way more difficult than I had planned.

School dragged on and on the next day. Keeping my wings pinned down wasn't going to be as easy as I'd hoped. They stayed confined, but they were suffocating. It felt like I was trapped in a straightjacket. The more I thought about it, the more I was aware of their need to be free. But I had to get used to this. They had to get used to this. I couldn't let them roam free. It just wasn't going to happen. Not possible.

I found Kai and Declan huddled together in the clearing, speaking in angry hushed tones. When I looked at them side-by-side Declan was a few inches taller than Kai. Though they were both well built, Declan's figure was more intimidating, bulkier.

163

Declan looked down at Kai or I suppose it was more of a glare, but Kai didn't shrink in the least from his stare. If anything, he looked fiercer glaring back as they spoke vehemently.

"Hey fellas, am I interrupting something?"

Their eyes jerked toward me as if surprised by my presence. It wasn't as if I had been *that* quiet.

"No, of course not." Declan tried to smile, but it didn't reach his eyes. In his eyes I saw traces of fear.

"Is there something I should be worried about? Is everything okay?"

"There's nothing you need to worry about, Calliope."

Kai scowled at Declan, clenching his jaw tightly, an obvious stance of disagreement.

My forehead scrunched. "It doesn't look like nothing to me."

"It's nothing," he reassured.

Kai crossed his arms. "Declan and I have very different views of what exactly 'nothing' is."

"We're not going to quarrel about it in front of her, Kai," Declan hissed. "Why are you pushing it?"

"Why do you think she can't handle it?" Kai shot back.

I liked Kai's confidence in me, but Declan's uncertainty made me worry that maybe it was something I didn't want to know. They faced each other, nearly chest to chest. I really didn't want to have to break up a faery brawl, so I decided to intervene before it got that far.

"Okay, boys, knock it off, and how about you let me decide what I can and cannot handle."

They continued their stare down with gritted teeth. "It should be her decision. You can't take that away from her," Kai pressed.

Declan sighed heavily. "Fine." He broke, and moved away from Kai. "But *I* will tell her."

Kai was satisfied enough that he grew a snarky grin. "Fine."

Declan straightened his shoulders. "Some fae came too close for my comfort today, so we had to steer them away."

"Declan hasn't had anyone get that close to you before and—" Kai interrupted.

"And it riled me up a little bit," Declan cut him off.

Relief settled inside of me. At least it wasn't any more information about me that they knew and I didn't, or that Favner had finally located me. "Now, that wasn't so bad was it? I think I can handle knowing about a couple of faeries adventuring out my way." They stayed silent, which always seemed to speak volumes with them. "But I'm guessing these faeries weren't as harmless as you two?" I questioned.

Kai narrowed his eyes at Declan, urging him to give it up.

"They were Keepers of Favner. His top two in command."

"Which means Favner knows one of two things." Kai looked pointedly at me. "Or both. That Declan and I are leaving Faylinn and hiding something from him or that you are alive."

"And Favner can't know I'm alive because then I'll be deemed as a rogue faery and forced to go back?" I questioned. I still wasn't completely clear on what Favner's beef was with me.

"Exactly," Declan stated, eager to end the conversation. "What did you come here to talk about today, Calliope?"

With all the testosterone drama I'd almost forgotten about my wings. "They came in." I shrugged.

"Your wings?" Declan asked.

"Well, let's see them." Kai relaxed first, letting the corner of his mouth quirk up.

"No." I took a step back.

"Oh, don't be such a troll. Let's see those big beautiful wings." Kai came closer, but I held my ground this time, meeting his confidence head on.

I suppose he was trying to insult me. Trolls must be cowards. "I don't want to take them out. I finally figured out how to strap them down comfortably." Or as comfortably as it was going to get. "It'll take me another hour to strap them back in if I show you now."

It was only partially true. The main reason I didn't want to show them was because I knew they would gawk and talk about them for the entire afternoon and I couldn't bear to hear them examine every little inch of me. Not today. Not ever. But really not today.

Kai rolled his eyes and folded his arms defiantly across his chest, pinning the vines under his hand. "Fine."

"Don't listen to him, Calliope. You don't have to show us anything you don't want to."

"Thank you, Declan," I acknowledged. "I only came to give you the news. It's just one more step to faerydom that I figured I would share with you two."

"So you just use us for faery information and then leave," Kai said. "I see how it is. I feel so violated."

I gave Kai an annoyed glare, one that I'm sure he was getting used to and I was becoming a pro at.

"Calliope," Declan prompted, ignoring Kai. "How do you feel about your wings?"

I hadn't been able to give myself five minutes to think much passed what an inconvenience they were. When I thought about it though, they really were pretty. A little cumbersome to hide underneath my clothes, but they were truly magical. The wings finally made me feel magical. "I like them. Definitely better than my ears. My ears make me feel like a *troll*." I eyed Kai.

Declan chortled and shook his head. "You don't look the like a troll, trust me."

"Trolls are hideous," Kai agreed.

"*Obviously* trolls exist," I muttered dryly.

Declan gave me a rueful shrug. Why wasn't I surprised? For all I knew every other creature from my bedtime storybooks existed in my backyard without my knowledge. All the monsters hiding under beds and in closets really did haunt every child's night.

"How about Vampires?"

Declan and Kai laughed. I took that as a no.

"Werewolves?"

They shook their heads, smirking at my game.

"Mermaids?"

Declan scrunched his eyes, thinking.

"Maybe?" Kai said. "I think I saw one once, but I normally stay away from large bodies of water."

"Fallen angels? Demons?"

Kai and Declan shared a look as if they were asking one another through their eyes. They turned back to me and shrugged.

"So, it's just trolls and faeries, huh? Oh and Pixies."

"Other creatures are out there. Sprites, gremlins, dwarfs, elves, brownies... but we don't really converse with them," Kai said. "They have their own territories in Faylinn and keep to themselves."

I put my fingers to my temples and rubbed. It was going to be a few days before that information set in.

"Okay," Declan said, assertive and moved toward me. "I think you need a little break. Yes?"

Was it that obvious? "Always, but it depends on what you call a break."

"Let's get out of here today," Declan offered, leaping swiftly from the ground to the top of the boulder.

"Get out of here? The clearing?" Kai asked, excitement rising in his voice.

"Yeah. What do you say, Kai, think we could show Calliope the wonders of the woodlands?"

A grin that was way too mischievous for my taste sprouted on Kai's face. "Oh, yes. I think it's about time the little princess learns what it's really like to be a faery."

I eyed them as Declan and Kai shared a glance. Were my ears and wings not enough of an indication? What else was there to know?

"Would you like to do the honors or shall I?" Declan asked Kai conspiratorially.

"For her first time maybe you should." Kai measured me with his eyes, making me feel self-conscious in a whole new way. "Although I could use a good laugh."

"What are you two talking about?" I probed. I don't know why I bothered asking when they started talking all cryptically like this. My opinion all of a sudden didn't matter and they took pleasure in making me squirm.

"It's better if we don't warn her," Kai said.

"Don't warn me about wha—"before I could finish asking my question, Declan snatched me up in his arms and soared up into the canopy of leaves, landing agilely on the highest branch within a matter of seconds. I looked down and immediately regretted the decision.

"Holy crap!" I cringed, gaining back my stomach. "Yeah, a little warning would have been nice."

The forest floor came in and out of focus as it struck me how high up we were, the branches crisscrossing below us like a woven basket. Declan's chest shook from laughter. It suddenly dawned on me that I was pressed against his bare chest, clinging to his neck.

"You should see the look on your face," Kai said from a branch on the tree next to us. "It's priceless."

"Can you put me down please?" I asked.

"You think you'll be able to balance well enough?" Declan asked, uncertain of my equilibrium. If he was so concerned about that why soar into the trees unannounced?

"I'm a faery shouldn't that come naturally?" I peered down at the limb he had us suspended on and watched as it lightly bounced under our weight. It didn't look strong enough to be holding the both of us.

"Were you able to walk your first try as a toddler?" Kai asked.

I scowled over at him briefly and then asked Declan, "So, I'm just supposed to let you carry me from limb to limb as you leap through the air, fifty feet off the ground? *That* sounds harmless."

"I won't drop you," he assured.

"Will you at least let me try?"

The way Declan and Kai underestimated me was frustrating. I realized I was new to this, but how hard could it be? I couldn't be *that* incompetent. My faery instincts should come naturally, right?

"I think we better start lower to the ground for that."

He stepped off without warning, sending my stomach into a whirlwind as we dropped to a branch below, about twenty feet from the ground. I caught my breath. Declan's arms steadily released me, standing me upright. I straightened my shirt over my stomach. This limb was a lot thicker than the one up higher, which gave me a little more confidence. Kai landed on the opposite side of me on the same branch.

"You got this?" Kai asked, doubtfully.

"I can balance just fine," I contended. I kept my arms straight at my sides, extending my hands to keep steady. It wasn't as difficult as they were making it seem.

"It's not the balance I'm worried about. It's the leaping or... falling. You may not quite recognize your proximity to the next branch. It'll come with practice, but if I were to tell you to jump to that tree across from us, would you be able to make it?"

"I don't see why not. You guys make it look easy enough." I stood straighter, squaring my shoulders, poised.

Kai swept his hand in front him to let me pass and get closer to my target. "Be my guest."

"Kai, don't encourage her," Declan stepped in. "Calliope, don't get overconfident. You'll have to learn one way or another, but be careful as you make that first leap. Try to estimate the distance in your head and measure the power you think you'll need behind the jump."

I steadied myself on the edge of the limb, curling my toes, gripping for balance and focused on the closest branch with the least amount of foliage blocking my landing.

"Focus on your target," Declan advised. "Then leap."

"But don't overestimate," Kai interjected.

"Don't underestimate it either," Declan added.

"Will you two just be quiet?" I scowled. "You're making me nervous."

They smiled sheepishly and quieted down.

"You can do it, Calliope," Declan encouraged softly.

I didn't let myself think anymore. I took a deep breath and leaped over the moss covered logs and rocks below, landing on the opposite tree. I made it, but what I didn't plan for was how round the limb would feel under my feet. I couldn't catch my balance before I was falling forward. With no time to think or scream, my hands reached for a branch to latch onto, but all it did was tear at my palms as it was ripped from my grasp. Arms latched onto my waist before I hit the ground and I found myself in Kai's arms, which set me gently down.

"Seems easy enough, right?" he said, smirking. I glared at him, but softened it when I realized he'd just saved me from being further injured.

"Not bad for your first time. My first time I didn't even reach the destination before falling," Declan said when he landed behind me. "At least your feet touched the branch. Now you know what to expect."

I winced when I opened my palms. "Ouch," I muttered.

"What did you do? All you had to do was fall. We were here to catch you," Kai reprimanded, stepping closer to me.

"Well, my human instincts kicked in to save myself before falling to my death. Heaven forbid I impulsively reach for a branch."

"Here, let me see." Kai reached out for my hands.

"No, don't touch! It stings!" I pulled my hands protectively to myself, cradling them against my stomach.

"Don't be such a baby. Let me help you," Kai urged. Something in his husky voice made me want to stop fighting him. A small part of me wanted him to touch me, to feel his hands on mine again.

Kai was only inches from me now as he placed his hand on top of one of my scraped palms, gently applying pressure as he cupped it with his other hand. His fingers softly grazed my torn skin. The heat radiating between our hands churned my stomach. I peered up from under my eyelashes and saw his eyes concentrating on our grip. As if he felt my gaze on him, he lifted his pulsating eyes and caught my stare. Warmth spread in my cheeks, but he didn't smirk. He held my gaze for a few seconds, then cleared his throat and motioned with his indigo eyes for me to look back at my hand. It tingled slightly for a moment before he lifted his fingers and my skin was perfect again, only the residue of blood left over. The cuts were healed.

"How did you…?"

"Another one of our fae qualities," he said. "How do you think we can live so long? You think we've really dodged that many accidents?"

"Can I do it?"

"There's only one way to find out." He nodded to my other hand. "Try it."

I put my healed fingers to my other palm, but nothing happened. "It's not working."

"Are you even trying?" Kai rolled his eyes and reached over, putting my hand back over my palm with his hand laced on top, our fingers intertwined fitting seamlessly together. "Imagine sewing up a tear or patching up a hole." He looked at me, urging me to try. I don't know how he expected me to concentrate with the feel of his skin warming mine, his body only a breath away.

I looked back at my bloodied skin and tried to focus. The Keepers watched my every move, studying everything I did or said. I'd still become a science experiment, only in a completely different way than I expected.

The tingle never started and I was about to give up again when Declan's low voice came from behind my shoulder. "Close your eyes. Sometimes that helps." So I did as he instructed and pressed my eyes shut, picturing my hand sewing a rip in my sweater. When that didn't work I pictured a needle and thread actually stitching up my skin. There was a surge of what felt like electricity shoot through my hand. When I lifted my hand, I was as good as new.

"I did it!"

They both looked at me with approval.

"Bravo, Princess, you've just fulfilled your first enchantment," Kai said with only half the mockery as usual.

"I'm going to take that compliment and run with it."

"You should." Kai lifted a crooked grin.

Later that day Declan looked to the sun. It hung in the sky just above the shade of trees, making its descent. "I need to make it back to Faylinn by sunset. I must go."

"Oh." A twinge of sadness weighed on me at the thought of having to end the day. "Evening shift, huh?"

I'd settled for practicing my balance in the trees for the remainder of the afternoon. They showed off, of course, flipping from branch to branch and swinging from vine to vine. It was actually pretty fascinating. Almost like watching Cirque Du Soleil fae men style. I didn't want the day to end. It was the first day in… in… I don't know how long that I relaxed and miraculously had fun.

He nodded and shifted his eyes to Kai. "You good here?"

"Oh, ye of little faith."

"Well?" Declan said. "I never know with you. Sometimes you stick around, sometimes you don't want to."

"I'll be around for a little while tonight."

"Good," Declan said and turned to me. "Be safe walking home, Calliope."

"I will. Thanks, Declan. For everything today."

He bowed his head, lifting his strong hand in a wave and sauntered west into the depths of the woodlands. I watched until his chiseled figure was swallowed up by the surrounding lush green.

When I shifted my eyes back to Kai, he was watching me strangely. I couldn't put my finger on the blank stare of his deep blue-iris eyes. His scrutiny unsettled me so I decided it was time to go.

"I should go, too." I started to make my way in the direction of my house.

"Stay." Kai said hesitantly, as if he didn't know why he said it. Then his face cringed as if he wished he didn't say it, but didn't take it back.

I looked back to him. "I can't."

The corner of his mouth quirked up in a smile, but it didn't quite meet his eyes. "You can't? Or you won't?"

A stupid part of me wanted to stay. But why? He'd never done anything but insult or mock me. His rare moments of kindness were there, but mostly he left me anxious. "It'll be dark soon and I should be in the house before dark," I stumbled over my words.

"You don't trust me, do you?" He tilted his head to one side, studying me.

"It's not a matter of trust, Kai," I said truthfully. "In all honesty, my mom doesn't know about me yet. If she sees me walking out of the trees past dark she'll freak."

"As opposed to you walking out of the trees during the

day," he said dryly.

"During the day at least I could say I was just exploring, taking a walk or something, but there really is no good excuse if I come traipsing in the house late at night from the backyard."

He folded his arms over his chest. "So, you'll tell your friend Cameron, but you can't tell your mother, a woman who already knows about the existence of the fae, that you're a faery?"

"My dad has asked me not to."

His face changed as if he thought he had it all figured out. "Ah. The loyalty card."

"What's *that* supposed to mean?"

"You're loyal to your father." He shrugged.

"Well, yeah… he's my dad. But I'm loyal to my mom too. She just has a lot on her plate right now. We'll tell her when the time is right."

Kai rested his eyes curiously on me and for a couple seconds neither of us said a word. It hadn't occurred to me that we were only about a foot apart when I felt us drifting closer. When had he gotten so close?

I blinked and the fury started to build inside of me. "Would you stop doing that? You promised you would never do it again."

Then he blinked and the moment was gone as he sauntered away from me. "Do what?" He smirked.

"Enticement. You keep using it and I don't appreciate it."

He chortled, clearly pleased with himself. "Sorry to say, Princess, but I haven't used Enticement on you since the first day we met. I told you I wouldn't."

He had to be lying. But as he smiled at me smugly I could see the truthfulness in his eyes.

"I'm afraid this is just my natural charm. I'm better than I thought."

I bit the insides of my cheeks, feeling the blush redden them. "Whatever. Don't flatter yourself."

I could see the satisfaction in his eyes. "Have a good night." He stepped further away, starting to leave.

"Wait. That's it?"

He looked to me with a tilted grin. "What? You want me to sit here and beg for your presence? Sorry, Princess, I don't grovel." He turned from me again and began his walk away.

No. He didn't get to turn his back on me over and over. And no, I didn't expect him to grovel; I just didn't like him always having the last word. He didn't get to walk away this time. I ran in front of him. He nearly stumbled back, but was caught by his quick reflexes.

"Can I help you?" he said sardonically polite.

"You're so infuriating!" I announced and clenched my fists. Was that really my best comeback?

"One of my better qualities, if I do say so myself."

"No, you don't get to do that." I fervently shook my head. "You don't get to agree with me while I'm insulting you."

"You should really practice a little more on the insults, Princess. You haven't quite mastered the art." He smirked maddeningly. I wanted so badly to smack it off. Just to see what he would do. "I know a great teacher if you'd like some instruction."

"Uh! You drive me crazy!" I stomped my foot. *What.* Was I three?

"Why thank you." He bowed in his head.

"Why? Why do have to act so above everything all the time? Why don't you take anything seriously?"

176

Kai folded his arms over his uncovered chest and lifted an eyebrow, but didn't reply to me. His silence burrowed deep under my skin. He opened his mouth to speak, but then as if he thought better of it closed it again.

"You can't answer a simple question?" I persisted.

He licked his lips and bit his bottom lips, contemplating an answer. I wanted to kiss that bottom lip and the realization of that thought hit me like a ton of bricks. I was going crazy. It was official.

I fought the ridiculous urge. "Well?" I pressed.

His voice lowered when he spoke. "You make it so easy to toy with you. Some faeries would eat you alive."

I recoiled at the severity of his tone. I couldn't tell if he wanted to seem playful or menacing. If he was going for menacing, that won. I'd give him a blue ribbon.

"One day you'll figure it out."

"Doubt it, since I plan to stay as far away from Faylinn as possible."

"You'll give in one day. You won't be able to fight it any longer. You simply don't have it in you."

He was goading me. I knew it and it was working. I lifted my hand to smack him, but before I got the satisfaction he grabbed my wrist and pulled me to his chest. His fresh breath grazed my face and I gasped. His form met every inch of my body, chest to chest, thigh to thigh.

"We'll work on your hand to hand combat some other day. It's definitely not at the level it should be by now," he said, his voice low and husky.

My breath caught. My eyes were level with his lips and the temptation to inch just a little closer was too much to hold back. I watched his lips press together as he swallowed then open them

177

slightly. His warm breath washed over my face. I lifted my eyes to meet the depths of his that could swallow me whole. He blinked once, but that was all it took to sever the connection, pulling me out of the trance.

I let out the breath I was holding and grunted. Yanking my arm from his grip, I turned and stormed away. *What in the world was I thinking?*

"You know, retreating isn't really helping your case," he hollered, but I didn't listen to him. I wasn't going to let him affect me anymore today. It had been too perfect of a day to let him ruin it now.

SIXTEEN

The next morning I woke to the calming pitter-patter of rain on the windowpane. Water darkened the asphalt as I drove down the road to school. The leaves glistened from the moisture, enhancing their color. As soon as I pulled into the parking lot the rain started to come down in buckets. I shoved my hood up and booked it to the front doors.

At our lockers Cameron watched Isla and Lia with a bored look on his face as they were deep in some conversation, animations flying every which way. I smiled at him and was rewarded with a smile in return. Pulling back my hood, I shook off the droplets as I turned to my locker.

"Calliope," Cameron hissed.

Cameron never called me by my full name. That should have been my first clue. When I looked back at him his eyes were afraid as he was desperately trying to be subtle and motion to his ears. It took me only a second, but that second could have meant everything. I flipped my hood back on and searched the hallway

179

to see if anyone saw. Thankfully, everyone else seemed to be involved in their own worlds, racing to class, joking and talking with friends. My eyes drew back to our crowd and Lia gave me a look, raising her eyebrow. My stomach sank. Tell me she didn't see them.

"Callie, you look like you're searching for a stalker. What's your deal?" she asked.

I was so worked up I couldn't get myself composed enough to say anything to her. I swallowed and took a deep breath, trying to calm my wired nerves.

"Jake's eyeing you, Lia," Cam said, diverting her stare. She scanned the hallway and a slow smile grew on her lips with an eye roll.

"I'll be right back," she excused herself.

I thanked Cameron with my eyes and then Isla was dragging him away. "We should head to class," she said. "Bye, Calliope."

Cameron shook his head and gave me a you-are-so-lucky look. I couldn't agree with him more. Screw being on time, I raced to get to the bathroom to fix my hair.

Though the hood messed with my hair, it also protected my hair from the rain. I don't know how I would have redone my hair to cover up my ears had it been soaking wet. It only took me a minute and then I heard the warning bell from the bathroom. Once I stepped out the door I nearly collided with Lia.

"Whoa, Callie, take it easy. What's with you today?"

"Nothing. I'm fine." What else could I say? *My fae ears were poking through my hair. I didn't want to frighten you or the rest of civilization.*

"You're not fine. I know when you're fine and this is not fine."

She was reading me too closely now. She couldn't pass off

my strange behavior as wallowing in self-pity anymore. I had to find an escape route.

"We'll talk later. I've got to get to class." I barely escaped and then sprinted to get to class. I couldn't even worry about the fact that she was watching me as I darted away. I made it there in record time. Hopefully, no one else noticed my super speed.

With the rain flooding the lawn, everyone was required to eat lunch inside. The four of us found an empty quad and sat against the wall.

"Let's hang out after school today," Lia said to me. "This rain has convinced me I want some rain boots and look how cute Isla's are."

I trailed her coveting gaze to Isla's black and purple plaid rubber boots.

"Thanks, Lia," Isla said, smiling broadly. "That's really nice of you."

I thought about the Keepers. Declan wasn't going to be there today, but after last night, ate at me knowing that Kai could sense his strong effect on me. There was a part of me that wanted to surprise him and go out when I knew Declan wouldn't be there. And I kind of didn't want Declan to be there when I talked to Kai. There were a few questions I wanted answered.

"Maybe Saturday. I've got some stuff I need to do after school today."

"You're passing up a shopping outing? For what? What could be better?"

If only I could answer that honestly. She might give me a free pass if she knew the real answer. "Nothing's better, just more pressing. I can't keep procrastinating my English Lit essay. Mrs. Harrison wants a five-page paper about Hamlet. I can barely write a paragraph." Which wasn't a complete lie, just not the full truth. The essay wasn't due for another week.

"We never really hang out anymore," she pouted.

"What are you talking about? We just…" I stumbled through my memory, but she was right. I couldn't remember the last time we hung out. Every free chance I got I went to see Declan and Kai. "This weekend. It's you and me."

She pursed her lips and eyed me. "I'm holding you to that."

"Deal."

The rain let up a little. It was more of a faint scattered sprinkle now, the clouds above a gray haze. I lifted my hood back over my head to shelter me from the mist as I walked out of the sliding glass door.

The clearing was empty when I arrived. I gazed up into the limbs, searching for his figure in his usual spots, but he wasn't there. My courage was starting to lessen. I had hoped to catch him off guard. I didn't want to have to call out to him, asking for his presence. I just wanted him to be here.

When I turned to leave, movement caught my eye. I shifted my gaze to the right, deeper into the trees. Behind the haven of nature Kai had his arms arched, an arrow headed straight for my chest. I heard the stretch of the string on the bow, ready to release the arrow. His shimmering eyes were focused and determined. My eyes widened in response, but I couldn't even think to move, scared still.

"Calliope," Kai said, startled.

There was a hitch in my breathing. That was the first time Kai had called me by my real name.

His stance relaxed as he lowered his weapon before holstering it in place on his back. "Do you realize I almost just killed you?" The alarm was apparent in his voice. "Why are you dressed in all dark colors, creeping around like you don't belong here?"

I looked down at my dark grey hoodie and jeans and shrugged. "I wasn't creeping around. Do you go around pointing arrows at every unfamiliar figure? What if I had been Cameron?"

"I waited to see your face. I wouldn't kill just anybody." He let out a heavy breath of air. "Soggy sludge, woman."

"Excuse me?" I chuckled.

"What are you doing out here? You do remember that Declan's not here, right?" He moved toward me, his dark green top soaked by the rain, shifted over his torso.

"I know. I came to talk to you actually."

Kai blinked and composed himself. "Well, you might as well make yourself useful while you're here." He looked up and then motioned for me to come to him. "The ground's soaked." When I didn't move he said, "I wasn't *actually* trying to kill you, you know. You can trust me."

I thought about hesitating a little longer just to mess with him, but instead I walked to him. He swept me off my feet before I could protest and landed in the tree next to us, setting me upright beside him on a limb thick enough to hold the both of us. He offered the seat closest to the trunk, so I could lean against it and I accepted it gratefully.

Kai pulled out some twigs that had been stripped of their leaves and handed one to me. "I might as well teach you how to make arrows. It's one of the ways we survive."

I sat quietly and as patiently as I could as he instructed me on how to shave the tips and trim them just right as to not cut off too much or not enough. I gazed up at him a few times without speaking. His brow creased in concentration as he paid extra attention to detail. It was strange the way we sat so silently, not provoking one another like usual. We hadn't really been alone since the first time we saw one another. I tried to push away the nerves that were spreading through me at the thought of us being alone. There wasn't a soul for miles.

"Kai," I prompted cautiously. He hummed in response. "Is Declan's father still around?"

Kai gave one shake of his head without meeting my eyes, not offering anything more.

"What happened to him?"

"I don't know."

If I was wise I would have just let Kai be and not bothered to ask him any further questions, but my need to know grew stronger. They seemed to know everything about me, while I knew nothing about them.

"Does he not talk about him? Did you never know him?"

He sighed. "It's none of my business to pry into Declan's life if he doesn't want to share. If he wants to talk, he'll talk to me."

What was it with guys? Human or fae they were all the same. They never asked each other questions about their lives. They saw it as prying or meddling rather than caring or concerned.

"How long have you known Declan?" I prodded.

"My whole life," he said shortly, focusing on sharpening the tip of his branch as if his life depended on it. I suppose it did in the long run, but I knew he couldn't be *that* interested in the twig.

I set down my arrow. I hadn't been making much progress anyway. "And he's never mentioned him? Did he die? Disappear?"

Kai set the twig in his lap with an irritated sigh. "Why are you so concerned? You don't care about the fae in Faylinn. Why do you care about this?"

"What?" I set my eyes firmly on him. "Why wouldn't I care? And who says I don't care? I just don't want to be bound like you."

"And you think you get that choice?" He lifted an eyebrow.

"I've already made that choice. It doesn't mean I don't care. It just means I'm not ready to leave my life here."

"How lucky for you," he muttered.

How did we even get on this topic? How did this get turned on me? I wasn't letting him off the hook this time. "So, you haven't cared enough to ask about what happened to his dad?"

"He doesn't know and neither do I." His gaze intensified, but he lifted his arrow and began carving once more. "And I'm not the nosey type."

I decided to ignore that last comment. I wasn't being nosey. Wasn't it important to understand your friend's background? Who was I kidding? I knew what I was doing was wrong or I would have asked Declan himself, but my need to know outweighed my conscience. "When did he disappear?"

Kai exhaled and peered up at me. I could see he knew I wasn't going to let up. "A little before Nyssa's death," he surrendered.

"Nyssa was Declan's mother," I clarified. "Do you think the same thing that happened to the other fae happened to him?"

"Probably," Kai said gruffly and went back to his twig.

"Do you have any theories?"

Setting the arrow abruptly in his lap, he glared at me. "Do you ever stop asking questions?"

I met his stare, unwavering. There were moments when staring into his vibrant eyes that affected me more than other times. This was one of those times, but I was determined to hold my ground, willing myself to be unaffected. "You're going to accuse me of not caring about Faylinn and then criticize me for asking questions and being concerned about what has happened to them, what's causing them to disappear? Pick an angle, Kai."

"I simply don't understand what makes you tick. You're unpredictable."

"Pot calling the kettle black."

His head tilted, perplexed. "I'm sorry?"

"Never mind. You keep avoiding my questions," I pointed out.

"Yeah, this is why Declan is in charge of teaching you and I'm not."

"Fine. I'll stop asking questions and leave you to making your arrows." I got to my feet and dusted off my jeans. He was being testy today anyway, too ornery for my taste. "Thanks for the lesson on arrow crafting," I muttered and turned to leave, staring over the edge, wishing I had an easier exit strategy.

"No, don't go." A low snarl rumbled in his throat and he glared down at his lap as if he was scolding himself for speaking up. "I have a theory," he bit off the words like he didn't know why they were coming out of his mouth. "But I don't know how it would be possible."

I sat back down without saying a word, afraid that if I encouraged him to explain he would stop.

"Did Declan teach you about the other kingdoms?"

I shook my head. "There are more of us?"

"Thousands more. They live all over the world in kingdoms like Faylinn. Faylinn is basically the homeland, but others branched off years and years ago."

"Why?"

Kai shook his head, cutting me short. "We're getting off track here, Princess."

Princess. So we were back to that. Though I didn't want to in that instant, I bit back my retort for him insisting on calling me that. One has to pick her battles and this was one I probably lost on day one.

"Sorry. Okay. So what about the others?"

"Well, when Favner took over he sealed off the passages to the other kingdoms. They can't come in and we can't go to them."

"Do you know many faeries from the other kingdoms?"

He nodded. "Yeah... acquaintances, friends. We used to trade between the kingdoms, what supplies they had and we didn't and vice versa. We didn't have the same ideals, but we worked together."

"So, you think other kingdoms are breaking in and taking Faylinn's fae?"

He shook his head. "I think as punishment for defying Favner he has banished whoever he pleases to another kingdom, sealed them off from their families, our people. He's cut off the communication and has forced them to live a solitary life."

"But you think they get to live?" I asked earnestly, hoping that was true.

"What's a life without your family? Without those you love? Surrounded in a world where everyone hardly knows you," he said intensely, completely unaware of how true his declaration was to me.

"And you wonder why I have such a hard time accepting the possibility of going to Faylinn?"

"But you wouldn't be forced to live without your family. You could still visit them whenever you wanted." He spoke rapidly, leaning into me, getting ahead of himself.

"I'm sorry, but are we talking about the same kingdom? Because unless I'm mistaken, Favner doesn't really seem like the type to allow visitation rights."

Kai opened his mouth. Hope I'd never seen before shined in his eyes, and then it shut off as he bit down on his lips, gritting his teeth.

Yeah, that's what I thought. He knew I was right and he could no longer criticize me for wanting to latch onto my human life, savoring every moment I could.

I made sure to get right back on track. I wouldn't let him change the subject or leave me hanging this time. "So, why do you think that he banishes them and doesn't kill them?"

"He's not afraid to hide someone's death. If one of our own dies he won't hide that from the families. Whether he tells the truth about their death, that's a different story. But when a faery disappears, it's as if they've been erased, as if they haven't existed in the first place and we're simply supposed to accept their fate."

"But why would the other kingdoms let Favner pawn off our fae to them? If you used to work together with them, why would they turn on you?"

Kai shrugged and went back to shaving his branch. "Like I said, it's only a theory. I don't know the logistics or how he's getting away with it. I just have a gut feeling."

I watched him; his dark wet curls falling over his eyes. In the misty light today his eyes reflected off deeper blue with subtle purple hints. It was unfair that any living creature could be so perfect. He looked up then and caught me staring. My cheeks flushed and I immediately reverted back to working on my pitiful looking arrow, not wanting to see the arrogance in his eyes. His low chuckle made his amusement apparent at my expense.

The lingering raindrops sporadically slipped from the canopy of leaves, lightly trickling down on us. "Why did he seal off the passages in the first place?" I asked through the stillness.

He sighed. "He said it was for our protection. But I think he did it for assurance. He knows no one in Faylinn can or will try to overpower him, but other leaders have the power. He wants to be sure that doesn't happen. He knows he doesn't deserve the right to be king. Rather he feels entitled to it, but I don't believe he deserves it."

"Maybe you should make a change then."

Kai laughed, but there was no amusement in his tone this time. "Yeah. Maybe someday."

SEVENTEEN

I was finishing up some physics homework that I'd definitely procrastinated when there was a knock at the front door. I opened it to see Cameron with his shoulders slouched.

"Cam," I said, taken aback. "What's up?"

He wasn't smiling and an immediate pang of concern pricked my heart. "Can I come in?"

"Of course." I stepped aside and let him walk passed me. He made himself comfortable in our family room; plopping on the couch I had all my homework on. He didn't even seem to notice the mess surrounding him as he leaned forward, his hands folded over his knees. I sat next to him, moving the books and paperwork out of the way.

"I think Isla's cheating on me," he said calmly, but eerily calm.

"What? Why would you think that?"

"I saw her walking out of Garrick Jensen's house yesterday. He hugged her way too long at her car before she got in."

190

My blood boiled. Isla was *not* about to cheat on the one person *she* didn't deserve. But I decided to give her the benefit of the doubt. "She and Garrick have been friends since middle school, haven't they?"

He winced. "It was the look in her eye when I saw her walk out. She looked like she was trying to be cautious. And she ignored me all day yesterday. Whenever I saw her in the hallway she'd start walking in the other direction, like she was trying to hide from me."

"You need to talk to her, Cam," I advised.

"She won't answer my calls or text messages," he said, exasperated.

That didn't sound like a woman cheating. It sounded like a woman scorned. "Have you ever thought she might be mad at you for some reason and that she was venting to Garrick?"

He threw his hands up in the air and fell against the couch. "Then why didn't she come to me? Why did she go running to him? If the problem is between us I should be the first one to know about it."

"Because she's a girl, Cam. She's probably hoping you'll figure it out on your own."

He sighed. "Mind games, Cal. I *hate* them. Why can't girls just say what they mean? Why can't they all be like you?" I blinked. I didn't know how I was supposed to take that. "You make it so easy. You tell me up front when you think I'm being a jerk and I tell you when you're being a drama queen. We keep each other in check."

"Because that's what friends do. We're not afraid to hurt each other's feelings. We do it for the benefit of one another. We trust each other enough to tell one another those things."

"So, why can't she trust me?" He looked at me with his

191

ocean eyes, so earnest and defeated. I wanted to curl him up in my arms and kiss away his frustrations.

I sighed and leaned against the couch beside him. "Cam, it's probably not because she doesn't trust you. She's just mad that you can't figure it out on your own. A lot of girls do that. We think guys should just be able to get it. But guys are idiots, no offense."

"None taken." He draped his arm over my shoulders, tugging me to his side.

"You just need to find a way to confront her. Go over to her house if you have to and talk to her. But maybe give her some space to cool down. Wait, no. The longer you wait the more upset she'll probably get. Just go see her now. I don't know why you didn't do that in the first place."

"Because I knew you'd know what to say." The weight of his eyes peering down at me was palpable.

A deep breath escaped me. I couldn't keep our eye contact. He was so blind. If I wasn't careful I would let my feelings show, so I kept my gaze down in my lap and picked at my fingernails.

"It's probably all a misunderstanding. You just need to have a one on one conversation with her."

He nodded, his head now resting on mine. "Thanks, Callie. You're so wise."

I chuckled sardonically. "Yeah, right."

He shifted and put his fingers under my chin, giving me no choice but to look at him.

"What?" he asked.

"What?"

"You just sounded off." He peered at me, searching my eyes.

I swallowed. *Please don't look at me like that.* That look wasn't fair. He didn't mean it. Not in the way I wanted him to. "No I didn't."

His thoughtful gaze remained. The touch of his fingers on my chin did things to me that I didn't want to feel anymore. "You don't talk to me anymore." His voice was quiet.

I rolled my eyes. "What are you talking about?"

He dropped his hand, but kept his probing stare. "You don't. I feel like you hide stuff from me sometimes."

Don't let yourself be so transparent, Calliope. Don't let him know the biggest secret you've kept from him for years. He's not yours. He never will be. You've accepted that. Haven't you?

I shifted my eyes to get their uncaring blinders back up, to show him indifference toward his feelings for his girlfriend, to show indifference toward his feelings for me.

"Do you not recall my latest deep dark secret that only you know about?"

He faintly chortled in response. "Right. Does your change have to do with that? Is there something else you haven't told me?"

That I love you. Why was it easier to tell him I was a freaking faery than to tell him about how I felt?

I shook my head because I couldn't form a response believable enough.

By the look in his eyes I knew he didn't believe me, but he also wasn't going to force it out of me, which I was grateful for. "I'm going to go talk to Isla now." He stood up.

"Good idea." I followed him to the entryway.

If I had been a backstabbing, double-crossing wench, I could have easily turned that situation in my favor. But, of course, lucky me, I have morals. And I love Cameron too much to screw him over like that.

193

"What are you doing today?" He opened the front door.

"Well, I'm going to finish this physics homework and then I'm headed out for a quick round of Faery 101."

He chuckled, shaking his head. "Have you ever thought about what a surreal life you have?"

I smirked and laughed, but not because I found him humorous. "Every day."

He unexpectedly pulled me in for a hug. "Your life feels so foreign to me now." There was something off about his usual carefree tone. "I don't like it."

"You know me better than anyone else," I assured.

He squeezed me tightly and nodded into my neck. "But everything's changing," he murmured so softly I wasn't sure if he actually said it and slowly pulled away. "I'll see you tomorrow." The sadness was gone from his voice. Maybe it had never been there to begin with.

"Okay."

I watched his back as he walked away from me.

The sunlight was at its peak, high above the canopy of trees. I squinted and moved across the small clearing to get under better shade. Declan and Kai had situated themselves among the large rooted tree, sharpening their daggers and creating sturdier sheaths. They hadn't really spoken much since I had arrived. Normally, they were balls of energy, waiting to be released.

"You guys are awfully quiet today," I mused.

Declan looked up at me. "Why don't you give your wings a breather? You know you're safe out here, Calliope."

"Your clothes must be suffocating them," Kai muttered and

194

bit down on the handle of his bone carved knife as he reformed the sheath in his hands.

"I release them in the comfort of my bedroom, thank you very much," I snapped at Kai. "They get plenty of free time at night." I felt like we were talking about a pet I was neglecting.

"Don't they get uncomfortable?" Kai asked.

Of course they did, but I didn't want to tell him that. "They are fine."

"That can't possibly be true."

"I should be applying for colleges soon," I announced to steer the topic away from my wings.

"College?" Declan asked abruptly. "When? Where will you go?"

"Wherever I'm accepted."

"But when?" Declan pressed.

"After I graduate in June. The semester will start at the beginning of September. That's sort of how college works."

Declan and Kai looked at one another. They didn't speak, but their eyes were fighting.

I looked away from them and concentrated on leaping between the scattered rocks and boulders. "It's not as if I'll be that far away. I'll come home every month or so or when I have time. You both knew I planned on living out my life away from Faylinn. I haven't made it a secret that I don't want to go to Faylinn. I've been safe so far. No one has discovered me and I think I'll be able to keep it up. Besides, you guys will probably be so busy guarding Faylinn since you won't have to worry about me that you won't even notice when I'm gone. Think of what a relief it will be to not have to come see me every day."

I realized after a minute that I was talking to myself. They were silent. They were never silent. I peered across the clearing to where I'd left them. Both Kai and Declan were frozen in place, their heads slanted to the side as if they were lost in thought, their faces anxious. But they weren't looking at me. They weren't paying attention to me at all.

Declan's head snapped to the west. I followed his gaze, but didn't see anything, only the thriving world of the woodlands, sprung to life.

"Liam… Owen," Kai whispered barely above the breeze. At least I think that's what he said.

Declan nodded once. "They're back." He looked to me. "Up. You need to hide, Calliope. Time to use your fae abilities. Jump."

"But I…" I faltered.

"Now, Calliope," he urged, fear crystal clear in his deep oceanic eyes. "Go."

I didn't think. I leaped. In less than a second I found myself balancing on a slim limb high up in the branches, I shifted uneasily trying to keep from falling. Then Kai was at my side, taking my hand in his, catching me. He knocked his head to the side, directing me to follow him, but he didn't let go of my hand, keeping a secure grip on me.

We leaped high above the wild ground through the full branches, dodging inconveniently placed vines and boughs. Kai lead the way, guiding my every move. It felt indescribable, the way my body knew how to glide soundlessly. I thought I needed more training to become as stealth-like as Declan and Kai, but it was as if my body knew this was the time to perform. Our rhythm was exact as we soared. When his foot landed, mine landed. When he flew higher, I was right behind him.

My hand felt warm and secure in his grasp. I found myself liking the feel of our hands intertwined, knowing he would never let me go. Unexpectedly, I realized I didn't want him to let me go.

When we were at a distance that Kai felt was safe he stopped and let my hand drop, my security fading away. The branch was wide enough for us both to stand on as he paced back and forth and breathed heavily, his breath more relieved than exhausted.

I was the first to break the silence, but I kept my voice quiet even though we were miles from where we had started. "What was that all about?"

He let out a breath of air as if he'd been holding it the whole way. "Favner's Keepers. Liam and Owen."

"The ones that came close to us before?" He nodded. "How do you know it was them?"

His jaw clenched before he spoke. "They have a certain... stench."

"What? Why?" I stepped closer to the trunk, feeling uneasy about balancing on the thinner end of the branch.

"Their preference for raw meat," he said, hushed. He kept alert, scanning the forest floor below us and beyond.

I shuddered. "And you smelled that?" I uttered, breathless.

"As Keepers our senses have to be heightened," he replied automatically, stating facts.

Kai went eerily still and his ears perked up in the direction we'd come from. He was motionless. There was a crunch that sprang up from the forest floor no more than forty feet away and I was instantly in the shelter of Kai's steady arms. He placed a hand over my mouth. *As if I was going to breathe a word.*

A gruff voice came from somewhere below us. "Someone's been in these parts of the forest. I knew I sensed it before. It's stronger than last time."

I let my eyes drift to two figures beneath, their backs toward us. One of them was all muscle with black wavy hair sweeping the tops of his shoulders. He looked as if he could bench-press a cow. His arms arched out, too hulk-like to rest by his sides. His head scoured the lands from left to right. For all I knew they could smell us.

"Favner won't be pleased when he finds out. Who do you think is foolish enough to try and escape?" the thinner of the two said. He kept his hair pulled back in a long blonde ponytail that fell down his sculpted back. He wasn't as large, but he looked as if he could definitely hold his own in a fight.

"I don't know, Owen. But we will find out. They won't get past us for long."

The hulk that I'm assuming was Liam, lifted his head to the trees, his eyes scanned from one branch to the next. If he turned even a couple feet we would be spotted.

I swallowed the heavy lump in my throat, but didn't breathe a sound.

Though I was scared for my life, I was highly aware of Kai's uncovered warm body pressed to mine, the firm ripple of his contours forming to my back. His chest rose up and down at the same time as mine. I felt the stable cadence of his heartbeats thump against me. His grip around my waist never loosened, his fingers clutching my hip like a lifeline.

"They must have gone further east." Liam began walking away. When the other didn't follow, still surveying the limbs up high, convinced we were near, Liam bellowed, "Come, Owen."

I barely heard their movements through the leafy groundcover as they trudged away. My heart pounded rapidly in my chest, my breath pumping swiftly through my lungs.

Kai's voice brushed my ear as he lifted his hand from my

mouth. "They're gone." But neither of us made a move to separate. He rested his hand on my shoulder and then gradually let his fingers trail down my arm. I closed my eyes and let out a shaky breath, thankful to be out of danger and completely taken aback by the way his touch affected my body. My head fell back in relief against the curve of his shoulder with my eyes shut. I felt him go still, but then he let out a slow breath, relaxing.

His finger lingered at my wrist, barely grazing the skin as if he wanted to take my hand once more, but was holding himself back. I felt him breath in and out against my back, the warmth stroking my neck. "Are you okay?"

About what exactly? Your closeness or the fact that we just barely escaped death? I took a deep breath, hoping that would give my voice a chance to collect itself. "I think so."

He sighed. "Calliope—"

The branch suddenly shuddered slightly under our feet, clenching my stomach. When I looked up, Declan stood with an expression of relief fixed on his face.

"Thank the Fallen Fae. I lost track of Liam and Owen a mile back. I was sure they had found you."

Declan's eyes drifted between Kai and me, our bodies pressed firmly against each other. Kai released me and my knees wobbled beneath me. Declan jutted his hand out to steady me before I fell from the bough.

"You question my ability to protect her?" Kai's tone was challenging.

"No, I simply know how good those two are at tracking rogue faeries and by some miracle we escaped them," Declan amended, keeping my hand firmly in his.

When I caught my breath I said, "I didn't think anyone liked Favner. Why would they return rogue faeries to him? Aren't you all on the same team?"

"He has a handful of followers. Those who figure if you can't beat him, join him," Declan said.

"A bunch of worthless cowards," Kai said vehemently, unable to hold still any longer.

"So, they could find me," I said. "Favner could force me to come to Faylinn."

Kai scowled, refusing to meet Declan or me in the eye. He kept his eyes fixed in the direction Liam and Owen disappeared.

"We won't let that happen, Calliope," Declan said, but his tone wasn't as reassuring as I would have liked. "It's why I've been around for the last five years. I've been able to keep you in hiding for that long and I will do it for as long as it takes. If that is what you want."

"But why? Why have you chosen me to protect?" I questioned, taking my hand away from Declan's tight grip. That question seemed especially pertinent in this moment. "There must be others out there who could use the protection too."

"Your father was a good friend of mine, a mentor," he said with finality. "We can talk more about this later, Calliope. Right now what I'd really like is to get you in the safety of your home where they can't get to you."

Kai finally released his eyes from the search and said, "Good idea," agreeing for once.

They escorted me back, walking a few steps behind me, conversing in hushed voices. It sounded important so I didn't want to interrupt. We reached as far as they could go and Declan told me to keep safe.

"I don't want you coming out to see us on your own anymore," Declan said.

"But, how else will I get to see you?" I searched back and

forth between the two towering figures. I suddenly felt very small and insignificant.

If I couldn't go see them anymore did that mean I couldn't come near the forest anymore?

"We can signal," Declan assured. "If we need you we'll use Kai's flute. We'll play a short melody for you to recognize it as us. And if you need us all you have to do is say our names. Our given names."

"Your what?"

"A given name. They aren't handed out lightly, but I know you will guard our names and only use them when necessary," Declan said.

Kai answered my blank stare. "Every faery receives a given name when they are introduced into the world. If you know the given name you can have complete control over that faery. So, you can see how your given name falling into the wrong hands can be a very bad thing."

"All you have to do is say the name and we will be summoned to you," Declan said.

"You won't have a choice?"

They shook their heads.

"I don't want that kind of power," I faltered.

"The time might come when you will want that kind of power, Calliope," Declan said. "I know you won't use it unless absolutely necessary and that is why I feel comfortable enough to share mine with you. You won't abuse the power."

"But what if something happens and for whatever reason I can't say your names? What then?"

"You'll always be able to find me," Kai said from behind Declan. I looked back at him. There was no hint of arrogance in his eyes. They bore into mine with a genuine intensity.

201

"Kai will keep you just as safe as I would," Declan said, interrupting my thoughts, but I could hear an uncomfortable undertone in his voice.

"I know." I realized in that moment I trusted that they would take care of me. I trusted them with my life.

"No matter if you say my name and I'm in Faylinn, I will hear you. I will come as fast as I am capable."

I acknowledged him with a nod.

"My given name is…" he leaned down and whispered in my ear. I knew that Kai could still hear him, but I could only assume he did it for further protection from anyone else around who could be listening. "Declan Alastair."

When he spoke the name it made a significant impression. Without fully understanding the meaning, somewhere inside me I knew this was a precious honor.

Kai leaned down to me next, his quiet breath brushing my ear. "Kai Rodric." He pulled away and said, "Now get inside." He nodded to my house.

I looked between my two guardians, two men who I felt closer to now than ever.

"Bye," I said and walked from the trees onto our grass. The lights inside my home beamed like a beacon, but it almost seemed more surreal to come back to my human life than to exist in the fae world now. I peered cautiously through the windows before deciding it was safe. No one was in sight. I closed the sliding glass door quietly behind me.

"You're coming in awfully late tonight," Dad's voice came from the darkness in our living room.

I gasped. "Dad, why are you creeping in the dark?"

"I watched the sunset and never bothered to turn on the light," he explained.

I moved toward the back of the couch and flipped on the light on the side table. "You really should warn a person before you just start talking from the darkness."

"Why are you coming in so late tonight?" He leaned back in his recliner; his legs rested on the ottoman at his feet.

I peered at the clock on the wall. The hands indicated that it was nearly eight o'clock. "Kai and Declan were teaching me how to maneuver in the trees." I kept Liam and Owen out of the equation. If Dad learned about them, he'd never let me set foot in the forest again. "I'm getting pretty good at it."

"You've been out there for almost four hours, Calliope. I thought we had agreed you would be inside before sundown."

"I know. I'm sorry." It wouldn't help my case if I told him during sundown that we were being chased by professional rogue fae hunters. "It won't happen again."

"You're lucky Mom's still not home." Just as the words passed his lips, I heard the faint groan of the garage door opening. "I told her we hadn't eaten yet. She's bringing Chinese."

"That sounds good."

He motioned to my bedroom. "Go change. Put on some pajamas or something, unless you want her asking why you have twigs in your hair and dirt on your face." *I had dirt on my face?* I wiped my hand across my cheek and he smiled softly. "There's no dirt on your face, but you really do have leaves in your hair."

I raced from the room when I heard the side door creak open.

"Hello?" Mom's voice echoed through the house.

"Hey, Melody," Dad greeted as I closed my bedroom door.

I couldn't sleep that night. My thoughts were swirling in a

whirlwind and my room felt like it was a sweltering sauna. When I turned to check the time on my nightstand it blinked 2:37 am. I needed air. Heaving myself up from my bed, I went to the window and opened it. My wings fluttered, enjoying the breeze that rushed in almost as much as me. I took in a deep breath of the cool freshness.

The night was quiet with the exception of cricket chirps and leaf flutters. My eyes gazed down at the lining of the trees to the mystery of what could be lurking there now. The Keepers were probably out there scouting for whatever or whomever they were so worried about.

Once my body was satisfied I turned to go back to bed, but then I heard voices, hushed low voices.

"Lurking again?"

"You are one to talk."

"We both know I wasn't lurking. I've always been around."

My eyes scanned the trees, but it was too dark to decipher their figures. I knew it was them. I didn't need to see the bickering Keepers for confirmation.

"Well, you can take a break for the night. Sit back, put up your feet up. You've been working *so* hard all day," Kai's tone was patronizing. Was it strange that I knew his voice?

"And why do you feel like you need to all of a sudden protect her around the clock?"

"It's no secret to you who she is. She needs protecting."

"Well, for the last five years I think I've done a pretty good job." Declan's voice was frustrated.

The fact that they knew more about me than I knew about myself rattled me. Were there really still secrets that I was being shielded from? Did everyone think I was that fragile that I couldn't handle the truth?

204

"Yeah, you have, but now Favner isn't going to let her go. When he discovers and I mean when, that you didn't get rid of her..." Kai trailed off, but it wasn't hard to figure out what the end of his sentence was going to be.

"It doesn't mean that you should be here." I could barely hear Declan's voice, but it was bitter.

"What is this really about, Declan?" There was a long pause. I almost thought Declan wasn't going to answer. "What?" Kai repeated, more adamantly.

"You don't get to swoop in here now," Declan's voice raised. "I've watched over her for years. Protected her. If anyone gets a chance to be with her it should be me, not you."

I shivered, but not from the cold.

"If you wanted that chance you should have taken it. You've had how many years?"

"She didn't have the Sight, Kai," Declan contended. "If I'd shown myself to her she would have bolted away, screaming and crying. You remember how she reacted when she saw you for the first time. I didn't want to frighten her."

"And prowling in the shadows outside her bedroom window wasn't supposed to frighten her?" I could hear the smirk in his voice. I could picture the look he would have—one eyebrow raised as he tilted his head patronizingly.

There was a thump and then a low curse under someone's breath. It sounded an awful lot like a fist hitting a tree trunk.

"You don't get to make the decisions around here," Declan muttered.

There was a heavy sigh.

"In case you haven't noticed," Kai said. "*You* are the favorite."

"But you ignite something in her that I can't," Declan

replied softly.

"Hatred?" Kai's amusement was apparent in his tone.

"You and I both know it's far from hatred."

What did they know about what ignited inside of me?

They were silent for a few minutes, but I waited, too absorbed in the conversation to leave the window just yet. A gust of wind ripped through the trees. I wondered what they were doing. Had they always guarded my house so closely at night? Or were they on higher alert with the arrival of Liam and Owen? I sat down against the wall under my window, my head resting against the windowsill.

Declan broke the peace of the night. "It's passion, in case you were wondering."

"I wasn't." Kai paused before he said, "You don't really have to worry about me, you know."

"It's all up to Calliope in the end. She gets to decide what she wants. But we both know we may never get a chance. You know the law," Declan said, subdued.

The realization set in, bile rose in the back in my throat. The law. It had been staring me in the face since the beginning, but it never clicked when Declan had mentioned it in terms for me. I would only be allowed to marry within my colony. Even if I wanted a future with Declan or… Kai, it would never be possible.

"Cameron still owns her heart. I think he always will."

"That won't matter when all is said and done."

"You weren't there that day he came," Kai contested. "She sparkles around him, Declan."

Someone sighed again.

"Then you better fight like hell because it doesn't look like anyone's going to give up anytime soon," Declan's deeper voice cut through the night.

"Don't worry about me. She's all yours." Hearing Kai's words sent an ache through my chest. *But why should I care?* "We could never work."

"You know it won't matter in the long run anyway. It's a nice thought, but we both know an actual life with her is impossible."

I couldn't listen anymore. It was all enough information to drown me in anxiety. Declan was supposed to get rid of me. Bonding arrangements put us in chains. I could never be with either of them even if I wanted to. And Favner wanted me dead. *Why?* How did he even know about me?

EIGHTEEN

"How's my favorite faery?" Cameron popped up next to me in the hallway on my way to Physics. After overhearing Declan and Kai's conversation last night, I couldn't fall back asleep for a couple of hours. The wheels in my head wouldn't stop spinning. I couldn't have gotten more than three hours of sleep.

"Can you *not* call me that in public?" I said, hushed.

"Oh, c'mon, Cal. It'll only make people suspect something when you respond like that. Just be cool." He nudged my shoulder to try and loosen me up. I guess it didn't work. "Hey, are you okay?"

I let out an overwhelmed breath of air and rubbed my tired eyes. "I don't know. I learned a couple new things last night that I'm trying to come to terms with. And with all the changes, I just don't feel like myself anymore. I'm not Calliope anymore. I'm freak faery girl. That's what they would call me if they knew what I was, isn't it?"

"I'd come up with something much more clever than that."

208

Cameron winked.

I let myself chuckle a little and it made me yawn.

"You've done really well at hiding your wings," he whispered to me. "I thought they'd be a lot more noticeable, but with the combination of those flowy shirts and your backpack, you'd never know unless you were looking for it."

"The backpack kind of hurts sometimes. It rubs them raw."

"So don't wear the backpack. I honestly can't see them," he said reassuringly.

I shifted the backpack, "Where's Isla?"

He shrugged. "Turns out she wasn't cheating, just mad at me. We worked it out."

I figured they'd made up when I saw them kissing in the hallway yesterday morning. I thought it would start hurting less with time to see them kiss, but as it turns out I was wrong. Coming to terms with the fact that I was never going to be the one in his arms was a lot harder to except than I anticipated. I knew I needed to accept it. It was apparent I'd never be his, as I wanted him to be mine. But deep down I just couldn't make myself.

"But then she got mad at me again this morning because she thought I should know the difference between what her hair looks like today and what it looked like yesterday."

I laughed. "She went and got it highlighted yesterday, Cameron. And they took off a couple inches of her hair."

"Is it really that big of a difference?" he asked incredulously. *Boys.*

I laughed again. "Only to the females. We notice things like that. I mean, with how much you stare at her, I would have thought you'd notice too, but boys will be boys."

"Great." He chuckled softly. "How do I get myself out of

this one?"

"She'll get over it," I said encouragingly, swimming through the sea of people in the swarming hallway. Cameron latched onto my belt loop, trying to keep from losing me in the masses. He let go when he was at my side again.

"She seems to think I've been missing a lot of stuff lately," he continued our conversation.

"Like what?"

"Well, the reason she was mad at me last week may or may not have been because I forgot it was our three month anniversary," he said sheepishly.

I chuckled. "I've never understood why dating couples make anniversaries out of everything. *It's been two month since our first kiss*," I said dreamily. "*It's been five months since you told me you loved me*." I smirked at him and saw that he was laughing too. "Is it because it's a triumph that it's lasted for so long or...?"

He laughed. "You tell me." When I didn't reply he said, "No, seriously, please, tell me. I need to get out of the dog house."

"Flowers. Chocolates. Mixed tape. Jewelry. Love notes. Stuffed animals," I prattled off all the typical romantic gestures I could think of.

"You'd want all that stuff?" he sincerely asked.

"Me?" I thought about it for a moment. I'd never had a guy get me any of those things before. "Honestly, no. Those gifts are a cop out. All I'd want is just the affirmation that I meant something to you, that I mattered. A heartfelt apology. It's easy to merely say things or make gestures. It's another to actually mean them. Maybe tack on a bouquet of wild flowers or something. Not a dozen roses. Too cliché. Just be thoughtful."

When I looked up at him, an unreadable mask covered his

familiar face. His momentary gaze unsettled my insides, releasing the butterflies from their cages to fly wildly. I broke the staring contest first, unable to confidently look him in the eye when he watched me like that.

He cleared his throat. "Thanks, Callie." The warning bell rang as I reached the door of my physics class. "Ah crap... I'm going to be late!" he said and lifted his hand, booking it down the hallway. I chuckled and found my seat.

When I got home from school I had one destination in mind. I wanted answers.

"Princess," Kai crooned infuriatingly when I stepped into the forest. I had barely even passed the borderline when Kai stopped me.

"Where's Declan?" I cut to the chase.

"Hello to you too."

I didn't respond to his sarcasm. I simply stared at him, waiting for an answer. Today he actually wore a light beige shirt, one of their billowy hand sewn tunics, the collar left untied. Sometimes I wondered if they didn't wear shirts simply to see my face every time I saw them without one. Though I'd gotten a little used to it, it didn't change the fact that they were still half naked and flawlessly built. I was able to keep my composure better when they were fully clothed.

"Probably moping up in some tree." He shrugged. "And I thought we told you not to come searching for us on your own anymore."

I ignored that last comment. I had actually kind of forgotten. "Isn't that normally your post?"

"Didn't you hear?" He cocked his head to the side. "Declan and I are trading places today. He mopes. I gallivant off into the sunset." Kai circled around me, causing my head to spin by following his movements so I stopped. I stared straight ahead, crossing my arms in front of me, trying to suppress a smile at his joke.

"Maybe if you weren't such a prick to him all the time he wouldn't have to mope up in a tree."

"A prick?" His indigo eyes nearly crossed in confusion as he twisted his face in front of mine, forcing me to look at him. "Like a rosebush thorn?"

"Forget it."

He turned back to his task of balancing on some vine-covered rock and gracefully hopped to the next. A bow and a tube filled with arrows were strapped to his back.

"I heard what you said last night."

Kai shifted his gaze back to me without losing his balance. "Eavesdropping, were you?"

"If the two of you were having such a private conversation maybe you should have taken it further into the forest," I chided. "My hearing has sort of improved over the last couple months. You know, one of those fae abilities you two informed me about."

"How much did you hear?" He sounded bored with our conversation already, but I knew he was uncomfortable with everything that I could have heard. He pulled the bow and an arrow from his back.

"Enough to know that Favner doesn't exactly want me alive."

Kai spun slowly around, his expression unchanging. He stared at me blankly.

"Would you like to expand upon that?" I prompted.

"You want every little frilly detail about how a faery king wants you dead?" he said brusquely. I shuddered. Did he have to put it so bluntly? He didn't even try to soften the blow. "What would be the point in trying to hide the obvious? You should be scared. You deserve the warning. You shouldn't take that threat lightly. Favner isn't the faery to mess with. Even I know to stay out of his way."

"Why didn't you two ever mention it to me before if he's such a threat? Shouldn't I have been on my guard all this time?" I said accusingly.

"Declan didn't want to frighten you," Kai said and turned to shoot his arrow. "There's nothing you can do. So, we've done our part out here and kept you safe." It landed in the center of a trunk twenty feet away.

That sparked a thought. "What did you mean by Favner finding out that Declan didn't get rid of me? Why would Declan need to get rid of me?"

"So you heard that part too, huh?" Kai seemed a little uneasy, but tried passing it off as indifference. He kept his back to me.

"You two don't exactly quarrel quietly."

"What would be the fun in that?" He spun his head back and flashed a crooked smile my way, fluttering my heartbeats. He wasn't allowed to get me flustered right now. I didn't need a distraction from the conversation. Couldn't he be serious for one minute?

"Why was Declan supposed to get rid of me?" I repeated, determined to get a straight answer.

"As much as I love being the bearer of all bad news, I think Declan should get to explain that one to you." Kai turned back to his target practice.

"Well, where is he?" I inquired. "You never answered my question."

"Beats me." He shrugged indifferently, his back to me. His next arrow landed in the same tree, right next to the first. "I'm not *his* Keeper. Just yours."

"You don't have to be my Keeper. I never asked you to stay."

Kai paused before answering. "You didn't have to." He dropped his stance and turned back to me. His liquid iris eyes peered at me. They really looked at me. Not with sarcasm or malice. Not playful or mischievous. His eyes appeared solemn, gentle… meaningful.

I swallowed and cleared my throat, breaking away from his gaze. "What am I supposed to do?"

He sighed, breaking his trance. "Nothing."

"I need to do something. I can't just sit back and relax now. What do I need to know?" I persisted.

Kai sighed and gestured for me to take a seat. I situated myself beside the nearest tree. "Faeries tend to be particularly fond of the chase," he said.

I swallowed back any fears. "And Favner is fond of chasing me."

Kai nodded. "Most of us are, apparently," he said under his breath, but I don't think he expected me to comment.

My eyes shied away from him, looking to the fallen leaves scattered along the ground. I couldn't find the confidence to look him in the eye. "Kai, I don't want any part of your world. If Favner knew that, would he leave me alone?"

"Not if he knows that you didn't die. I'm not sure how well Declan covered his tracks."

I swallowed. "Declan was really supposed to kill me?"

He set his jaw. "Yes."

"This is unfair. I didn't do anything. My father left the faery world and had me. So I'm a rogue faery. Is that really worth killing over?"

"Calliope." Kai exhaled. "Your father hasn't been the most forthcoming about his life in Faylinn."

I stopped before replying. It was only the third time he'd ever used my actual name. He said my name with care, as if it was something he wanted to hold on to, something that could mean something to him.

"Will you please tell me? I'm tired of the secrecy, Kai. It's exhausting."

Kai shook his head, still not looking smug or cocky. He peered at me earnestly. "Has your father told you *anything* about his life in Faylinn? The history he left behind there?"

"He told me he was a faery and that he met my mom and decided to join her in the human world. She was more important to him than that world," I prattled off the Reader's Digest version of my dad's explanation.

Kai leaned into me, over his legs. "Well, he left out one minor detail." He paused, causing me to shift in my skin. I could see the battle play out in his eyes as he struggled with an inner decision. Apparently one side won, whether it was the good or bad side I didn't know until he spoke. "Declan is going to kill me," he said under his breath. "She apparently was more important than his kingdom."

I stopped breathing momentarily. "*His* kingdom."

"Before your father met your mother, he was the next in line to become the King of Faylinn. He tossed away his birthright to be with her." His words may have sounded callous, but his tone was gentle.

Kai's words suspended in the air between us. He kept his position, his face mere inches from mine.

I sat back, the realization setting in. "Which makes me threatening to Favner because…" The pieces were falling into place.

"You are the one faery who can take away his throne. You are the last rightful heir to Faylinn. The last of the *True* Royal bloodline."

I was the heir to Faylinn? No, I'd barely wrapped my head around the fact that I was a faery. I was not their faery *freaking* princess.

"When he finds out you lived, he'll be obsessed with finding you," Kai said. "To be rid of you for good."

"Kai…" I broke off, not knowing what to say. "Why didn't you two tell me before?"

"Umm… Do you have amnesia or does your initial freak out about actually being a faery come to your recollection?"

I didn't answer him as the mere thought of being fae royalty still tried to find a place in my brain.

"I wanted to tell you, but Declan wanted to protect you," he explained. "He figured telling you about your inheritance would really send you over the edge. He wanted to gradually introduce you into this world. The more comfortable you are with it, the easier it will be to transition into our world. We haven't wanted to push you into doing anything against your will."

My anger suddenly surfaced. "So, even though numerous times I said I didn't want anything to do with Faylinn he still expected me to transition? What? Were you two going to gag and kidnap me—force me to go with you?"

"No!" Kai protested, offended. "It was nothing like that."

216

"Then what?" I stood. "What makes you think I want to be a faery queen?"

"I don't!" He jolted up beside me. "That's why I never told you, Calliope. I don't want to force you into anything you don't want to do! You deserve more than that!"

I opened my mouth to speak, but nothing audible passed my lips, so I closed it. Since when did Kai care so much?

He took a step closer to me, but I moved away. I needed to walk off my shaking legs. "My dad. I have to talk to my dad." I paced in front of him.

"Let me walk you back," Kai offered, taking another step toward me.

"No," I denied him. "I need space."

He nodded and stood still, watching as I escaped for the borderline.

When I walked out from the trees, I instantly felt knots in the pit of my stomach. My mom stood with her arms folded across her chest in the open doorway, a probing look in her eyes.

Perfect timing.

NINETEEN

I nearly retreated back into the forest, into the security and protection of my trees, but I pushed on. My eyes darted around the yard like a cornered animal, unable to hold my ground. Every time my eyes found her, she was unchanging, watching my every move. I swallowed back the rising heavy lump. She didn't need to say anything. Her eyes spoke volumes. She knew. She had to know.

"Calliope," she said steadily, with more coolness than I think she felt in that moment. I hadn't quite reached the deck.

"Hi, Mom." Maybe she didn't know. Maybe I was overreacting, painting a picture in my head that didn't exist.

"You were in the forest," she stated matter-a-factly, not questioning why.

I nodded, lifting a foot to step up onto the deck. I wasn't sure if she saw something in my eyes or if it was a gut feeling but she screeched, "Finnian!"

Her shouting stopped me. I remained motionless on the

deck steps. It was like watching sand trickling through an hourglass in slow motion, the distress in her eyes, the anxiety of waiting for him to reach her. He finally swiftly strode into the room behind her.

"What? What is it?"

His eyes met mine, trapped by my mom's stare. I saw the blood drain from his face as realization set in and the scene before him made sense. When she reluctantly turned to him, seeing his deer caught in headlights look, it was all confirmed. We read one another like a book.

"You knew?" she gasped.

"Melody," he started.

"You knew!" her voice rose to a near shattering glass decimal.

I winced.

He sighed, our cover blown.

"Mom," I tried. It was hard for me to see passed the death glare she gave him. My father just might die tonight.

"Calliope, I need you to be quiet right now," she said shakily, trying to keep it steady. "You two, over there now."

Dad and I followed orders, not daring to argue, and sat closely on the couch in the family room, seeking comfort in numbers.

This was her courtroom now, and we were on trial. Let the questioning begin.

"Finnian, how dare you keep this from me? How dare you risk the safety of our daughter!" She pointed an accusing finger from him to me whenever she spoke about one of us. She had

219

only been lecturing us for about fifteen minutes, but it felt like a lifetime.

"She figured it out on her own, Melody," Dad defended himself. "I've only been her support system. I didn't want to worry you if nothing else came of it."

"But it did!" she cried. I wanted to leave and I got up to escape, but she caught me. "Don't you dare think about moving." I immediately sat back down, but she wasn't finished with him yet. "You didn't think that this was nothing coming of it?" She lifted my hair from my ears and I felt instantly bare and uncomfortable. "Does she have wings too?"

He looked down which was definitely the wrong move. At that point it was as if she couldn't take one more hammer falling. She stormed away—a breath of her perfume trailing behind—without a word.

It was a weird feeling. I'd just been chewed up and spit back out and chewed up again, but all I felt was relief. It was finally out in the open. I wouldn't have to hide in my room all the time anymore. If I wanted I could walk freely in our home without being paranoid that someone would see the points of my ears or feel restrained by the bustier holding down my wings. They suffocated more and more each day that I couldn't release them.

"I think she took it rather well," he said after a minute and I had to laugh.

"We should have told her sooner, Dad."

"I know," he said, humbled. "But you were adjusting so well that I didn't want to disrupt the process."

"And you thought this was a better plan?" I asked wryly, peering up at him.

"Well…" he shrugged. "She'll come around," he said and pulled me under his arm, kissing the top of my hair. "The trial is next week. If we could have just held off for another few weeks this would have been avoided. I just hope she doesn't let this affect her ability to function."

He really cared about my mother. Of course the love my parents had for one another went without saying, but he risked the doghouse and most likely the silent treatment and a few nights of sleeping on the couch so she could have peace of mind. Granted telling her from the beginning might have gone over a little more smoothly, but he wasn't concerned about himself. He had good intentions even if they weren't executed properly.

The reason I'd come storming out of the trees in the first place bubbled to the surface. I unlatched myself from him and stared him down.

"What now?" he asked, sensing my frustration.

"Why did you give up your kingdom?"

He sighed heavily as if he knew that was going to come out at some point. I really wished it had come from him.

"That was kind of a large detail to leave out, Dad. Why didn't you tell me?"

He pressed his lips together, looking thoughtful. "The less you knew the better. We were able to stay hidden without the knowledge of Faylinn and my history there. It was easier this way."

"Well, I'm obviously not hiding very well anymore, now am I?"

He stood up, leaving me seated. "Calliope, I chose to stay with your mother because she was my life. I was no longer tied to my kingdom. The string secured me to her, but I didn't leave my kingdom to Favner," he said with a trace of regret in his voice. "I left it to my brother. He had always wanted Faylinn and I wanted your mother. I didn't think my inheritance was relevant at the time and there was never the right time to tell you."

"You have a brother?" I asked in surprise. "Then what happened to him?" After I said it, I knew it was an insensitive question.

Sadness fell across his face. "I can only assume the same thing that is happening to all of the other dwindling fae."

"I'm sorry, Dad."

He nodded his acceptance. There was a moment of silence and I gulped back my sorrow for him.

"So, you left Faylinn for Mom," I breathed. "Now I'm a faery princess and I'm just supposed to go on with my life as if nothing happened. How?"

"I'm not saying that at all. I don't even know how to protect you anymore. You're not safe in Faylinn, but if anyone finds out what you are here, you won't be safe here either."

"Is that supposed to bring me comfort? Because you are not doing a very good job of it."

Something dawned on him. His expression changed. "It makes sense now. Why faery blood runs so strongly in you. You are drawn to Faylinn because it's falling apart. You are the rightful heir. It knows it won't survive without you. That's why you can't stay human. You're meant to be a faery."

"Whoa... No, no, no, no, no," I said, pulling away from him "*You're* the rightful heir. If anything they need you, Dad. Favner is rotten. They need a better ruler. Someone who knows how to care for a dying realm."

"Maybe you should think more about what you are saying, Calliope. You seem awfully concerned about a place you learned about mere months ago."

"Of course, I'm concerned. Innocent people..." I cleared my throat. "Faeries are dying or disappearing because of him.

Faylinn isn't the same place you remember, Dad. The way Declan talks about it…" The pain in Declan's eyes flashed in my mind and I winced.

My dad's eyes had that all-knowing glint, as if he knew something I didn't. "You'll make the right decision in the end."

"You think it's *my* responsibility to take care of this?"

"You are the true heir," he stated. "It will only keep haunting you until you accept that."

"But that's not my world. I don't know anything about it. I don't know the history. I don't know the rules of the land or even the faeries residing there. I would be worthless at taking charge."

"It will come to you," he said, promising.

I let my eyes rest firmly on him as understanding set in. "This is the real reason why you didn't want to tell Mom," I said, feeling a little bitter. "You knew she would figure it out and tell me. Were you ever going to tell me?"

"In time I would have when it became necessary."

"It was necessary from day one, Dad."

"I never asked for any of this to happen, Calliope. I tried keeping you from Faylinn. Your entire life that has been my only concern, but my feelings don't matter. Faylinn is more powerful than you. It's more powerful than me. It will keep fighting for you."

"And I'll keep fighting back," I said with finality.

I went to bed that night without seeing Mom. She locked herself in their bedroom for the remainder of the evening. My dad had to sleep on the couch. I offered him my bed, but he declined it.

My wings curled lightly around me as I lay in my sheets, as if they had a mind of their own and knew I needed the comfort. Their soft embrace caressed my body. In their warm strange sense of security, I drifted off to sleep.

The house was quiet when I woke up the next day. Dad wasn't anywhere in the house and Mom stayed holed up in their room.

At lunch, I walked out of the school to sit on the grass and breathe in the open air. I just needed one moment of peace, one moment of clarity. Was it too much to ask for?

"Hey," Lia said cheerfully, wrapping her arm around my waist in a side hug.

I flinched back without thinking. It wasn't as if she could have felt the wings, but I couldn't control my reaction. I was already too on edge.

A defensive look painted across her face as she lifted her hands in surrender. "My bad. Note to self. Don't touch Callie anymore. I'll just add it to the list underneath: Don't mention the hair or clothes. No swimming. And treat nature with respect."

I shied away at "the list". Had I really become so defensive about everything? "Sorry. I didn't mean to do that," I apologized.

"Calliope." Her voice was firm. "There's something you're keeping from me. You know you can trust me, right? What's been going on with you lately?"

"Nothing," I denied. "I don't know why I did that. I've just been a little jumpy for some reason. Today's just not a good day."

"Are you pregnant?" she whispered close to my ear.

"What?" I stepped back. "No!"

"You can tell me if you are, you know?" she said

sympathetically. "I wouldn't judge you. Life happens. I'd support you no matter what."

I shook my head. "Lia, why in the world would you think I'm pregnant? Who would I be doing it with?"

"Well, you're wearing baggier clothes and you don't like people to touch you. And your mood swings are kind of giving me a headache," she said these things as if she thought it was obvious.

Great. I'm glad I've been so pleasant to be around. "I'm not pregnant, Lia," I insisted, hoping it would reassure her and get her off my back.

She planted herself in front of me, compelling me to look her in the eye. "Callie, then whatever is going on with you, you can tell me. You know that, right? I won't judge you. Anything you say won't scare me. I'm your best friend."

"There's nothing to tell." I shrugged to add emphasis. Shrugging seemed like the right thing to do at the time. "I'm fine."

Lia looked betrayed, but I couldn't bring myself to tell her anything. "Well, when you finally decide that you can trust me, you know where to find me." She turned her back on me and walked away, leaving me officially alone.

What just happened? Why was everything falling apart?

I felt the tears climb up my throat and scratch behind my eyes, but I took a deep breath and clenched the tear ducts. I would not cry at school. Not in front of everyone. This wasn't that big of a deal. I tried to play the mantra in my head to calm myself. *It's not that big of a deal. It's not that big of a deal. It's not that big of a deal.*

"Hey." Cameron appeared in front of me. My gaze refocused and he was peering at me with such concern that the tears threatening to escape fell down my cheeks without permission. "C'mon. Let's get out of here."

"I can't ditch," I murmured.

"What's one period? I'm sure your parents can write you a note. They'll understand." He drew his thumb across my cheek, brushing away the tears.

"You can't ditch."

"My dad will get over it," he said softly.

He wasn't going to back down, so I nodded and sought solace under his welcoming arm as we walked out to the school parking lot.

His jeep rattled back and forth as he took it off-roading down a path near the canyon. He let the silence fill the car, knowing I needed the time to collect my thoughts and breath. When we were nowhere near civilization he stopped and motioned for me to get out with him. I followed without question.

As we walked up an off the beaten path sort of trail, I started to hear the trickle of water. We reached a small grassy pasture with a miniature waterfall, water seeping tranquilly through the boulders.

"Release them."

"What?"

"Your wings," he said. "Let them be free. I know they need it." He saw my apprehension. "I won't look if you don't want me to."

I hadn't shown them to him yet. I hadn't shown them to anyone. It was never the right time, and if I was being honest, I was too nervous. Showing the wings would be like revealing a part of my body that should be kept covered. It felt intimate to me for some reason. They were a part of me now, and showing them would make everything real. But I did as he said because I really did need to let them stretch out. I carefully pulled down the bustier and set it on the nearest boulder. The upper wings reached out through the sleeves of my tank top while the others spread out the bottom. They fully unfolded and it felt so relieving just to have them fly free, like stretching out a tight muscle.

Cameron didn't say anything, so I looked to him for confirmation that this wasn't going to be his breaking point— that this wouldn't be the point where he would officially flee from the sight of me.

"You're beautiful."

I couldn't stop the blush.

"We're going to need to make you some shirts with slits so they can be free more often."

"What would be the point? I couldn't show them off anyway."

"For moments like this," he said as if it was obvious. "Don't tell me that when you go to see Tweedle Dee and Tweedle Dumb that you keep your true self hidden."

I chuckled, but didn't deny his accusation.

"Callie." He shook his head. "No wonder you're so on edge. You can't let yourself be you anywhere you go. Even in the presence of your own kind. And look at you. Why would you want to hide?"

I sighed. "Because Cameron, I'm not who I thought I was. Nothing about what I knew has been true. Every time I turn around someone throws another grenade of information at me. I'm a freaking faery princess!" The words gushed out of my mouth like word-vomit. I couldn't hold them back. And they sounded ridiculous.

His mouth dropped. "What?"

I fell against the trunk of the nearest tree and slid down, too exhausted to stand any longer. "Yeah. My father was supposed to inherit Faylinn when he met my mom. I'm apparently the *rightful* heir now."

He chuckled. "Do you realize how many girls would kill to be you right now?"

I tossed my hand in the air, brushing him off. "If girls really knew the pressure it put them under they wouldn't feel the same way."

"Maybe, maybe not. But you're here moping because you're royalty."

"I'm *not* moping because I'm royalty," I countered. "It's all just a lot to take in, okay? What if your mom came up to you and said, 'Oh, Cameron, by the way, your father is an elf from Santa's workshop and I'm an alien from outer space, so that makes you—"

"Something really messed up," he cut in.

That stopped me in my tracks and the laughter bubbled over. I *really* laughed, freely. He joined in and sat beside me, nudging my shoulder.

"There you are." He smiled warmly. "I knew you were in there somewhere. You've really got to loosen up, Cal. You're too young to have a heart attack."

I leaned my head against his shoulder, basking in his familiar company. He reached his arm around me, being careful of my wings, and let me relax under his friendly embrace. We sat there without speaking for a while. It was exactly what I needed. Just to have a silent support system. To know I wasn't alone in this.

Sunlight filtered through the leaves above us, fluttering

patterns in our laps. Cameron reached over and traced the lines dancing on my bent knees, tickling my stomach.

"Do you think I can still have a normal life? Do you think I can stay here and live like everyone else? Go to college. Get a job. Get married." I paused. "Have a family?"

When he didn't answer I gazed up at him.

Cameron's eyes moved from my legs and scanned my face, making my feelings for him rise to the top. He bit his bottom lip. "I don't see why not," he said. "You've mastered your tactics for covering up so far. If you want to keep it up, I don't see why you couldn't live like a human if that's what you really want to do."

"I do," I said earnestly.

He broke our eye contact and looked to the ground. "Yeah... I don't really think you're cut out to be royalty anyway. You're too much of a commoner."

I shoved his shoulder, untangling myself from him. "Will you take me back home? I really need to talk to someone."

Cameron sighed. "Back to Tweedle Dee and Tweedle Dumb, huh?"

"Well, it depends on who is who," I said, getting easily to my feet.

"Well, I haven't met Dee yet, but Dumb is obviously the one who thinks he knows everything."

I chuckled. "Dee it is, then."

When we pulled up to my house my mom's car was parked in the driveway, which did not ease my burdens. *What was she doing home already?*

"Does your mom know yet?"

"She found out last night." I looked to the house, already dreading having to face her after last night. "Saw me walking out of the trees just before dark."

229

"Ooooo," he sucked in air. "That must have been a fun one to explain."

"You have no idea."

"See you… later?" He was about to say tomorrow when he realized it was the weekend. "That is if you live to see another day."

I smirked and lifted my hand to wave, but stopped. "My car," I realized.

"Isla and I will go get it and bring it back to you."

"She won't be mad that you ditched school with me today?" I know I would be if I were her.

"If she is, she'll have to get over it." He shrugged.

I smiled again. "Thanks, Cam."

"Anytime, Callie."

When I walked in the front door, my mom stepped into the entryway at the sound of the door closing.

"I got a call from the school," she said. "You weren't in your last period class. I tried calling your phone, but it kept going to voicemail. I was worried about you." She looked like she was trying to control her distress. I appreciated it, but I knew I deserved whatever lecture was going to be sent my way.

"I was with Cameron. We were up the canyon so the reception must have been bad."

She nodded. "And you ditched because…?"

"I needed to get away. Ever since… this." I gestured to myself. "I've been a little overwhelmed and distant from Lia. She got really upset with me today, so Cameron took me to get some fresh air."

"And you couldn't just come to our backyard?"

I shrugged. She nodded. The silence carried on between us, neither of us really knowing what to say.

"Cameron knows?"

I nodded again.

"Does Dad know he knows?"

I answered with the shake of my head.

"Does anyone else?"

I shook it again.

Mom walked over to me and rested her hands gently on either side of my shoulders. "I want you to know I'm not mad at you. I was upset last night because it was a shock and I am upset that your father kept it from me, but I can only imagine how scared you must have been." My shoulders fell; feeling the weight of everything settle in. "I wish I could have been there for you. Can I be there for you now?" I nodded and she took me into her arms. "I'm scared too, you know," she whispered into my hair. "I don't want to lose you."

Being hugged by my mom was exactly the strength that I had needed. There was something about her touch that even on my worst day could comfort me and make me feel like everything would be okay. Of course, eventually it would. Even if it didn't feel like it right now. In the distant future we'd look back at this time and laugh at our misfortunes because that's just what you do. That's all you can do. At least that's what I've been told.

When we pulled apart I asked, "Do you mind if I go?" I pointed to the forest, anxiousness beating in my legs.

She pursed her lips. "Who are you visiting with in there anyway?" her motherly tone back in place.

"Declan and Kai."

She pursed her lips. "I don't think I know them."

This seemed silly. I had been spending time alone with them for months now. And they were the ones that have been keeping me alive. If there was anyone that I should be allowed to hang out with it should be them. "Dad does."

"I guess that's good enough," she said, skeptical.

"I promise that you can trust them."

She nodded, though I could still see the concern in her eyes.

I kissed her cheek and headed to the back door. "Thanks, Mom." I knew she knew it was for more than letting me escape.

TWENTY

Entering the trees was becoming such a natural thing. I didn't have to bother to watch where I stepped or even call out to Declan. I knew where I would find him if he wasn't in Faylinn. The familiar roots wound in and out of the ground like a serpent. And there he was, sitting in the crevasse of giant roots, stringing a new bow. It was comforting to know I could find him.

Could I have both worlds?

I refocused and remembered why it was that I'd come in the first place. Though I could have been subtler, I didn't want to beat around the bush. I was so tired of beating around the bush. "You were supposed to kill me?"

Declan looked up at me, then glared into the trees and sighed, knowing Kai must have been the culprit.

"Why does everyone keep hiding things from me?" I said heatedly. "I can handle the truth. Tell me the *truth*, Declan. All of it. Please," I added.

He didn't look up at me, but he had stopped stringing his

bow. "Remember when I told you that the Royals have a special ability? One that no regular faery has?"

I nodded, recalling that day he first told me about Favner. It felt like a lifetime ago. He hadn't gotten a chance to tell me about it since Kai had so conveniently interrupted us as usual. When I realized I nodded and he hadn't been looking at me I said, "Yes."

His head stayed bowed, glaring at the forest floor. "Favner has the ability to command us without giving us a choice. It's an ability that can be controlled, but he chooses not to. It's how he's gotten us all to be divided as we are. Whatever he says we are forced to do whether we want to or not. It's called Supremacy."

"So, he controls your minds." He lifted his aquamarine eyes to me and nodded. Their vibrancy took away my breath. "But, if he commanded you to kill me how am I still alive?"

Declan exhaled. "There was a group of us. Three of us, actually. Foster, Warren and myself. The three of us were in Favner's chamber when he ordered us to find you, but he commanded Warren to do the actual deed and bring your body back to him." Declan paused, stood and began to pace slowly in front of me, peering up at me occasionally. "When we found you, you were with Finnian and he was pushing you on that tree swing in your backyard. You were about thirteen and the life inside of your eyes was so full. You were just starting a life."

His loyal gaze connected with mine and his light oceanic eyes consumed me before he turned from me as if he couldn't say this to my face. He strode over to a log and sat facing the opposite direction, the light shining through trees, cascading shadowy figures on his back.

"I couldn't let Warren finish you off, especially in front of Finnian. Back in the day I knew Finnian to be the strongest warrior, but as a human he would have been defenseless against us. I couldn't bear the thought of ending you and seeing the look on his face as it was done." I saw his shoulders rise and fall as he took a deep breath. "So, I turned on Warren. He was stronger than me, but by some miracle of the fallen fae I was able to defeat him. I remember the look in his eyes as he lay on the ground. It was as if he wanted me to kill him."

I was about to speak, to comfort him or thank him, but he continued with guilt in his voice. "Getting rid of Warren wasn't the worst part. Foster saw the whole thing and stood by. He was only about fifteen, if you compare it to human years, but he was loyal to Favner. He was about to run off and reveal what I had done, so I did what needed to be done."

Declan didn't need to explain. I went to be next to him. He stared off at nothing, only the stillness of the woodlands, so I grabbed his hand in mine. Words wouldn't suffice for what I wanted to say, so we simply sat there as I held his hand and stroked my fingers over his. He didn't react, merely sat still, the only sound between us were his quiet breaths.

"How did you get away with it? When Foster and Warren didn't return with you and you didn't have my body, how did you explain that?"

"I told him that on our way back we were attacked. Favner's biggest rivalry kingdom is the Rymidon Kingdom. Kai mentioned he told you about the other kingdoms?" I nodded. "Honestly, they are not truly our enemies, but it was my only out. Favner believes they have a grudge against us for being the largest kingdom with the most power since we are the homeland." Declan shook his head in exasperation. "I told him that we were ambushed. I obviously didn't go back unscathed after battling with Foster and Warren. I had my fair share of cuts and bruises so my lie was believable."

I swallowed. "And what did you say about my body?"

"I told him they took it. It was my life or nothing. I said they would have finished me off too if I had tried to escape with you."

"And he never once questioned you?"

"I saw the uncertainty in his eyes, but he didn't see what I could possibly gain by killing my fellow fae. I had served beside Warren for many years. He didn't think I had it in me." Declan exhaled and murmured softly, "*I* didn't think I had it in me."

I saw a tear escape from his eye, but neither of us bothered to brush it away.

"So, you've traveled from Faylinn every day and protected me for the last five years to keep me from a man who wants me dead," I clarified, feeling overwhelmed by his dedication and bravery. The risk he had taken to be here after all this time.

Declan gazed over at me with his electrifying green-blue eyes glistening. "I could never let anything happen to you." His eyes trailed over my face, from my lips to my eyes and back. Our faces inched closer and closer. There was no thought to our actions; his lips were about to graze mine, but stopping him never crossed my mind. Did I want to stop him?

"This is where the two of you have run off to?"

Startled by the female voice, I let go of his hand and we both turned to face the voice. I not only saw Kai who stood with his arms at his side, an unreadable expression on his face, but a woman. No. Another faery. She was beautiful. Her lengthy light brown hair was rolled into dreadlocks and flowed all around her. A thin cream band wrapped around her forehead, keeping the hair from her flawless face. She was fierce. Her eyes were golden. They even sparkled like gold.

How long had Kai been standing there?

"Kai, if Favner even knew… no, forget Favner. If Mom knew that you were leaving Faylinn on your free time, that this is where you have been…" She trailed off, too exasperated to continue. "They are going to kill you."

Kai's face changed back into his indifferent guise. "Who? Favner?" He swatted his hand. "I already knew that."

"Then how could you be so foolish? And Declan… I thought better of you." She looked pointedly at Declan who actually looked ashamed.

If she hadn't looked so young I would have mistaken her for their mother. But she was obviously not a mother. She was Kai's… sister?

"And who's she?" She darted her hand to me, accusingly. I cowered behind Declan. This girl was going to tear me to shreds with one look.

Weren't faeries supposed to be all colorful and sparkly? She was anything but. Her clothes were all neutral with only slight color accents here and there. Declan scolded me several times before. I was mixing them up with Pixies. *Us.* I was mixing *us* up with pixies.

Declan spoke now. "She's none of your business, Allura."

Allura looked hurt for a split second before plastering the lethal looks back on. "It is my business if she means you two are being put in danger. Is she human?"

"How did *you* manage to get away, Allura?" Kai asked impishly, dancing around her, flicking her hair. She swatted him off.

"That doesn't matter. What matters is that if you two don't come back to Faylinn and stay in Faylinn there is no hope for either of you."

"There is no hope if we do go back, Allura. You know

237

that," Declan said. "We've been gone for too long."

"Wait. When was the last time you guys went back to Faylinn?" I asked, stepping out from behind Declan.

"It doesn't matter," Kai said.

"It does too!" I replied.

Allura's amber eyes locked on me and changed instantly. It was as if Allura had truly seen me for the first time. She gasped. "You... you're..." For the first time since she opened her mouth, she was at a loss for words.

"Go ahead, Allura. Spell it out," Kai taunted. "Would you like me to spell it out for you?"

"She's..." She pointed with a hand clasped over her mouth. All of her fingers had twine laced between them and woven down around her wrist, adorning them with dangling tiny blue flower petals—faery jewelry, I could only assume.

"Yes," Declan finally put her out of her misery. "She's Finnian's daughter."

"How did she know?" I asked timidly.

"It's hard not to, Princess," Kai said, turning his wry gaze on me. "You're practically the female version of him. Just twenty years younger."

The moment he said princess, his nickname for me didn't seem so snarky anymore. I still didn't like it, but he hadn't been doing it simply because he thought I was a priss or to annoy me. Well probably to annoy me a little bit.

"How—" Allura sputtered, still unable to string a sentence together. I assume she didn't know what to ask. She wasn't anything I'd pictured the women would look like. Allura was draped in what looked like a tweed romper and a dark brown burlap vest. A strand of pale green vines was tied around her waist, accentuating her figure. Her delicate wings peaked out behind her. They weren't much different from mine: four delicate petal-like wings, but Allura's were a faint dusty blue.

"Well, you see, Allura, when two people love each other very much, they get together and—"

"Shut up, Kai!" Her heated gold eyes glared at him. I understood her frustration. Apparently I wasn't the only one he could infuriate in less than two minutes. That was truly a talent. "I know the process. What I want to know is how it's possible that *she's* a faery." She pointed at me once again.

Declan stepped in. "We think it's the Royal bloodline. Faylinn wants its true heir back."

Her eyes shifted between the two of them. "And what... You two have been here protecting her? How did you find her? Where does she even live? What are you two going to do when Favner finds out about her?"

"Favner already knows about her. He thinks she's dead," Declan explained.

Allura looked so confused, I almost felt sorry for her. She seemed so strong and fierce at first, as if nothing could break her. Her expression changed as if a light bulb had brightened in her head. Or I guess it was more like a firefly. "You can save us," she finally said. "I knew I felt a change in the winds."

"What?" I asked.

"Yes!" She leaped forward. "If we bring you back to Faylinn and everyone sees you, they will know who you are like I did. Favner will be forced to step down!"

"What do you mean you sensed a change in the winds?" Kai interrupted, stepping toward her.

"The Sowers feel it. The True Sowers. Something brewing. Something significant. No one knew what it was. Change. War. It hasn't been talked about outright, but there has been chatter."

"They know," Declan said.

"Favner?" Kai hissed.

"Maybe. No. I don't know. But the rest of the fae. They sense Calliope as the new heir. They just don't know it yet," Declan clarified.

"Wait. What?" I interjected.

"I don't think it's as simple as Calliope storming the castle and taking over, Allura," Declan said.

I was ignored once again. I was being talked about as if I wasn't there.

"Of course, it is. No one wants him to rule, but no one else is brave enough to go up against him. You are the only one that can save us!" Allura set her eyes upon me with so much certainty in her sparkling eyes. There wasn't even a hint of doubt.

I opened my mouth to speak, but struggled for the right words to say. My father and I already had this conversation. I didn't know anything about Faylinn and I loved my human life. I was still able to live among humans and be who I wanted to be, who I planned to be. What if I had a life waiting for me with Cam? Was I supposed to drop all of that and become someone's queen? No. I didn't need that sort of responsibility. I couldn't handle that kind of responsibility. I would fail them.

The three of them faced me now, a kaleidoscope of colors in their eyes so bright and earnest. They believed in me. They believed I could do this for them. How could I let them down? But how was I supposed to lead them?

"Stop looking at me like that," I demanded. Their confidence was too much.

Immediately the three of them looked away from me. Then there was a gasp. "She has the power," Allura said in awe as she looked cautiously back to me.

"What power?" I searched their faces.

The Keepers went quiet as they looked to one another once more, as if sharing their thoughts through eye contact. What were they? Telepathic?

"Your Supremacy," Declan finally explained. "You don't quite know how to control it yet."

I sucked in a breath of air. All different occasions were coming back to me, rolling in my mind like a film reel. It made sense. Every time Declan and Kai would get that pained look in their eyes like they didn't want to answer me. It was my... Supremacy.

"You were born to rule Faylinn," Declan said gently, visibly sensing my unease.

"I can't," were the measly words that slipped out of my mouth. "I'm sorry." I shook my head and escaped toward the forest's borderline.

"Calliope!" I couldn't be sure whose voice it was. My thoughts were too clouded. There was no stopping now. I couldn't bear to see their eyes looking at me with such confidence. I wasn't the one they needed. Someone else in Faylinn could do the job. But it wasn't going to be me.

One of the other fae was bound to be a better leader than me.

I bolted down the hallway to my room and shut the door behind me, locking it. Like a coward. It was exactly why I would be a terrible queen. I ran from conflict. I didn't know how to resolve problems. I ran from them.

There was a knock at my door. "Calliope?" He couldn't have had worse timing. "Sweetheart?"

"Not right now, Dad," I grumbled. "Please," I added as an afterthought.

"Is everything okay?" he asked through the door.

"I really don't want to talk about it. Please just go away," I said more adamantly.

I heard his footsteps trail away. *Thank you.*

I flew onto my bed and buried my face in the comfort of my pillow. My tears soaked the cotton as they fled from my eyes. I didn't want to have a pity party for myself, but this was overwhelming. There was too much pressure. Pressure not to let anyone down. Pressure to do the right thing for me. Pressure to make the right decision for everyone else.

Maybe for someone else this would have been an easy decision. They could go blindly into Faylinn thinking that being a faery queen was awesome and that they could do whatever they wanted. All the rules were at their fingertips. But how realistic was that, really?

Every little girl dreamed about becoming a princess, but when becoming royalty meant more than crowns and frilly dresses it was a lot to consider. When it meant leaving behind everything that mattered to you and starting over, then what? Did the fae really think it was wise to put their lives in the hands of a seventeen year old who is completely unprepared?

And, yet, even if it was my choice—everyone always has a choice—was it really my decision to make? I couldn't be so selfish as to only think of myself now. This decision would affect thousands of faeries. Shouldn't the faeries of Faylinn get to vote on if they wanted me to rule?

There was another knock at my door. "Go away, Dad," I persisted.

"Honey." It wasn't my dad. It was my mom. "Will you please let me come in?"

My heart softened. She would understand. She wouldn't

want me to go either. My mom could make the decision easy for me. She could force me to stay.

I opened the door to let her pass inside. "Thank you," she said, following as I went back to my bed. "I think Dad has brought me up to speed on everything going on." She paused. "But do you want to tell me what's got you so upset?"

My eyes focused on the window facing the trees. "They think I'm the one who can save them from Favner. They want me to be their queen."

"And I take it you aren't too keen on that?" She plopped onto the edge of my bed.

"I think it's absurd. I don't know how to run a faery kingdom. I barely know how to run my own life! I couldn't get Cameron to fall in love with me. Lia refuses to speak to me. I don't even have colleges picked out yet. And faeries want me to run their kingdom. I'm so overwhelmed! My life has crumbled to pieces!"

She spoke gently. "Do you think maybe your life is falling apart because you're choosing the wrong path?"

I gaped at her. She didn't continue. She simply stared at me waiting for an answer. Was she siding with them?

"You think I'm not meant to stay here with you and Dad?" I choked.

She exhaled. "Calliope," she said softly.

"You do! Of all people I thought you would understand. I thought you would make this decision easy for me!"

"Calliope," she said with that parental firmness, cutting me off. She grasped my hands underneath hers. "*No* one wants you to stay here more than I do. *No one*. This was my worst fear after I found out I was pregnant with you. What if they found us and took you from me?" She swallowed. "That thought ran through

243

my head over and over again for years. Though Dad was completely changed, what if you carried a gene?"

She lifted a trembling hand to the bridge of her nose and squeezed. I stayed silent holding onto every word of my untold story.

"Year after year I waited for a change, some sort of sign that you were a faery and year after year of no change I felt a little lighter. I know it's one of the reasons Dad didn't want to tell me. He knew the fear that they would come for you would eat me alive."

Mom brought her gaze up to mine. "Only another mother can understand the love a mother has for her child. I've had an unbreakable connection with you from the first time I saw your tiny heartbeat, from the first time I felt you inside of me." She clenched her teeth and swallowed back tears. "But, you don't belong here anymore," she barely whispered.

I didn't want to believe her. I didn't want a new life. But everything inside of me was confirming what she said to be true. I was a faery trying to play human in a world that I no longer belonged in. I gritted my teeth, realizing I'd been denying it for so long, refusing to believe what was right, that I suppressed what I knew would happen all along. But this new element added a whole new playing field.

"Of all people, I wish it weren't true," she continued. "You are my daughter. My only child." Her hand rested on my cheek, tenderly securing me to her touch. "Do you know how much I want to save you from anything that could hurt you and never let anything happen to you? I selfishly let your father leave the kingdom for *me*. I know how to be selfish and take what I want. But, honey… you don't belong to me anymore. Faylinn is a powerful place and it wants you badly." She lifted her hand from my face and gestured to the grove of trees. "*They* need you."

The tears speckled my face. She reached over and wiped them away with that never failing loving glint in her eyes as a tear fell down her cheek.

"You have nothing to be scared of. Faylinn would be lucky to have you as their queen. They know what they are missing. Do you?"

I sat wordlessly, taking it all in. She kissed my forehead before leaving me with my never-ending thoughts. I think the reason I'd been so scared when they presented me with the position was because I knew I eventually would accept. Why fear or deny something you know would never be possible or happen to you?

Do you?

Those words echoed in my mind all night. That night when I finally fell asleep, I dreamt about an unfamiliar place, far in the depths of the forest. It's enchanting village hidden behind a sturdy wrought iron gate. The gate glowed as if beckoning me forward, begging me to enter, pounding a beat of life.

A giant black creature appeared, guarding the entrance, preventing me from passing. Fire blew from his mouth between sharp teeth, intimidating anyone who tried to enter. When I came upon the dragon, I pulled a dagger from a sash at my waist, ready to defend myself. He looked down at me and I could almost see the humor dance across his big ferocious blood-red eyes. "You think you can defeat me? Do you?" he roared, laughing throatily. "Do you?"

As he scoffed, underestimating my nerve, I stabbed him in the gut. He bellowed and crumpled to the ground, his massive figure disappearing in front of my eyes.

Do you? I thought in my head, triumphant.

TWENTY-ONE

The next morning when I went to the clearing Declan paced back and forth, moving over fallen trunks and rocks, without missing a step. I stood silently, watching the pondering look on his face. He was concentrating extremely hard on something. I took another step forward, standing in a stream of sunlight. The rays beamed off my yellow wings that I had finally set free, reflecting a shimmer from the dew on a tree branch. One of the rays caught Declan in the eye, causing him to lose his footing and trip forward. He lifted his aqua eyes to me.

"Calliope," he breathed, surprised. He hadn't heard me coming, which was saying something. I was becoming more stealth-like. I was officially all-faery.

His eyes grew wide as they took in my wings, but couldn't say another word. He gravitated toward me.

My wings fluttered effortlessly behind me, reveling in their true environment. "If I come to Faylinn, how will I know what to do?"

"It will come to you," he said. My father's words echoed in my mind. "If nothing else, I think you have a pretty wise man you can turn to."

I smiled humbly. "Faylinn loved my father, right?"

He nodded, assertive. "Faylinn was at its liveliest during his family's reign."

"What if they don't accept me like you think they will?"

"There is no way they could deny you," Kai's voice descended from his favorite branch. I looked up to him and he smiled. A genuine smile. Butterflies twirled in my stomach. I tore my eyes away.

"Then I want to go. I want you to take me to Faylinn," I said with finality.

Declan pulled me into his arms before I could react and spun me around. His grip made it difficult to breathe, but he was laughing. I couldn't interrupt his delight. I invited his delight with open arms. The moment I made the decision to go, I had that intuitive feeling in the pit of my stomach that it was the right choice.

"This isn't going to be as easy as Allura was making it seem, you know." Kai was down on the ground with us now.

Declan stopped and set me down, the smile vanishing from his face. "No, it's not," he agreed. "We must get in undetected first."

"That's nearly impossible. There are five to six Keepers at every post."

"Well, how did Allura escape undetected?" Declan questioned.

"She never told me," Kai said. "I assume since you've been gone she's gotten friendly with another Keeper."

Declan shifted uncomfortably. Since Declan had been

gone? "So, you and Allura were…" I let the sentence allude to whatever it was they were.

"No," Declan denied immediately. "I mean… we were never anything official. We are friends. Have been since we were kids."

"Oh." There was a twinge that settled in the base of my heart. Was I jealous? It wasn't as if either of them hadn't had a life before me. I didn't have the right to be jealous. I loved Cam.

Kai stepped in between Declan and me, moving the direction of the topic back to the issue at hand. "So, you understand what this means? Accepting to come with us?" he asked me.

"I suppose I have to do whatever it takes. Whatever gets thrown my way, I'll have to roll with the punches."

Kai laughed. "Roll with the punches. A line you want to hear from your future queen."

"Kai," Declan warned.

"It's fine," I amended. "I realize I'm not exactly queen material. I get that I'm not what you had in mind, but you'll have to take me or leave me. You all seem to believe I'm your only hope."

"Don't get me wrong, Your Highness." I rolled my eyes and bit my tongue as a crooked smile tugged at Kai's mouth. "You'll be able to take over the kingdom and rule the way it should be run. I have faith in that. I simply worry for your well-being." The way he said that he worried about my well-being was sincere, as if I actually mattered to him. But what did I care of how Kai felt about my well-being? "I like your wings, by the way."

I felt my cheeks flush and looked away.

"Kai and I will have to set up a strategy, some sort of plan to get by the boundary undetected, so it may be a few days before we leave," Declan said.

"A few days," I repeated to clarify. Surely, I hadn't heard that correctly. "I still have like six months until my graduation. You want me to leave before my senior year is even over?"

They both looked at me as if I was slow.

"Did becoming Faylinn's queen mean something different to you than it did to me because…" Kai peered at me in puzzlement.

Declan spoke, "Calliope, what Kai is trying to say is that if you have chosen Faylinn, why would finishing out the year be necessary?"

I shrugged tensely. "I don't know. I just didn't imagine leaving so soon." I began to pace uncontrollably. "I still haven't even told Lia what I am. How am I supposed to leave now? What is everyone going to say about me? Will they all think I disappeared? Oh, the rumors…" My head began to spin. It felt like I might faint if I didn't sit down.

I noticed there was silence and it carried on after I stopped babbling. They hadn't answered me yet and I knew that was a bad sign. When I peered up, they were looking to one another, as if trying to decide who was going to be the bearer of bad news. I really didn't like their silent connection. I didn't even ask. I simply glared, letting the fury burn through my eyes and they knew it was time to speak up.

"Fae magic works in ways that causes humans to eventually lose their memories of faeries," Declan said. "It's for our protection."

"I would be erased from their memories?" I asked, incredulously.

"It's a chance," Kai said. "Out of sight, out of mind sort of thing."

"You still have human blood running through you, so it might not have any affect. They haven't had any issues with remembering you thus far," Declan said.

"But it's still possible," I pressed.

They both nodded solemnly. At least they had the decency to appear apologetic.

"It's possible," Declan said quietly, measuring my reaction to see if this would be my breaking point. I thought that I'd already reached it, but they kept throwing curve balls.

I didn't have much of a choice anymore. I was kidding myself into thinking I could have a normal life as a faery in this world. The physical changes were becoming too unnatural, and it was exhausting trying to constantly hide them.

"When do we leave?" I questioned, without inflection. I might as well get straight to the point. It was the only thing left I needed to know.

"I suppose we can leave when you feel comfortable, but I would urge you to make the decision soon. I'm not sure how much longer we will be safe here," Declan cautioned.

I stopped and looked at him. "I thought you said Favner didn't know I was still alive."

Declan rested his hand on my shoulder, wanting to comfort me. His rough fingers brushed my bare shoulders. "I would like to believe that, yes, but I would still like to be sure, and the longer this drags out the more suspicious he could get. Allura isn't the only one who can sense a change."

"It's Thanksgiving. I would at least like to have a few days with my family for the holiday before we go." I said assertively.

"Is three days enough?" Declan asked.

I swallowed. "Three days?"

"The magic number," Kai said wryly, trying to lighten the

mood and failing miserably.

I sighed, surrendering. "Okay. I'll be ready in three days."

Without having much time, I had to make things right in my human life. It almost felt like a funeral, like I was dying and needed to get all of my affairs in order. I sort of was though, wasn't I? Calliope Willow Holbrook wouldn't exist in Walhalla. In three days it was very possible that I would cease to exist at all.

Being the Thanksgiving holiday, we had the rest of the week off from school. I thought about calling Lia before dropping by, but I didn't want to give her the option to turn me away. Lia deserved more from me. My dad was just going to have to deal with me revealing this to my closest friends. They were the only ones who had always been honest with me. They deserved the same in return from me. No matter the consequences.

I heaved a sigh, building up the nerve to proceed, before knocking on the front door of her house. It was about a minute before I heard the turning of the lock and Lia peeked her head around the door.

"Oh, are we friends now?" was her greeting.

"We've always been friends and you know it," I replied even though I knew she had every reason to be angry with me.

"You haven't really acted like it." She stood straight with her hand on her hip.

"I know, but I promise I have a good reason." I swallowed back my fears. This was Lia. She deserved the truth. She didn't deserve to be kept in the dark. It was as if I needed to keep reminding myself.

"Are you going to tell me that good reason? Or are we just going to stand here and have a staring contest?"

"Can we go somewhere private?" I asked.

"Come in." She sighed agitatedly and stepped aside, letting me pass into her entryway. "My parents aren't home, but we can still go up to my room if you really need the privacy."

I followed her up the stairs and prepped myself for what I would say. She closed the doors behind us and sat on her bed, waiting for me to explain. It wasn't as if I hadn't already told someone about this, so I didn't know why it was so difficult to gain the courage to tell Lia now. Maybe it was because I knew how her brain worked. She was a scientist. She'd want to know how it was possible. She'd want to run tests and log data. And what I am wouldn't be able to be explained logically. But this was Lia I was talking about. I could trust her. She wasn't going to turn me into her next science experiment… or someone else's, for that matter.

I hoped.

"Well…" she said impatiently.

I took a deep breath. "Lia, we've been friends for almost four years now. You know me. You know I'd never lie to you, right?" She nodded. "You know I'm not crazy. You know I would never do anything to purposefully hurt you or frighten you."

"Callie, just spit it out already."

"I'm not all human." The words spewed out of my mouth. I pulled my hair out of the two braids on either side of my head. "A couple of months ago I learned something about myself." I lifted my hair back into a ponytail, wrapping the rubber band around my golden curls to keep them back. My ears were completely visible now.

Lia didn't shy away from me, didn't scream. She simply stared, catatonic. What if I sent her into some psychotic break? I cautiously loosened the bustier and my buttery wings leisurely uncurled behind me from underneath my shirt.

"I'm a faery."

Lia swallowed and shifted cautiously back on her bed, away from me. Her mouth fell open as her gaze took me in. I knew it wasn't every day that your best friend revealed they were a faery, but I expected more of a reaction.

"Lia," I prompted.

She blinked. "You're. Not. Human," she said slowly.

I shook my head. A few expressions flashed across her eyes, but she blinked them away before I could pinpoint her thoughts. She stared at me now with a trace of fear and I hated myself for it.

"Lia," I hesitantly asked.

"Just give me a minute, okay?" Her chest rose rapidly while her eyes stayed glued on me, taking in my new appearance.

"Okay." I stood still, letting her observe me. It felt strange letting someone stare at me, even if it was my best friend, knowing I was being judged. I did in fact feel like I was being looked at as a science experiment. What if she wanted to take a sample of my wings or take a blood sample? No. She wouldn't do that. This was still Lia I was talking about. I waited patiently for about five minutes and then decided it was time to intervene.

"Lia, will you please say something?"

She rubbed her eyes, blinked, and cautiously took me in again. "You have wings," she whispered as if saying it any louder would give me fangs or devil horns. "And pointed ears," she observed a little louder. "Scientifically none of this makes sense, but there you are and here I am looking at you and... you're real.

You are a… faery?"

I nodded.

She folded her arms securely over her chest. "How?"

I pulled down my shirt the best I could without squishing my wings. I sat down next to her as carefully as I could, gauging her response and how uncomfortable with my proximity she was. When she didn't shy away I explained everything from the beginning, starting with my super human hearing and the pull to the forest. Her mouth dropped at all the places mine did when I learned them. She didn't try to interrupt once. Her silence was all I needed to know she was completely enthralled with the explanation of my behavior, like I was retelling a bedtime story. When I was finished she looked at me skeptically.

"You hid all of that from me?" Her forehead ruffled. "Why?"

"Because I was scared. I'm scared Lia. Wouldn't you be? It's all a little crazy."

"But I'm your best friend," she said adamantly. "You should be able to tell me anything. You should have told me from the beginning. I would have been there for you. I want you to feel like you can tell me anything. Every deep dark secret."

I shifted, uncomfortable with her tone. I understood that she was really upset with me, but it didn't make sense for her to be so frustrated.

"I'm sorry?" I tried.

"I forgive you," she sighed, looking me up and down, still examining me. Her eyes softened when she peered at my wings. "Can I touch them?"

I chuckled. "I guess."

Her hand reached behind me and gently stroked my wing like you would rub a flower petal between a couple fingers. A small warm smile appeared on her lips. "They're so smooth… like a rose petal."

"Yeah," I laughed lightly.

She sat back and sighed again. "Will you give me a minute?"

My brow crossed and I nodded. She got up from her bed and left her room, opening and closing the door behind her. She stayed away for about a minute before coming back in. I watched her linger in the doorway as I remained in the same spot on her bed.

"Lia?" I asked calmly.

"Just making sure you're still there and not a figment of my imagination or a dream." She closed the door behind her and sat back down on the bed. Her eyes lit up now. "So, tell me more about Kai and Declan. Are they hot?"

I rolled my eyes because, of course, that would be the next topic for discussion, but I said, "Unbelievably so."

"You like one of them, don't you?" she pried.

"Like them. As in like, like? No, no," I denied. Since the night that I overheard them, I tried to banish their words of affection for me because it wasn't possible anyway. There had been more important things to worry about. From day one they had been my mentors. My mind focused on them as separate individuals, my friends. Declan was kind and thoughtful, always willing to guide me. Kai, though maddening, was confident and witty, a silent pillar of strength that I could rely on. They had definitely sparked something inside of me, but it was pointless. We could never be anything anyway. "No, they are just my friends."

"Liar."

"I mean, sure they're good guys. They're brave and, yes, attractive and they watch out for me, but…" Did I care for

255

them? Yeah, sure. I cared about what happened to them. Did I think about them in a deeper sense? I didn't know. My feelings for them were so foreign. I'd only loved one person in my entire life and that was Cameron.

"They have protected you for years. That's commitment," she said.

"Well, Declan has. He has out of guilt. He was supposed to kill me," I reminded her. "Kai didn't come until just recently."

Lia didn't speak; she was lost again, taking in my appearance. "Now that I see it all together, your ears, your wings, your eyes… you're incredible."

I bowed my head, embarrassed by her scrutiny. I swallowed.

"This is going to take me a while to get used to."

I sighed in glorious relief. "I understand completely."

The only bit I hadn't tacked on yet was that I was going to Faylinn to stay. "Lia," I prompted for her to look me in the eyes, so I could get her full attention again.

When her eyes met mine and I didn't speak, she filled the silence. "What?"

I took a deep breath. "You remember the part where I mentioned that I'm sort of the next in line to rule Faylinn?"

I didn't need to explain. It clicked before I could even say it. "You're going to leave, aren't you?"

"Faylinn is where I belong now."

Her gaze softened, her eyes tilted down, forlorn. "When do you leave?"

"Friday."

"What?" Her cheeks flushed red. "That soon? What about the rest of the school year? And graduation? And your family? Can't you wait a little longer?"

I shook my head. "I can't. It's important that I leave soon."

256

"Matt will be home for New Year's," she said hastily. "He'll want to see you. You have to at least say goodbye to him. Wait until January to go."

"Lia, I can't. I have to go now. There's a… situation in Faylinn with the king there now. I have to go and help fix it."

"What kind of situation? It can't possibly be something that can't wait if you've already waited this long."

"It's not that simple, Lia."

"So simplify it," she pressed, troubled.

"Lia…"

She took a deep breath, calming herself down. "I'm sorry. I just can't stand the thought of you missing everything."

I clenched my jaw, fighting back the tears. "I know."

She was silent for a moment and her lip quivered. "Will I ever see you again?"

Declan and Kai's most recent revelation echoed through my thoughts. *Humans tend to eventually forget us for our protection.* "I hope so," I said, fighting the urge to cry.

Water built up inside her eyes. "Have you told Cameron yet?"

I could only shake my head. I couldn't think about saying goodbye to him yet. Two days. I still had two days to think about how to tell him. Plus it *was* Thanksgiving. I couldn't possibly bother him and his dad during the holiday. I imagine they'd probably end up at his grandparents anyway. His dad could barely make macaroni and cheese.

"What are you going to do about Cameron?" Lia looked at me sympathetically and began to shake her head. "He's going to have a hard time with this, Callie." Her words told me what I already knew.

"He'll be fine," I amended. He had Isla now. I wasn't

someone he relied on anymore. If anything, I relied on him. This would be harder for me than him.

She shook her head resolutely. "Calliope, you've been denying he would come around for so long that you've grown blind. This will tear him apart. Is he not a factor in your decision at all?"

"Of course he is," I insisted. "I'm not taking this decision lightly, Lia. I've been debating this for weeks. Aside from my family he's the one thing holding me back, but I can't let him dictate my life anymore. I have more important things at stake now than my love life."

"Losing you will kill him," she said softly, as if she was trying to hurt me.

I squeezed my eyes shut, tears streamed down my cheeks. "Thanks for that."

"He's already lost him mom. You're the closest thing he has to family aside from his workaholic dad. Did you ever think of that?"

I shook my head stubbornly and covered my ears. "Why are you being so cruel, Lia? Please stop."

Lia reached over and took my hands. "I'm just preparing you, Callie," she said. "I want you think thoroughly about every possible aspect. You think you don't matter to us. I see in your eyes the duty you already feel for this Faylinn place, but we, humans, will feel a part of us missing for the rest of our lives."

If you even remember me when I'm gone.

TWENTY-TWO

I hadn't gone back to the clearing since I told Kai and Declan I would go to Faylinn with them. Since it had been a couple of days, the pulsing crawled back into my body as a reminder of the forest. *As if I could forget.* It felt weird not seeing them, but I would be with them regularly soon enough. I needed the human time. It wasn't enough time, but I had to accept what I could get.

My stomach stirred as I looked down at my overflowing plate of Thanksgiving dinner. My mom's family crowded around the table—laughing and enjoying being around our extended family. Though every family member I'd ever known surrounded me, I felt more alone than ever.

"Calliope, you're not eating," Mom murmured across the table.

"Huh?" I looked up to my mom, her words just registering. "Oh." I took a big bite of mashed potatoes and smiled half-heartedly.

"How's that case of yours, Melody?" Grandma asked.

"Rodgers will get what's coming to him. I'm going to make sure of that."

"How much longer do you have to be in that courtroom with him?" Aunt Audrey asked, wiping food from my younger cousin, Lucy's, messy mouth.

"A couple more weeks."

Maybe three days was too long. I needed the trees and the open air. The noise level suffocated me. Aunt Audrey's kids screamed and giggled as they poked one another and spoke gibberish. My grandpa guffawed while listening to Uncle Griggs tell a story about a rooster and a tennis racket. At least that's what I think it was about. My cousin Kelli curled up in her chair with a cell phone, a smirk playing on her lips, unaware of the ruckus around her. Was she even old enough to have a cell phone? I wanted to be her—off in my own little world, happy and oblivious to the real world.

All of their voices were garbling together. I couldn't make out one voice from another. My throat was closing in. The pulse of my heart was sprinting. Finally it registered that my body was being pulled. It had never felt this strong before, like an anchor had thrown me overboard and tugged me to the bottom of the ocean.

"Calliope," Dad mumbled at my left. "Calliope," he repeated. I finally met his eyes, unsure how long he had been calling my name. "Honey, go get some air," he whispered, trying not to draw attention.

I was grateful for the release and excused myself. Mom watched me with a worried stare. I tried reassuring her with my eyes that I was okay, but I wasn't.

The relief didn't start until I passed the line of trees and even then it only brought it to a dull ache. It didn't release me completely. Maybe it was that I'd waited so long to come back or that the pull was getting stronger. Maybe it was that Faylinn knew my decision had been made and was ready for me. I wasn't sure. Though I would miss this life, I was suddenly grateful I only had one day left. I couldn't handle this feeling any longer.

"You don't have to go," Dad's voice drifted over my shoulder. He obviously misunderstood my breakdown.

I took a few breaths before answering. If I could just catch my breath, I could think straight again. "It's not that."

"You've been so quiet since yesterday morning. I thought maybe you changed your mind," he said.

I shook my head. "It's weird." I swallowed. "I feel so many mixed emotions that it's almost as if I wish they had already taken me. I feel like I'm dragging out the inevitable and Faylinn is upset with me. But then the other half of me wants to stake claim on my human life, a life that doesn't really exist anymore." It was so confusing.

He came up beside me, wrapping his arm around my waist and took a breath. "I lied before."

"About what?" I peered up at him. He watched the woodlands longingly. I wondered if he ever came into these trees just to remember what it was like, but I doubted he'd torture himself like that. Seeing the look in his eyes now, I knew simply being here now was tearing him in a million directions.

"When I said that I was no longer tied to Faylinn," he said. "I did feel more for your mother than Faylinn, but it wasn't an easy decision. I nearly stayed."

"But you didn't."

He looked down at me, a mist of moisture coating his eyes. "There's a separate love and pride that comes with running more than just a family. I didn't just leave behind my home, my parents

261

or my brother. I left behind thousands of family members and faeries who I'd grown to know and love over centuries of time."

His mouth twitched as he fought his emotions. "I loved Faylinn. I still do. And although this is a lot for you to take on, I know you are going to grow a love for Faylinn you didn't know could exist inside of you. My soul is still linked to it. It's the most magical place you could ever imagine." The watery haze glazing over his eyes escaped down his cheeks.

My heart was full, eager. I wanted to understand what he felt when he talked so fondly of Faylinn. I wanted to make a difference for those faeries he left behind. I wanted to know the love he felt for them. It was my responsibility to pick up the pieces now.

"You make me so proud, Calliope. No matter what happens. I will always be so proud of you."

I smiled meekly. "I'm going to need you every step of the way and you won't be there."

"I won't be far," he assured, pulling me tighter in his arms. "I won't be far," he murmured again.

After the farewells to my mom's family, my parents and I stayed up late talking, taking in every last waking moment we had. We didn't talk about faeries or Faylinn. We didn't even mention me leaving. We didn't want to taint the only time we had left. It was simply time for us to be us as it always was before everything changed.

I rolled over in bed that night, unable to sleep. Cameron's face lingered behind my eyes. We were leaving the next evening and I still hadn't told him. I doubted he was going to be happy with me, but I couldn't handle doing this any other way. I gave him up to Isla, but he was still my best friend. How was I supposed to live without him? I couldn't even touch the thought lurking in the back of my mind. What if after I was gone he forgot about me? Could I say I wouldn't regret going to Faylinn if it cost me the people I cared most about?

I knew that was why I really kept this from him until the last minute, for selfish reasons. He was the only one who had the power to change my mind. He was the only one who could convince me to stay. I had to wait until it was too late to change my mind.

I was supposed to meet the Keepers at sundown. The sun had just started to set. Orange streaked the horizon and I was still putting my things together. I called Cameron and asked him to come over about fifteen minutes before so I was expecting him any minute. I wanted to keep it short and sweet. It was easier this way. The goodbye didn't need to be dragged out. I told myself he would appreciate me for cutting the ties at the last minute rather than carrying out the inevitable goodbye for days, but deep down I knew that was a lie I told to make myself feel better for omitting the truth.

There was a knock on my bedroom door as I hovered over my empty duffle bag. Could I really not think of one thing to pack?

"Come in."

Cam peeked around the door. "Your mom let me in. She told me to come straight—" His voice stopped. "What... What are you packing for?"

"I'm going away."

"Going away? Like on vacation or…?" He saw the nervous look in my eyes when I turned around. "You're going to Faylinn," he clarified. I nodded. "Why? I thought you decided you could do this here? I thought it was decided you were going to stay here?" His voice grew louder, anxious.

"Things change. This makes more sense," I said and spun back to my duffle. I didn't know what I was going to pack in it. What would I possibly need? My cell phone wouldn't work and neither would my iPod. "And I don't know why you care so much anyway. You really don't need me anymore."

I decided to stuff it with my favorite clothes. I knew I would probably never wear them in Faylinn. They had their own clothes, clothes better suited for the woods, but I needed them. I just did.

"Do you even realize what you're doing?" Cameron took hold of my shoulders, stopping me from packing, forcing me to look him in the eyes.

"Yeah, I do. Don't act like you know better than I do. I'm not naïve."

"That's not what I meant." He sighed, aggravated with me. "I'm just worried about you. This is a big decision."

"Please, Cam, in case you haven't noticed I'm all grown up now. I can dress and feed myself and everything now."

"Don't do that," he said, dropping his hands and turning away in frustration.

"What. Don't do what? Make decisions for myself? Grow up? Get over you?"

There it was. I said it. *Why did I say it?* I hadn't meant to confess, but it was too late to take it back now. Cameron's face instantly twisted back to me and looked as if I slapped him.

Maybe it was that he couldn't believe I actually said it out loud or that he couldn't believe I could get over him. He was hurt nonetheless, but I didn't take it back.

We stood in silence for what felt like an eternity until he broke it. "Get… over me? When… When did you ever… I hadn't realized you ever…" He couldn't get out a complete sentence, which only seemed to enrage me more. Add the fact that he was such a guy that he hadn't even suspected my feelings sent me over the edge. I bit down on my tongue and turned away.

Humiliated was the tip of the iceberg. It didn't touch the feeling consuming me. Cameron moved closer to me, but I stepped away, red dusting my cheeks. He stepped toward me, cornering me against the edge of my bed, so I couldn't get away. I felt his soft palm on my cheek as he lifted my chin to face him, his face only inches from mine. *Please don't make me look at your face.*

"Why didn't you tell me?"

I clenched my teeth, desperately not wanting to have this conversation, and yet determined to stand my ground. I brought this on myself. "When was I supposed to tell you? In between make out sessions with Isla? Or maybe I should have done it before Jillian and Blair or maybe after Lia. There was that week right after Dana, before Myra." *Why couldn't I shut up?*

His eyes fell and he shook his head. "Don't do this, Calliope."

I wrenched my face from his fingers. "Take your pick. Tell me when you think would have been a good time." I bit my lips. I didn't know what had come over me, but the faucet wouldn't shut off. *Where was the water source?*

He exhaled heavily, exasperated. "Oh, I don't know, Cal.

We've been friends for years and there wasn't one time that you could have slipped in, 'Hey, Cam, I think I kind of like you'? All of the times we hung out. All of the times we spent in your room talking about life. All of the times we went out to dinner or to the movies. All of the times we spent driving on road trips. None of those times seemed decent enough?" His voice rose with every question.

"I was scared!"

"Did you never think maybe I was too?" he shot back. His gaze softened when he saw the tears filling my eyes. I couldn't look at him anymore. Not with that look of pity plastered across the face I knew all too well.

"Don't look at me like that, Cameron. I'm not this fragile thing. I figured out a while ago you'd never be mine. I've accepted that and now I'm moving on."

"You've accepted a life without me?"

"There *is* no life with you! Don't you see that?" His face fell, defeated. My eyes turned down, avoiding eye contact.

"Do you even know why my relationships ended in the past?"

That question caught me off guard. *But of course I knew.* He got bored with one and then went onto the next. But had he ever told me why any of them ended? He hadn't. Had I ever asked? Or did I just accept it when he moved on to the next?

I didn't answer.

He laughed bleakly as if I was missing something huge, right in front of my face. "Because of *you*. None of them could accept you as a part of my life." His voice trembled. "When they would all eventually ask me to choose—because believe me, Calliope, they all did—'*It's either her or me*'. And I would say '*her*'. *You.* It was always you."

266

He chose this time to tell me. *Now? Really?*

I moved back to face my bed. "And Isla?" I questioned quietly, staring down at the half empty duffle.

"She accepted you. She never questioned our relationship. Never asked me to choose."

And there was my answer. He didn't want me, merely a girl who would accept me as a part of him.

"I really care about these faeries," I softened my tone, deflecting his words. "They need me. *Me*. As much as I don't want to believe it and as much of a weight that it puts on my shoulders, I can't possibly deny them. So if that means I move to Faylinn and become a faery queen, I'll accept that too."

"So, you'll just abandon me? Leave your home. For them. They are *faeries*, Callie."

He had to throw exhilarant on the fire. "Don't insult them. Don't make them out to be some imaginary creatures. In case you haven't noticed, *I'm* one of them. I need to be where they are."

"Even if that means losing me?" he countered. "Losing everything we have?"

My stomach sank and I lowered my voice. "I already lost you, Cam. Isla is different. I can see that. You love her like you've never loved anyone before. And I've thought hard about this. Honestly, who is going to marry me, huh?" I paused, clenching that thought. "What will my children become? A quarter faery? Just another heir for Faylinn to go after? Could I really do that to them? Am I really willing to live a lie for the rest of my life?"

"I'll marry you," he said abruptly.

"What?" I snorted, disbelieving. "You're crazy."

"What if I love you?" he continued.

I shook my head. "No," I denied. "You don't love me. Not like that."

"How do you know? Just because I never confessed it doesn't mean I haven't felt it," he said, infuriated.

"If you loved me like that you would have seen it in my eyes. I'm an open book, Cam. You've said it yourself. You would have acted on it."

"What if I didn't act on it because I didn't want to risk this?" Cameron motioned between our bodies. "What if it didn't work out between us? What if a relationship ruined this?" He exhaled and swallowed. "I can't lose you. You're too important to me."

"I feel like I'm worth the risk," I said quietly. "If you wanted this, you would have taken it." Turning my back to him, I stuffed more useless junk in my bag. I needed to get out of here. *Now.*

This wasn't happening, not on the day of my departure. I dug my grave, now I had to lie in it. I had already accepted my fate. I knew where I was meant to be.

Cameron came up beside me, his fingers trailing down my cheek, urging me to look at him. For years I had wanted his touch. This touch. The meaningful kind. The kind that moved my stomach to my heart and claimed my breath. "I can't lose you now, Callie."

I swallowed, fighting back the water building behind my eyes. "You won't lose me. Not the important part. You won't lose our friendship."

"What if I want more than friendship?" His sapphire eyes were earnest, piercing my heart. The heart that had always belonged to him.

"You don't," I disagreed, gritting my teeth and closing my

eyes to keep from looking at him.

"What if I do?" he persisted. "Now. What if I want this now?"

I swallowed the tears blocking my airway. The decision was already made. "Then I would have to tell you you're too late," I said softly, meeting his eyes. I had to show him I meant it.

"You're wrong."

There was determination in his eyes. Cameron snatched me into his arms before I knew what was happening and kissed me. It wasn't urgent or forced, but it was firm, demanding a kiss back. I didn't respond at first, but he kept his mouth on mine, working to ignite a spark. He knew I had it in me somewhere. Before I could tell myself to fight it, my walls were crumbling down and I was kissing him back.

It was pointless to fight it. Hadn't I wanted this all along? His lips were soft as they brushed against mine. My mind slowly became foggy and nothing else seemed to matter in that moment. Everything around us faded into a fog and I felt nothing—breathed nothing—but him.

His hands cupped the sides of my face and he quietly groaned into my mouth, deepening our kiss, drawing me closer toward him. I sighed in liberation, tightening my arms around his neck, breathing in everything that I knew to be Cameron. He whispered my name on my lips, opening my mouth with his. His tongue tangled with mine.

"Calliope?"

His voice pulled me back to reality. I stopped kissing Cam, pausing to compose myself before I spun my head to see Declan.

TWENTY-THREE

"Princess?"

I hadn't spoken yet. My voice was gone, my throat suddenly dry. What was he doing in my house? He stood fully clothed, bow across his chest and dagger at his side. He looked so out of place in my house. I shook off the moment. Something had to be said. I couldn't just stand there like an idiot.

"You know I don't like to be called that, Declan," I said dumbly.

I wasn't sure why I felt guilty. I hadn't done anything wrong. Declan wasn't my boyfriend. I hadn't committed myself to him or Kai. But looking into Declan's eyes of disappointment I suddenly felt like the scum of the earth. He thought better of me, highly of me even. I'd done something very wrong in his eyes.

"I apologize," he muttered. "I was coming to check on you. I signaled to you and got no response. It's long past sundown. I was worried, but I obviously had no reason to be." He was stumbling back, strangely ungraceful.

"Declan," I pressed. But he was gone, retreating away as swiftly as he could. There was a thud and crash as I heard him escaping.

The logic clicked. It was because he was away from the forest, in a structure filled with metal. He risked his life by coming into my home to protect me. And I was making out with Cameron.

Cameron said my name.

What had I done?

"Cal," Cam prompted once more.

I shook my head. "I can't." I kept my back to him and headed for the open doorway. I needed to talk to Declan, to explain or apologize or to say something—anything.

"Calliope," Cameron pleaded.

"No, Cam." I turned back to him. "You should be ashamed too. What about Isla? What are you going to say to her?"

His eyes focused on me with no hint of shame or regret. "That I'm sorry, but my heart belongs to you. It always has. I just never gave myself a chance to realize it."

"No." I shook my head, denying myself this moment—a moment that was supposed to be perfect and blissful. Cameron kissed me and confessed his love for me. I was supposed to be jumping into his arms and declaring my love back, but I couldn't. "No," I said more adamantly. "That should never have happened. That never happened."

"Calliope, please." The look of pain on Cameron's face twisted my stomach. I'd never done anything to hurt him before. We'd gotten in fights before, sure. But never had he left me feeling this absolute shame. He looked at me as if I'd betrayed

271

him. I had never betrayed him in my life. I had never even considered doing anything that might slightly harm him.

"I'm sorry. I can't. I just can't be with you," I said, choking on the approaching tears. I couldn't keep them at bay anymore. They came rushing like a tidal wave. "Maybe if we could turn back the clock to three months ago, I could see myself with you and we could have been happy. But things have changed, Cam. I've changed." I swallowed. The realization set confidently in. "I'm sorry. This isn't what I want anymore." There was no future with Cameron anymore. There never could be.

The look of helplessness twisting his face was more than I could bear. I turned and bolted. I had somewhere I needed to be.

"Declan!" I ran into the darkened trees, swatting away the drooping vines and random branches. He couldn't have gone far. "Declan?" I stumbled over the rocks and stumps cloaked in wet green, recklessly in need of reaching him. "Declan, please!"

What had I done? What must he think of me now? I wasn't blind. I denied it in my mind, but I wasn't an idiot. Declan cared for me and this was how I repaid him.

A figure stepped out from behind a trunk, I nearly fell trying to stop myself from slamming into him. But it wasn't the face I was expecting, the face I hoped it would be. I was now face to face with those deep, vibrant violet-blue eyes, glowing in the dim night sky.

"Kai," I choked.

"My Queen," he greeted. "Looking for your Keeper?"

Though it was a new way of addressing me, I didn't even bother scolding him. "I need to talk to Declan."

"Well it turns out you did something pretty awful. He doesn't want to see you."

I took a breath. "You're lying."

"I'm not sure I want to talk to you either, but *someone* has to keep you from running into a trap." He folded his arms and leaned his shoulder coolly against the nearest trunk as he eyed me.

I combed my fingers through my hair. "It just happened. One second we were talking and the next it just happened. I didn't mean for it to happen like that. It just did," I blundered.

"Wait, what? You and Declan?" Kai's arms fell to his side as he straightened up, alert.

"What? No." *He didn't know.*

"What happened Calliope?" His tone was probing, yet hesitant as if he didn't really want to know. He feared my answer.

I opened my mouth, but bit back the words. Did I have to apologize? I shouldn't have to explain myself to him. I didn't owe Kai anything. I needed to apologize to Declan. He'd always been so loyal and kind and he'd just walked into the wrong place at the wrong time.

"It's none of your business."

"I'm afraid your business is my business, Princess," he said, irritatingly.

"Stop calling me that!" I spat.

"My apologies, it is Your Majesty now." He bowed deeply, not in respect, but mocking me.

"Stop!" I screeched even higher.

"My, my, what a temper she has. She's a feisty little one. I *like* it."

I spun around and saw a dark silhouette several feet away, leaning against a large oak, his arms crossed over his chest. My

273

eyes adjusted to the darkness to take in his appearance. His ears pointed out from the disarray of hair that stood on end; so blonde it was nearly white. A dark brown cape tied around his shoulders. He brushed it back and stepped forward. He was undeniably handsome.

Kai moved in front of me, blocking my view. "Favner," he said.

That was *Favner*? But he was so... so... normal. I mean, aside from his dreadfully good looks and the fact that he was a faery; he wasn't huge by any stretch or vicious looking. From the way he was described I half expected him to be breathing fire. But this man was lean, a couple of inches shorter than Kai, and didn't look like he could harm a dragonfly.

I tried peering around Kai, but he shifted in front of me as if sensing my curiosity.

"Don't underestimate him," Kai whispered, low enough for only me to hear.

I stayed hidden, but lifted my eyes around Kai to see Favner. Kai couldn't honestly expect me to just sit back now. Favner stepped away from the shadow of the tree followed by two large shapes. The sound of something being dragged through the leaves trailed behind him. Liam and Owen came into view, devilish sneers formed on their malicious faces as they hung back, flanking Favner's sides.

"Liam. Owen," Favner said shortly. That was all the instruction they needed. They came around one side of him and threw a body to the ground in between Favner and Kai. She grunted as she hit the dead leaves.

I felt guilty for heaving a sigh of relief that it wasn't Declan.

"Thank you," Allura snapped, but with half the bite I knew she could have dished, "for your never failing kindness." She spit

274

on their feet, which rewarded her with a harsh smack from Liam. She choked, spitting blood, and warily sat up, tucking her legs underneath her and glaring at him.

"Allura," Kai said, breathless.

Allura's beautiful face was broken and bruised. Her thin headband, once naturally circling her head like a halo was broken, spilling her dreads over her tormented amber eyes. Filthy and torn, her clothes were barely draped around her body to cover her up.

"Look what I found wandering in my woods." Favner spoke as if he was talking about the weather and smiled as if he won a prize.

"Kai," she wept. "I'm so sorry. He was going to hurt Violet." The words fell rapidly from her split lips. "I couldn't let him touch our little—"

Favner's palm met Allura's cheek with a *crack* and she fell to the ground, but this time she didn't make an attempt to get back up. I'm not sure she could if she tried.

"Don't *touch* her," Kai fumed, stepping forward. I could practically hear the grinding of his teeth. He took another step but stopped, seeming torn. *Go to his sister or protect the future of Faylinn?* From behind him I could only hear his shallow breaths and feel the heat radiating from his back, his fists clenched tightly at his sides.

Favner disregarded Kai's words. "Kai, aren't you going to properly introduce me to your young lady friend? I do believe it is the only respectful thing to do for your king. You simply can't hide my subjects from me."

I could feel Kai tense. He hesitated for a few moments, but thought better than to keep me hidden and begrudgingly moved to the side of me.

Favner grinned, vile. "You are beautiful aren't you? No wonder you've been able to take my best guards away from me. Who wouldn't want to protect someone as precious as you?"

My voice failed me.

"Kai," Favner prompted once more. I wasn't sure what more he could want from him. He'd already taken his sister, displayed her beaten body at his feet.

Kai roughly cleared his throat. "Favner, this is Calliope. Daughter of Finnian," he introduced me with venom in his tone. It wasn't hard to detect it, but Favner was oblivious to his disgust. Or he was unconcerned with Kai's feelings toward him.

Favner scanned every inch of my body, inspecting me in a way that made me feel naked. He stripped me of my confidence, making me feel smaller than an ant. His eyes were different from Declan's and Kai's. They were different from Allura's. The three of them had bright eyes, pleasing to look at, while Favner's were dark yellow like oozing pus. I felt nothing but evil seething from them.

"What have they been hiding from me for all of these years?" he mused, tapping the corner of his mouth.

Kai made a growling sound in the back of his throat, something very inhuman.

"No wonder you weren't taken care of when you should have been. I can't say that I blame Declan now." He licked his dark red stained lips and bit his lower lip. "You're simply too divine to toss away. I would certainly hate to have to dispose of you now."

I could tell it took everything for Kai to hold his ground. He wavered on his feet, debating his next move, but kept me in his sight.

Favner continued, "So let's compromise, shall we? I have a

proposition. You interested, precious?" I didn't respond to him. I knew he was going to propose whatever he pleased no matter what I said. "Rule by my side." He held his hand out to me, trying to entice me forward.

"And if I say no?" My voice came out confident, not at all as shaky or unsure as I felt.

"I'll simply finish the job that should have been done years ago," he declared my death indifferently, as if my seventeen years of life meant nothing. "No difference to me. It would just seem a terrible waste of you." He clucked his tongue. "But the choice is yours."

I looked up to Kai, but his eyes were set on Favner. His fists still clenched at his sides so tightly they shook. His jaw tightened as he tried to keep his composure. He never blinked as if blinking might cause him to miss something.

I looked down at Allura splayed over the soil and dead leaves, who still hadn't moved. My fate would be hers or worse if I didn't respond in his favor.

"If I say yes?" Favner was getting closer to me, but I kept my feet planted. I wouldn't show fear or weakness. I wouldn't let him see how terrified I felt inside, though my revulsion was clawing me from the inside out.

"Then my dear, we'll ride off into the shadow of trees to reign as the King and Queen of Faylinn and live happily ever after. We'll drink, eat and be as merry as we'd like." He reached out to touch me and twirled a piece of my hair around his fingers. "It feels just as soft as it looks." His metallic breath fell across my face, painfully bitter. "The things I could do to you to change your world." His words slithered through my veins, sly as a snake waiting to strike.

That was the last straw and I was airborne, flying backward

and landed in a mess of wet leaves. Kai had shoved me out of the way. I watched from the ground as he towered over Favner. But Favner was unafraid.

"Back down, Kai," Favner ordered. But Kai stood unafraid, planting his feet more determinedly.

Favner's face contorted. He snarled and his eyes grew more intense as he focused on Kai. A small triumphant smirk turned the corners of Kai's mouth as if he just discovered a dirty little secret. And then he flew at Favner.

"Liam. Owen." There were no other directions, but it was the only piece of encouragement they needed. Before Kai could reach Favner, Owen snatched up Kai's arms, pinning them behind his back while Liam landed a blow to his face. I flinched.

"Unwise decision, my friend," Favner said, without a hint of emotion.

Kai stared up at Liam, without a trace of fear. Liam hit him in the stomach and Kai doubled over, letting out a heaving grunt. Owen's booming laughter rose above Kai's muffled groans, revealing in the power they had over him.

"Please! Please, stop!" I begged.

"Is that a yes, precious?" Favner didn't take his eyes off of Kai.

My eyes shifted between Kai and Favner. Kai met my gaze, agony contorting his face. "Don't," he mouthed, blood dripping from the corner of his split lip.

I shook my head at Kai absently.

"I'm running out of patience, precious. You have one minute to take me up on my offer and then the deal will no longer be an option."

Liam's fist met the other side of Kai's face and landed another strike to his stomach. I winced against the sound that seeped from Kai's lips.

Where was Declan? I needed Declan *now* and then my thoughts finally connected. "Declan Roderic," I said in barely a whisper.

"What was that, my dear?"

"Yes," I choked, trying to buy my time. *What if he didn't come?*

"I'm sorry, what was that?"

"Yes," I said firmly, my eyes darting from Kai's crumpled figure to Favner. "Yes, I will be your queen, just make them stop. *Please!*"

Liam slipped in another punch before Favner stopped the torment. And it was over. Kai dropped to his knees, coughing. "No, Calliope. Don't." He coughed up a pool of red liquid. "I'd rather die."

I ran to be by his side and put my hands to his battered face, willing him to heal.

"Calliope, come," Favner commanded.

I didn't respond. I was concentrating too hard on repairing Kai's battered face. He was just beginning to heal. His indigo eyes poured into mine, looking so conflicted. "I'm fine," he murmured, holding his stomach.

"No, you're not."

"Calliope, don't provoke him," Kai faintly pleaded.

"I'm not," I lied.

"Calliope," Favner barked. "Come or Kai won't be so fortunate the second time around."

"Go, Calliope." I hesitated. "Now," Kai said firmly and grimaced.

I exhaled shakily and got to my feet, savoring one last glance at Kai who wasn't nearly ready enough to defend himself.

Glaring at Favner, I walked to stand in front of him, as close as I could force myself to be. Liam and Owen hovered by Kai, ready and waiting to act at the slightest of Favner's commands.

"You heard her, Kai," Favner said, all too pleased. "We'll be a fine pair, you and I, precious." He approached me, closing the gap and encroaching on my personal space. He took my hand in his, slowly lifting it to his mouth. I suppressed the impulse to flinch as his cold lips kissed the top of my hand. His devious eyes watched my reaction as he pressed his lips to my hand again. I took a deep breath, struggling to keep my face blank. Declan wasn't coming. My fate was sealed.

TWENTY-FOUR

"I think it would be wise of you to take a step back, Favner," Declan's voice boomed from behind us. His brawny figure appeared out of the darkness and stood close to where Kai kneeled.

Favner snickered. "Declan, my oh so faithful Keeper. You are good, but not that good. Attacked by the Rymidon Kingdom," he scoffed. "How did I not see the lies before? Did you really think you could hide her from me forever?"

Declan took in the scene around him. He gritted his teeth when he saw Kai. As his eyes wandered across the ground they found Allura's still body and immediately grew wide. He sucked in a husky breath of air, but instantly collected himself.

"She's the rightful heir," Declan dismissed Favner's previous words. "Which means she's the rule maker. She's the one everyone will have to answer to. You'll just be one of her pawns, a puppet to control."

"Oh, you think?" Favner's eyes shifted over me and rested

steadily on my eyes. "Calliope, come," he summoned. I couldn't defy him. Kai's body had, had enough and I couldn't bear to see Declan's fate turn out the same. I looked apologetically at Declan, trying to convey to him just how much it pained me to obey Favner. I moved my feet begrudgingly to be near his side. Favner sneered, pleased with himself and slipped his arm around my waist, possessively yanking me to his side. "That's it, precious. I knew we would get along marvelously."

I could feel Favner's eyes on me, but I couldn't force myself to look at him. How could such a striking man be so revolting? My skin crawled where his arm touched me. His fingertips brushed the bare skin at my waist, making me want to cringe away. I involuntarily shuddered.

"Calliope," Declan urged. "Use your Supremacy."

I didn't know how. I never knew when I was doing it. It just came to me. "I can't," I said, powerlessly.

"Yes, you can," he insisted.

"Enough," Favner said. He looked to Owen and Liam and they slowly approached Declan with evil boiling from their eyes. Liam lifted his fist quicker than my eyes could process, but Declan sidestepped and ducked away from the oncoming blow.

"You didn't think I was going to make it that easy for you, did you, Liam?" Declan taunted. Liam swung again and missed.

"Don't get cocky, Declan. I've beat you once, I can do it again," Liam retorted.

Declan smirked. Declan never smirked.

"Join the fun, Owen," Declan goaded, keeping his eyes focused on Liam. "I promise to go easy on you."

"Declan, don't be stupid!" I cried, wanting to reach out to him, but I was glued to Favner's side under his solid grip.

I should have kept my mouth shut. At my voice, Declan

attempted to shoot me a reassuring look, but that gave Liam a perfect opening to land a shot. Declan's face jerked to the side, but he didn't cry out. He didn't have to. His face said it all.

"Lesson number one, precious. This is what happens when fae disobey strict orders," Favner said callously, but I could hear a smile in his voice. He was relishing every minute of Declan's suffering.

It was a rough dance as the three of them dove, leapt and struck one another. Declan was surprisingly quick, but not always quick enough. I shifted my gaze between the scuffle and the ground, wincing at every strike taken.

"Please," I pleaded. "Call them off." But Favner made no move to stop. He simply knocked his head back with pleasure. "Let him go," I begged. Tears streamed down my face as helplessness overcame me. I searched deep within me. I'd done it before. My Supremacy had come so easily in the past. I never had to think about it. *Why wouldn't it come now?*

Favner aggressively snatched me up into his arms. "You're mine now," he seethed, his warm breath sweeping across my cheek.

I jerked in his arms to free myself, but his hold was too tight, too strong. His fingertips dug into my arm and leg as he began to sprint away.

I shrieked for help and then we were falling to the ground. I tumbled out of his arms and my head met a boulder. Numbness was all I felt before the pain hit me. I blinked back the water in my eyes and attempted to sit up. Wetness slithered through my fingers when I raised my hand to steady my head. I brought my fingers in front of my bleary eyes to see red trickling down the skin. Out of the corner of my eye I caught sight of Kai hovering over Favner.

"She isn't yours to take," Kai warned, his hand clasped around Favner's neck, pinning him to the earth.

Favner grunted. "She doesn't deserve my place. She couldn't handle the politics that come with being the ruler. She might be the heir, but she knows nothing of our kingdom. She knows nothing of the fae," he spat.

"And you do?" Kai snarled. "Don't act as if you care. Don't you dare pretend to know the first thing about our kind. She is already twice the leader you ever were."

Favner released a strangled growl of laughter.

I nervously searched for the other scuffle, but when I found them no more than twenty feet away, Declan was no longer a part in the struggle. Liam and Owen stood dumbfounded, searching their surroundings for Declan but, when they saw Kai's chokehold on Favner, they sprang into action, flying toward Kai.

"Don't move!" I shouted, freezing the guards in place. "Stand back!" They slowly stepped away from Kai, glowering at me with their vivid fae eyes.

I did it. *I did it!*

"How did she do that?" Owen grumbled, dumbstruck, to Liam. Liam let out a huff of air, crossing his arms firmly over his chest, shooting daggers from his eyes at me.

I turned my attention back to Favner and Kai on the soil. When I saw the cream blade in Kai's hand I knew he had his dagger. It was pressed against Favner's throat.

"You don't have it in you," Favner said, so sure of himself. "Neither did Eldon. Like father like son."

"Don't you dare say his name," Kai sneered, pain crushing his voice.

"Eldon was a loyal one. Loyal to the very end," Favner taunted. "Just not to me."

Declan materialized and moved to be alongside Kai while I watched from a safe distance. I'd never seen such a face on Kai before. His eyes burned with disdain. Would Kai actually kill him? It wasn't as if Favner would bat an eyelash to killing either one of them. If Kai freed him there would be no peace. There would be no release from his power. The fae would continue to suffer under his reign, enduring every day imprisoned.

Before I caught sight of them, Liam and Owen had shifted from where I bound them and were gaining on Kai. "Stop!" I demanded. And they did, but I wasn't sure how long it was going to last. I couldn't keep my concentration on them and watch Kai. Declan pulled back from Favner and drew his dagger, aiming it at Liam and Owen, securing their placement once more.

I had only taken my eyes off of Kai for one moment, but Favner had escaped his grasp and now stood toe to toe with him.

"Liam," Favner bellowed.

My anger was beginning to surface. What a coward. I found myself walking toward them. "What, Favner? You can't fight like a man? You have to use every power you possess to dominate in a struggle? You can't fight Kai yourself?"

He shifted his stare from Kai to me. Never had a stare been so sharp. Then the back of his hand connected with my cheek and I fell to the earth. Immediately I knew why Allura hadn't moved after Favner's last blow. Numbness flowed from my head down through my limbs, paralyzing me, cutting off every breath of oxygen.

"No!" Kai shouted. "Get away from her!"

Wetness trailed down the side of my face, but I couldn't move. I watched from the ground, only catching glimpses of their feet springing across the soil. The numbness gradually began to ebb and I clenched my eyes closed against the stinging, breathing in deep. I heard the clank of weapons. A gruff voice hollered in agony while another grunted in triumph, but there was no way for me to decipher which sound came from who.

After gaining the strength to lift myself from the ground, I wiped the trickle slithering down my face. But it was no longer just a trickle. Crimson smeared my entire hand. I looked up and saw Kai and Favner in a swift dance as their feet vaulted from trunks and boulders, diving at one another, never quite making contact. Neither of them were marked or looked winded. I wasn't sure that the grunts had come from them. I swiftly shifted my stare and discovered the other fight between Declan, Liam and Owen. Blood stained Declan's sleeve, but he was still fighting fearlessly. He had overpowered two fae guards before. I prayed he could do it again.

After realizing I was smack-dab in the center of the action, I scurried back to get out of the way and watched the two battles unfold in front of me. Favner gained on Kai, nearly landing a swipe to his face, but, thankfully, Kai was quick. He dodged every strike Favner made.

It was like a train wreck. I didn't want to watch, too afraid of the outcome, but I couldn't tear my eyes away from them. My heart gave a jolt at every possible blow Favner tried to make, strangling my every breath. While absorbed in the struggle, I was suddenly aware that Favner wasn't using his supremacy. Why hadn't he been able to control Declan or Kai?

A cry tore through the air and Kai flinched back. Almost instantly blood seeped from his shoulder and Favner looked arrogantly victorious. I sucked in a breath of air. Then I heard the knife sink into Favner's flesh and he dropped to his knees, grasping his stomach. Kai tore the dagger from Favner's stomach and held it up to his throat.

Favner shifted his seething eyes to me and sneered. "You have *no* idea what you're getting yourself into, little girl. If you were smart—" he choked and his voice grew weaker, "you'd back down now. Run back to daddy and let the grownups take care of the important affairs of our kingdom. This is bigger than you realize."

"Shut up!" Kai shouted and shook Favner.

Favner snickered and turned back to Kai whose eyes were closed. "Why won't you look at me, Kai? Look me in the eye," Favner demanded. My heart tensed, clinching my breath. What if that was his only way to control him now?

"No, Kai! Look at me!" I hollered impulsively. "Look at me!"

Kai's control waivered, but he finally peered over at me, keeping Favner firm in his clutch. Our eyes locked. In that moment something passed in the space between us. A string linked our lives, intertwining every part of me that I never realized wanted to be touched by him. I wanted nothing more in that moment but for him to live. I could feel the Supremacy slowly dwindling, the connection gradually severing, but his eyes stayed fastened to mine. He was holding my heart and I don't think he even realized it.

I couldn't watch for fear of losing Kai's gaze, but out of the corner of my eye I saw a flash here and there of Declan battling with Liam and Owen. I couldn't use my Supremacy on them as much as I wanted to, as much as it pained me not to. A booming yell tore through the air, but I couldn't tear my eyes from Kai. *Please don't let that be Declan.*

"If I'm going to die I want you to look me in the eye as you do it. No cowering from me," Favner goaded. I watched Kai's arm shake. "Your father couldn't kill me either. You would make

287

him proud." The tone in Favner's voice almost sounded caring, like he could have a heart, but it was weakening. "You turned out to be a coward just like him. It's too bad I killed him so he couldn't see how much like him you are."

With every confession Kai's eyes drowned, being pulled further and further in the water, farther and farther away from me.

"I looked him dead in the eye as I did it too." He snickered breathlessly, no trace of remorse in his voice.

Kai's composure was cracking. At that confession I knew it was all over.

"Kai," I breathed as his eyes sunk to the bottom.

He unlocked our gaze, but not before a tear fell down his cheek. His grip on Favner must have weakened because suddenly Favner was on his feet a few feet away, ready to fight back.

"I only made him suffer for a few minutes until he bled out onto the forest floor," Favner taunted. "His heart kept fighting—even with the dagger still in it—as he repeated your mother's name over and over, begging for the mercy of your family."

"AHHHH!" Kai eyes grew wild as he flew at Favner with his dagger raised.

Favner dove to the side toward his dagger lying in the leaves, flipping and landing on his feet. The unadulterated determination in Kai's eyes scared me. He was not deterred by Favner's renewed energy. With Favner's heartless words, I now only feared that Kai's judgments might be skewed by his hatred. He tore through the space between them at lightning speed, slashing viciously.

Although Favner had gained some strength back, he was obviously still injured, unable to swiftly escape Kai's attack.

Favner wasn't as agile or as precise in his combat as they circled around one another. He sliced only air as Kai dodged all his attempts to strike. Favner cried out, clutching his bleeding stomach with his last attempt to wound and Kai saw his opening.

I heard the slice and a faint thud as the body dropped to the soil. A shiver coursed up my spine and I turned my face away.

Another gruff yelp echoed through the trees, but I couldn't look. I was frozen.

It was done.

I let out a suffocating lungful of air and looked up at Kai, kneeling on the ground over a motionless body. The woods spun around me, shades of green and brown blurring into one. But Kai's hunched figure remained front and center.

Kai gradually got to his feet, trembling as he did so, looking down at Favner's lifeless shape. He cocked his head back and cried out, forming the most unbearable sound. It echoed far and wide. Tree leaves rattled. Branches creaked. The wind howled with him. My heart couldn't handle it.

He unhurriedly peered over at me and let out a heavy sigh, slowly blinking his eyes. "My Queen," he breathed, attempting to pack the title with his typical arrogance, but not nearly hitting the mark. His head lowered. At first I thought it was in shame, but his stance was off as his torso bent forward.

Was he *bowing* to me?

After a moment he lifted his head to me. Tears welled up in my eyes with our gaze locked. Anguish coated his beautiful indigo eyes. But before I could go to him he bolted into the night, nothing but a Kai shaped hole in my heart as evidence of his existence.

"Kai!" I called out to him hopelessly. I made a move to follow, but pulled myself back to the present and raked my eyes around the grove.

Blood seeped from the corner of Declan's mouth. His chest rose and fell as he breathed heavily, having miraculously overpowered Liam and Owen. Their bulky figures sprawled out on the ground, red splatter painting the moss and leaves like a horrific mosaic.

I reached Declan and set my hand on his arm, but kept silent. My unspoken touch quieted him and he turned to me. He gently wiped the blood from the side of my face before I found myself instantly immersed in his arms, enclosing me in his warmth, his head resting on top of mine.

"Are you okay?" he whispered.

I nodded into his chest, unable to find the words to speak.

We stood there under the protection of the trees that were no longer daunted by Favner, holding one another, searching for relief. Where was the relief?

Declan pulled back and looked at me, tucking a wave of hair behind my ear and tenderly held my face. He opened his mouth to speak, but then his eyes rested just beyond my shoulder.

"Allura," he gasped and stepped around me. Declan stumbled over the ground, visibly not getting to her as fast as he wanted and finally dropped to his knees at her side.

Declan gently rolled her over, carefully brushing her tangled dreads from her battered face. "Allura," he pled for her to respond. "Please, Allura, open your eyes." Though her face was bloodstained and her eyes were swollen shut, she looked like an angel. "Allura, please. Don't die on me now." His voice cracked.

Declan shattered right before my eyes. Strong, collected, stable Declan was crumbling and I didn't know how to fix him. As he rocked a broken Allura in his arms he let out a crushing sob and whispered a repeated plea. "Please, please, please…"

I wanted to pull him away, to hold him and make the scene around us disappear. But all I did was stand there and pray to whatever God there might be to bring her back to him.

There was a reprieve when she groaned faintly. Her eyes trembled, struggling to open. Tears trailed from them, clearing through the grime on her cheeks.

"Allura," he breathed in relief at the token sign of life. "Thank the Fallen Fae." He held her to him, cradling her in his arms as she quietly whimpered. She weakly brought an arm around his neck, holding him closer to her in return. Their intimate grip on one another felt like a private moment, so I silently stepped away. There was more between them than he had led me to believe. I knew that now.

There was nowhere for me to go. Everywhere I looked I was reminded of what had just taken place, reenacting the fighting and slashing over and over again. I scoured the surrounding trees with my eyes, willing Kai to return. Maybe he would hear my silent plea and come back to me.

"Where's Kai?" Allura's voice rasped. I turned back to them. "Where's my brother?"

"He's okay," Declan assured, running a hand down her cheeks and wiping away the tears, careful not to touch the gashes marring her face.

Was that what he called okay?

Alive? Yes. But okay?

Allura sluggishly scanned the dead bodies around us to confirm Declan was telling the truth. "Where is he?" she insisted.

Declan gave Allura the short version of the events that transpired, starting when she passed out. I didn't hear any of it as I zoned out. I couldn't bear to hear the details repeated now. I had been there and watched it all play out, and yet it felt unreal.

Had that all just happened? It felt like a lifetime while it took place, but now it felt like a vivid nightmare.

"I should go find him," Declan murmured.

"I'll go with you," Allura said, trying to get to her feet and failing, wincing from the pain. Declan caught her and wrapped his arm around her to steady her, taking all of her weight on him.

The look on Kai's face and the heart wrenching sound he made was burned into my brain. It played over and over in my mind, like a merciless broken record. Now was not the time to bother him. "Let him be," I said quietly. He would need time. He deserved time.

Declan met my eyes and nodded respectfully.

A reverence blanketed the forest, quieting all the nature surrounding us. A look fell across Declan's eyes as he gazed at me, realization setting in. He smiled kindly then humbly took a knee, helping Allura kneel beside him. Allura lifted her mouth, trying to make an effort to smile. *What were they doing?* Their eyes lightly closed as they bowed their heads.

To me.

Favner was gone. I was Queen of Faylinn.

It was all over.

And yet it was only the beginning.

EPILOGUE
ONE WEEK LATER

Declan agreed it was best when I told him I needed to take a few days to recuperate and collect my thoughts after it became official. My inauguration to officially become queen was tomorrow. Or what did Declan call it? Faylinn didn't call it an inauguration. It was a... a Dawning. As dawn was the start of a new day, I was the start of a new era. My Dawning was scheduled for tomorrow morning.

I didn't hear from Kai after that day. He never came back to our spot. I worried about him. Though I knew he could take care of himself, my heart ached for him. How did you pick up the pieces after something like that? Learning about the reason your father no longer lived by your side, then looking into the eyes of the man who did it and taking that same action against his executioner. How did you put yourself back together? What if he couldn't?

Declan and I met on a daily basis as he filled me in on the happenings of Faylinn since Favner's take down. There was rejoicing and festivities of celebration, but soon that would end and guidance was going to be required. He told me of the talk of the fae as my existence became public. There was excitement, but mainly skepticism, which I knew would come. I was preparing myself for the booing and gnashing of teeth. I accepted it. It didn't make it any easier, but I accepted it.

"Declan, why couldn't Favner control you or Kai? It was as if his Supremacy wasn't effective anymore."

His aqua eyes looked at me kindly. "As soon as you decided to acknowledge Faylinn as yours, it became yours. You became the rightful controller of Supremacy. I think the only reason why Liam and Owen obeyed Favner was because they didn't know and they had been loyal to him for so long it had become second nature. The rest of us became free the moment you accepted us."

The weight of his words hit me with a heaviness I'd never experienced in my life. I realized the decision I made was not one to take lightly, but the full weight of my acceptance hadn't truly set in until he spoke those words. As soon as I acknowledged Faylinn as mine, it became mine. Their loyalty was to me now. Their lives were in my hands.

Before sunset Declan was going to guide me to Faylinn. I suppose it was crucial for me to be prepped and ready for my Dawning in the morning. I was going to be sleeping in a completely new place tonight. A place I was going to eventually call my home.

After deciding I needed a few days before going to Faylinn I was then reminded of the way Cameron and I had parted ways and I wanted to escape to Faylinn as fast as my feet would carry me. It was spineless, though, so I didn't do it. But it took a couple of days before I built up the nerve to show up on his doorstep.

"It's really happening?" he asked.

"I leave Saturday evening," I confirmed as we sat on his front porch swing.

We shared a moment of silence before he spoke. "Do you remember when I told you what the worst day of my life was?"

I nodded. How could I forget? Cameron's mom walked out on him and his dad when he was ten. He didn't tell most people why she left or that she even did, but when the day came that he felt confident enough in our friendship to tell me, that was the day I knew we'd be friends forever. Most kids didn't recover after something like that, but Cam did.

"This is a close second," he murmured, staring straight into the woodlands across from his house.

"Cameron," I breathed, lowering my head.

"I'm sorry. I didn't mean that in the way it came out," he said, laying his hand on my leg. "I just... I want you to stay and there's nothing I can do to keep you here. Not being able to have control over the most important things in my life makes me feel..." he trailed off.

"Helpless," I finished the sentence for him. "I know. Trust me. I know," I murmured.

"I love you, Callie, you know that? I know it doesn't change anything. I know it won't make you stay, but it's out there. I'll always be here, waiting in the wings if you decide to come back. No pun intended." We chuckled. "All of my cards are on the table and I have no regrets." He peered over at me, his light hair draping just across his blue eyes. His hand, still comfortably resting on my leg, squeezed gently.

295

I leaned in and lightly kissed him, barely brushing our lips, a whisper of a kiss. "I love you too, Cam. I always will."

My parents stood on the edge of the trees, delaying the goodbye more than I was.

"Are you sure it's not possible for you to come with me?" I asked, hopeful. A part of me was still in denial. I wasn't actually doing this by myself was I?

My dad shook his head. "They closed off Faylinn to me after I left. They saw my passing down of the kingdom as a betrayal. I won't ever be welcome there again." He peered over at my mom.

I nodded, though I felt, as queen, I had to have some power to be able to get him back, to make them change their minds. There had to be a way. I was on my own from here on out.

My eyes met Mom's and tears fell down her cheeks. She pulled me to her; embracing me so tightly my breath was all but smothered. We held each other silently, taking in our last moments. When I attempted to pull away she held onto me even tighter. I wasn't sure if she was going to let me go.

"Mom," I softly scolded.

"I know," she said. "I encouraged you. I told you it was the right decision, but I don't want you to go anymore."

"Now you tell me," I chided, only half-joking.

She released me, holding me at arm's length. "Why should they get to take you from me?"

"Melody," Dad murmured, resting a hand on her shoulder.

"No," she resisted, tearing her arm from his touch. "She's my daughter. My *only* daughter." I heard the tears rasp her voice.

"Mom," I breathed. Why was she making it so much harder on me? She had the power to make me change my mind.

"This wasn't how it was supposed to be," she muttered, putting her hands tenderly on my face. I didn't say anything. I couldn't bring myself to reply. There wasn't anything she could say to make this easier. She swallowed, struggling to gain her composure. "Okay," she exhaled. "I know. I know. You have to go. You should go. I'll stop blubbering."

Mom didn't blubber. She was the no nonsense parent. She clenched her teeth fighting more tears.

"Faylinn will be honored to have their rightful heir back," Dad said, bringing us back to the reason for our blubbering. "I'm so proud of you for making this decision. No father could be prouder."

I chuckled without humor, peering over at him. "They won't feel honored. They'll feel cheated. I have no idea what I'm getting myself into." The words Favner had spat rang in my ears. *She knows nothing of our kingdom. She knows nothing of our fae.* I felt so inadequate. I was just some ignorant seventeen-year-old *half-breed* with only the royal blood to tie me to the kingdom. *You have no idea what you're getting yourself into, little girl. This is bigger than you realize.*

"It'll come to you," Dad confirmed.

I gulped back my rising insecurities. "They told me that humans tend to forget fae... for our protection. Does that mean you guys will lose your memory of me?"

My dad shook his head. "Your mother and I won't. You are our flesh and blood. I can't say the same for Lia and Cameron. There really is no telling, but I assure you... we will always know who you are."

Gosh, I hoped so.

297

Before he said a word I felt him. I turned back to the woodlands to see Declan, hovering behind the first row of trees. He smiled warmly and nodded. That was my cue and now I wasn't ready. I hesitated when I turned back to my parents. It wasn't as if I wanted to drag this out, but I couldn't bring myself to leave, feeling the finality of it all.

"The fae are waiting, Calliope," Declan prompted respectfully. "It's time."

But I needed more time. This couldn't be it. This was coming too fast. I wiped the tears from my eyes and gave my parents one last hug.

"I will be back," I said into my mom's neck.

"I know," she said. "I know," she whispered as if to reassure herself.

I took a deep breath and turned toward Declan. He stood as a safe harbor, ready and waiting for me to take sail. His face brightened with encouragement and it filled me with a confidence I hadn't realized resided inside of me.

"I love you, Calliope," Dad called to me.

I gulped back the tears in my throat and nodded. "I love you back," I said over my shoulder.

It was time. I released my wings at last, letting them stretch unrestricted and wide. Declan bowed his head slightly to me when I stood before him and he lifted his palm for me to take.

"My Queen," he greeted with a smile and every part of my body tingled as those words echoed throughout my mind.

I accepted his hand as we began our journey to Faylinn.

MINDY HAYES

EMBER

a Faylinn novel

TURN THE PAGE FOR A SNEAK PEEK

PROLOGUE

Winter was upon us, and as the sun had just set, a bitter cold spread throughout the forest. I ran my hands up and down my arms to warm them against the brisk wind lashing my skin. He appeared from behind a tree, the moonlight shone on his face like a waterfall of gleaming mist. Startled, I lost my footing and fell to my knees.

He let out an irritated sigh and helped me to my feet. "Humans are so ungraceful. You should really attempt to work on that. After all this time one would think you would be an expert."

I glared at him, but kept my mouth shut. I knew better than to talk back. Although, it wasn't my fault that I couldn't control this body like I wanted to. It might have been a few years, but my body still hadn't completely adjusted. I knew it never would.

"What do you have for me?" he asked curtly.

"Calliope decided to go back to Faylinn in spite of the fact that Favner is dead. They left a few hours ago."

He scowled. "Well that happened sooner than I anticipated. Why didn't you prevent this?"

"There was no way for me to stop her," I tried to explain. "With Kai and Declan watching her as closely as they do, there was no way I could have prevented it without being obvious. You told me to do whatever I could inconspicuously, but if there was any chance that I would be revealed that I should step back. I did all you asked. At least she survived."

"Yes. That is what's most important." He brushed his long fingers along his chin, contemplating my answer. "We can still work with the timing."

"What about me?" I'd been his puppet long enough. My job was finally done.

"Now, now. Let's not be hasty. If my instincts are correct, there will be no way she will go long without going home. I need you to remain in place until that happens."

"But we had a deal."

Leveling his stare, he said, "And that deal is still in place until I get what I want. She will not last long without the guidance of her father. When she goes to him then you will have your reward."

"That could be months. You expect me to wait longer?"

"You've waited for this for several years, a few more *months* won't kill you."

ONE

Declan, we have to be close, right? I feel like we should have been there already."

It seemed like we had been leaping through the trees and over ravines for hours. It wasn't that I was tired. Surprisingly, my stamina was still going strong, but the anticipation of seeing Faylinn for the first time was *agonizing*.

Declan chuckled. "Your senses are spot on." He then shot down, out of sight. I stopped, nearly slamming into a trunk then dropped to the forest floor after him.

He stood, grinning at me with his hands on his hips.

"A little warning would have been nice," I said dryly. "That tree nearly took me out."

"But it didn't. You catch on quickly. Challenge is good every once and a while. You need to be aware of your body so you have an advantage if you need to make a quick getaway and lose someone hot on your wings."

"Hot on my wings? As in, hot on my tail?" I raised an

eyebrow.

His brow scrunched together. "Sure." He offered another smile and nodded his head to the side. "C'mon. We're here."

I remained in place. "All I see are endless trees and valleys."

"Of course that's all you'd see. We have to go through the Hedge first." Declan took another step and then was out of sight.

"Declan!" *Where the crap did he go?* I took a step forward, but nothing happened.

Then I saw Declan's head bobbing in the air a couple feet ahead, looking at me expectantly. "You coming?" His arm outstretched toward me, floating above the ground.

"You look unnatural, just a floating head. I think I'm going to be sick."

"Sorry." He stepped all the way back out through the invisible barrier. "Sometimes I forget you aren't used to all of this yet. Take my hand. I'll guide you through."

"That's it?" My brow furrowed.

"That's it."

I extended my hand, and he pulled me through what felt like water, but when we emerged on the other side, I remained dry.

Whoa. "And no one can get through that unless they are fae?"

He let go of my hand. "That's right."

We walked a few more feet, and the tree density lessened. The sun sunk just beyond the horizon. Faylinn came more clearly into view, dusted with a blue haze.

My body froze.

The kingdom rolled in the hills of the valley for miles. They hadn't disturbed the woodlands. They merely built around it, letting the nature be apart of their homes. Rich vines and moss crawled up the cottages, cloaking them in green, camouflaging them from the world. Perched in the limbs of the trees and scattered on the rolling grass, the chalets appeared to belong precisely where they were. It was beautiful, unlike anything I could have imagined.

"Welcome to Faylinn," Declan said kindly.

Before I could respond, men dressed similar to Declan and Kai in natural-colored cut-offs and tunics or bare-chests, began dropping from limbs and emerging from behind trunks. Vines wound up their left arms. Every one of them was equipped with a bow and arrows, as well as a sheath at their waist for their daggers.

Keepers.

One stepped forward and knelt one knee to the ground. "Calliope, this is Dugal," Declan introduced. "He's head of the watch for this shift."

"Your Highness." Dugal bowed his head in respect.

"Nice to meet you." I tried to smile to hide my embarrassment. When he didn't get up and every Keeper began to drop to one knee, I couldn't hold back the quiet chuckle forming in my throat.

"Declan, make them get up," I whispered urgently.

He ducked his head near my ear. "Just say, 'Thank you. You may all stand.'"

I repeated his words, and every Keeper stood tall once more, my eyes taking in the sea of colorful eyes staring back at me.

"It's been a long journey," Declan began. "I'm going to lead the Queen to her castle."

"Yes, of course." Dugal stepped out of the way, sweeping

his arm to the side to let us pass.

As we walked by them, one by one they regarded me with a gentle nod. I mimicked the gesture, not knowing what else to do. Waving my hand to acknowledge them didn't seem right. *I am so out of my league here.*

When we were far enough away I hissed, "Oh my gosh, Declan. I realize I'm the Queen, but couldn't you have simply referred to me as Calliope?"

"If you want me to call you that, I can do that. But when conversing with the rest of the fae, I suggest that you keep up with formalities so they know who is in charge."

"But it makes me uncomfortable."

"Well, that's simply something you will have to get used to," he stated without a hint of sympathy.

Okay, Kai. I sighed heavily in defeat and followed his lead as we walked down the hillside into the valley. Balls of light sprinkled the trees and dotted the ground, like the lights on the floor of a dark movie theater, forming illuminated pathways.

"What's creating the light?" I wondered aloud.

He tilted his head toward me and smiled. "Fireflies, of course."

I chuckled. *Of course.*

As we made our way through the land, one by one, vibrantly multicolored eyes found me. It wasn't instant recognition, but when I was recognized, mouths hung open and eyes gaped. Some bowed, some nodded courteously, but everyone watched. As the word spread while we walked deeper into the heart of Faylinn, faeries came out of their homes just to see me walk by.

I wanted to ask what they were staring at. My heart sped and my stomach knotted over the realization that I wouldn't leave until I became used to this. But the question was never asked because I knew. They all wanted to have a look at their new *rightful* heir to the throne. Apparently curiosity was a common trait in all living creatures.

Declan strode beside me with pride. I felt it in the way he walked and held his head high. He stood as a true protector. "It's okay to acknowledge them, you know," he murmured down to me.

"Yeah, I realize that," I whispered back. "Right now I'm trying to find the will in me not to fall or faint."

He chortled. "I understand. Just lift your hand in a small wave. You don't even have to look at them."

"As if that's not completely rude."

He gave me his arm. "I won't let you fall." I took it gratefully and did my best to nod at those we passed by.

A pair of indigo eyes met mine from a doorway in a giant hollowed out trunk, giving my heart a jolt. But when I looked into the face of the faery, they didn't belong to the face I expected to see. It was a woman in his place. There was a twinkle in her eyes when she smiled and bowed. I offered my best smile, hoping it didn't look like a grimace.

"I live up there." Declan's voice pulled me from her face as he pointed into the trees next to her house. High above the rest was a small hut perched in between a y-shaped trunk, cloaked in branches thick with leaves.

"You'll have to give me a tour tomorrow."

He chuckled. "I highly doubt there will be any time for that."

"What? Why?"

"Calliope, you have a lot going on tomorrow. The first day of your reign is going to be a big celebration. You'll be given the crown, and everyone is going to want the chance to meet you. Tomorrow will be reserved for the Dawning and a celebration. No one will work. The whole day will be dedicated to you."

"Please tell me that's a joke." His facial expression didn't change. "And what if I don't want to? What if I don't want a full day dedicated to me? Can't they just put the crown on me and call it good?"

"It would be a tad disrespectful to tradition."

I huffed a sigh.

We walked deeper into the heart of Faylinn and reached a grassy meadow. In the center of the pasture was the castle. Was it too much of an oxymoron to call it a quaint castle? The stone structure rose, captivating, above the village, but didn't tower like a monstrosity. It was created to set itself apart from the other charming cottages, but not to diminish the beauty of the rest of the village.

Ivy crept up the six staggering towers—three on either side—and sprouted along the arched entrance. Little square windows circled the top of the hourglass-like towers, perfect for watching over Faylinn. Nature encompassed every crevasse and corner of the castle as though the structure was built around the trees.

"Welcome home." Declan swept his hand in front of us, leading me toward the entry.

A tall man dressed in a khaki tunic and black britches stood to one side. "My Queen." He deeply bowed.

"Hi," I replied lamely.

"Let me introduce you to Evan," Declan said. "He will be your personal advisor. Any guidance you need, he will be at your disposal."

"It's wonderful to finally meet the daughter of Finnian."

His tangerine eyes sparkled under the moonlight.

"Evan's been serving by your family's side for generations."

"Oh."

Evan's radiant eyes softened. He didn't look his age. His face wasn't young, but he didn't look hundreds of years old either. Though I could see the years he'd lived in his eyes, so wise and experienced, he didn't seem more than fifty years old. "You come from a very influential family, my dear. It's good to see the line did not end with your uncle."

I gave him an appreciative smile. "Thank you, sir."

"Oh, no need for those types of formalities with me, Your Majesty. Please call me Evan."

I nodded. "Okay. Thank you, Evan."

"Evan," Declan interjected. "I think our Queen would like to be shown to her room."

"Of course." Evan stepped aside, dropping his head as we passed. "Have a good evening, Your Highness. I look forward to serving you and seeing you crowned tomorrow."

I waved meekly. "It was nice to meet you, Evan."

"Likewise."

I trailed behind Declan as he guided me through the halls. Strands of greenery snuck up the inside of the stone and tree trunk structured walls. Lantern lights flickered. I paused, watching the fireflies flit about inside the glass.

"Calliope," Declan prompted. "It's really not customary for me to be leading the way here."

"It's not like I know where I'm going," I retorted.

"True." He chuckled. "But, I would feel better if you would at least walk by my side."

As we walked, his arm brushed mine. I was grateful for his comforting company in this foreign place. He was the one thing that made me feel like I could eventually call this home.

The halls were dim, only illuminated by the moonlight that shown through the windows and firefly lanterns. Once we reached a wooden spiral staircase, he took my hand. "Your room is this way." He led me up behind him, keeping my fingers secure between his.

We passed a couple doors before Declan stopped in front of one and opened it, letting me pass before him. Light from the night sky cascaded into the room from the windows on the far wall. A queen-sized four-poster bed was nestled in the right corner. Vines dotted in pearly blue flowers curtained around the white bark bedposts.

Declan squeezed my hand before letting it go and set my bag down inside the door.

"This will be your bedroom. The washroom is through that arch," he said, pointing to a vined archway on the left side of the room.

"It's beautiful."

"I'm glad you like it." I felt his eyes on me as I surveyed the room. "I think I'll let you sleep. You have a long day ahead of you; dawn will be here before you know it."

I turned to him. "You'll come get me in the morning, right?"

A subtle smile grew on his face, and his aqua eyes lit up warmly. "If that's what you would like."

"Please."

He nodded and bowed out of the room. "Goodnight, My Queen."

I made a face, but didn't correct him. "Night, Declan."

The door closed, and silence blanketed the room. It suddenly dawned on me that I was truly all by myself in this unfamiliar nature-filled room. I'd never really been alone before. I wouldn't be saying goodnight to my parents. And though I'd seen them a few hours ago, I never felt more alone in my life.

There was a nightgown lying across the foot of the bed. It looked a lot more comfortable than the tank top and flannel pajama bottoms I brought, but I needed the comfort of something that belonged to me—something that tied me to home. After I put my familiar pajamas on, I crawled under the cream blanket below the branches and flowers. I already knew it was going to be a long night trying to fall asleep in a new place. I heard nothing but the sound of crickets and rustling leaves outside my window. I waited several hours for sleep to take me as the same thoughts circulated through my mind.

Faylinn is my home now.
This is my kingdom.

ACKNOWLEDGEMENTS

When I first started writing I was hugely unaware of what it would take to bring a story in my head to the public. I have an overwhelming amount of gratitude for everyone who helped bring Kaleidoscope to where it is.

Amy Van Wagenen and Karen Garcia, my second pair of eyes in the editing process, thank you for your countless hours and expertise that was put forth to make this book so much more than it was. I really appreciate you.

An enormous thanks to my girls: Kristen Grooms, Brandi Watts, Whitni Hess, Pam Townsend and my mother-in-law, who finished the book in its roughest form and all said, "I need the second one!" Thank you so much for your enthusiasm. It helps give me the desire to keep writing every day.

My critique partner, Brittany Smith, I can see this is only the beginning of a long rewarding friendship. Thank you for your eagerness to give honest feedback and guidance. I can't wait to see where our writing takes us!

Abbey Benson Photography and Sarah Hansen of Okay Creations deserve a world of thanks for helping to create the flawless image that is the cover. It's everything I had hoped it would be and more.

Jessica McLean, you are a rock star. Thank you for listening to my babbling and sometimes incoherent thoughts, but most importantly for your patience to put up with hair dye after hair dye to make a perfect Calliope.

To Lindsey, Kim and Jenny, who never once complained when I'd corner them and start brainstorming out-loud. Your willingness to offer advice and opinions means more to me than you know.

Kirk Ouimet. You helped make this possible. Thank you for your vote of confidence and giving me the opportunity to try and prove you right.

My best friends, Alix Ouimet and Sarah Beth Jolley, who have supported and encouraged my writing from day one—nearly five years ago—even though I know my amateur writing abilities in the beginning could not have been easy to read, you read through the horrific unpublishable novels and believed in me before I actually believed in myself. I love you more than my luggage.

I can't leave out my family who give unending support and love to last for the rest of my existence. I am who I am because of you. Thank you.

And there is no forgetting the husband. Ryan, without your constant, "Are ya done yet?" I may not have finally finished what I started. Thank you for never giving me a dull moment. I sure love you.

MINDY HAYES grew up in San Diego, California exploring her interest for singing and playing the piano. She first discovered her passion for reading when she had to make her first flight alone to South Carolina to visit her, then, fiancé. Mindy's love for writing followed shortly after. She and her husband have now been married for seven years and live in Summerville, South Carolina.

Visit Mindy online:
www.mindyhayes.com
www.facebook.com/hayes.mindy

Books by Mindy:
Kaleidoscope (Faylinn #1)
Ember (Faylinn #2)
Luminary (Faylinn #3)
Me After You (Willowhaven #1)
Me Without You (Willowhaven #2)

Made in the USA
San Bernardino, CA
27 December 2019